DELTA COUNTY BLUES

WINDS OF CHANGE
BOOK 4

GINA HOOTEN POPP

Publisher's Note:

This is a work of fiction. All names, characters, places, and events are the work of the authors imagination. Any resemblance to real persons, places or events is coincidental. To the extent that the image or images on the cover of this book depict a person or persons, such person or persons are merely models, and are not intended to portray any character or characters featured in the book.

This book is dedicated to my father.
Thank you for providing for me.
Thank you for protecting me.
Thank you for teaching me to stand strong.

ACKNOWLEDGMENTS

My gratitude goes to my family and friends for their support throughout my author journey. I love and appreciate every one of you. I would especially like to acknowledge my critique partners Linda Joyce, Jan Morrill, and Erin York for their thoughtful feedback during the writing of this story. I am so grateful to be surrounded by these three talented authors.

PROLOGUE

COWBOY LARSON

The need for approbation from one's fellow man is so strong no one is immune. This need for love and praise is as basic as our need for food and shelter. And, for some of us, that drive is more fierce than for others. It burns in our very soul. The need to be loved. The need to be appreciated. Maybe to be remembered long after we are gone. Leaving a stamp on the earth seems like a lofty mission when you consider all who have gone before us . . . and all who will come after. We're so tiny, so fragile in the scheme of things. But this drive to be noticed makes us go above and beyond. Yes, many of us are born with just such a desire. And as I sit here in this shady spot under an oak tree that was born before me and will surely outlive me, I ask myself why I feel this way. My late wife Saint once told me she thought it was my subconscious giving me a reason to live.

Perhaps she was right. She was one of those deep thinkers who can usually sort out what a person's all about within the first few hours of meeting them. I'm thankful she came into my life at just the right time.

A lot of what I do every day is for her . . . and for the fans of Mick's and my music. All one hundred million of them. Now I'm exaggerating here which my wife often said I do too often. And I would remind her that we all have some kind of fault. Whether it be lying, cheating, gossiping, gambling, murdering, exaggerating or just plain old self-righteousness . . . we're all infallible in some way. That's why we've got to forgive ourselves . . . and forgive each other . . . because we've all got some kind of vice or mental attitude problem. Think about it—when someone has done you wrong, you've got to get past it —because pretty soon you'll be doing something rotten yourself.

Believe me, I've given this a lot of thought, and that's why I'm such a good songwriter. My partner, Mick McLaren, will tell you he's a better songwriter. Maybe he is, but my songs sell more. Does that make me arrogant? Yes, I guess it does.

Anyway I've got to get to work. I'm trying to write a song to help Mick's nephew Rayne through a rough time. He's going to need it because if what I've heard through the gossip grapevine is true, he's in a world of hurt. Or maybe I should explain my thoughts on relationships to Rayne. Nah, I'll just write a song. Love and heartache. Hopefully, the song will help Rayne along with a lot of others as I'm sure most will relate in some way. And, of course, it'll help me and Mick if it turns out to be a hit.

PART 1

SOLDIER OUT OF UNIFORM

CHAPTER 1

Just Outside of Cooper, Texas
Wednesday Evening
September 17, 1958

AYNE

Staring down the empty highway, my mind had nowhere to turn but to the here and now. Not having anything to think about certainly was hard on a guy.

Jagged asphalt beneath my feet interlaced with ankle-high Johnson grass. Its tiny seeds clung to my boots and new blue jeans. Alongside the roadway, large cracks split the earth in the black clay soil. Gumbo soil, the old folks called it. Good for growing cotton. Not good for much else.

An ant crawled over the toe of my boot in an attempt to get back to its colony. Overhead, a bird cried out as it perched high on a telephone wire. Things I never would've noticed if I hadn't been hitchhiking on this lonely stretch.

Though I stood still, my mind wandered down an all-too-familiar path.

It seemed to me there were two ways of being in the world. Very secure. So secure that you eat, drink and sleep without even thinking about it. And insecure. A state that requires a person to keep thinking on their toes. Nothing stable. Nothing for certain. I'd learned to enjoy both as I'd found any situation could, and most often would, turn on a dime.

My thoughts continued on this way for some time as I wasn't going anywhere fast. I turned around to face the long road ahead of me and started to walk forward. But every once in a while, I stuck out my thumb and turned around, checking behind me for an oncoming automobile. My socked feet sweated inside my just-a-little-too-big boots. Dang, it was hot in Texas. Even in September.

But I must say, 1958 was turning out to be a good year in spite of the fact that years ending in odd numbers always seemed to turn out best for me. However 1958, despite the many changes it had already brought, was pretty good. Considering I didn't have any money, and I'd just lost my longtime girlfriend Jennifer. The little bubble-headed twit took off with my ex-best friend, Carl, who I was stationed with in Alaska.

"Good riddance. I'd rather be alone than with those two."

Can't believe Jennifer and Carl thought I would still be their friend. Even as I replayed their double betrayal in my head for the millionth time, my heart twisted in pain. Would it ever cease?

I tried to think of something else. Something pleasant. But that was hard to do. Because right now, right here, I needed to concentrate. My stomach had started to rumble, and I had nothing to eat in the AWOL bag swinging on my back. Sweat ran down my face. The back of my shirt was getting downright dank.

Maybe hitchhiking was a bad idea. Actually, no traffic was coming by, so I wasn't even hitchhiking—I was just walking backwards with my thumb stuck out.

After a few more seconds, I decided it was time to turn around and walk forward yet again. But just before I turned, I glimpsed a speck on the horizon signaling hope. Yes, a car. Some kind of big black automobile wavering in the mirage of heat that beat down on the Texas highway. As it drew closer, I could make out it was a hearse . . . a Cadillac hearse . . . and it was indeed slowing down—maybe to give me a ride. As it pulled up alongside me, the passenger window rolled down.

"Rayne, is that you?"

To my surprise, I recognized the voice. It was my old friend Marion. I hadn't seen him in more than five years, definitely not since high school. He'd filled out a little more, but he still looked the same with his shiny blond hair. Only the freckles across his nose had faded a little.

Dumbfounded and still a little drunk from the night before, I wasn't sure exactly what was happening. I mean even if Marion and the driver wanted to, they couldn't give me a ride because a coffin filled up the back. Marion must have read my mind. He jumped out and opened the back passenger door. Inside I could see a small jump seat.

"You're tall and lanky, but I bet you can fit here if you crouch a little," Marion said, sweeping his hand inside.

I still hadn't said anything at this point. However, I didn't want to seem unappreciative of his offer. I took my bag off my shoulder, swung it on the floorboard and hopped in. I barely fit, but I wasn't going to complain.

Marion shut the door behind me before getting back into the shotgun position where he had been sitting.

The radio played "I Don't Wanna See You Cryin'" by the Chordettes. It had an upbeat tempo and sounded kind of happy despite its title. I still didn't know what to say so I remained silent.

Soon enough Marion introduced me to the driver, who turned out to be his uncle from another city. Seems Marion had been visiting when he got the call to transport a soldier's body to his hometown so he could be buried. And, as fate would have it, that hometown just happened to be mine and Marion's. Therefore, I didn't want to ask who the soldier was because I was fairly certain it would be someone I knew.

Marion turned up the radio. "I like this song," he said. "But I really like the A-side of the record." Turning around in his seat, he said, "'Mr. Sandman'. You like that, don't ya?"

I nodded while wondering how in the Sam Hill Marion knew what song was on the A-side of a record.

Once Marion had turned back around in his seat, I twisted and looked at the coffin beside me. The copper handles gleamed. Someone had put out some money on this guy's funeral. Or maybe it was the government. Finally, my curiosity could stand it no longer, and I asked the question I didn't want to know the answer to.

"So who's in the coffin?" I tried to sound casual.

"It's a casket, not a coffin," the silver-haired driver said, staring straight ahead. "A coffin has six sides and a casket has four." He motioned the outline of a coffin with his hands while holding the steering steady with his knee. "But I knew what you meant."

"Uncle Norris has been in the business a long time. He likes to talk the details," Marion said, turning around again. "Rayne, the guy in the box is Gene Ratcliff."

I sucked in my breath. Gene lived down the street from us. He was older than me by about eight years, so we weren't close, but I still knew him. Knew his family.

Marion continued, "He was killed by friendly fire."

My heart jerked in my chest at the words "friendly fire." I never understood that term. I mean I knew it meant killed by your own people accidentally. But maybe a better choice of words would be "accidental fire" as a bullet that takes your life is certainly not a friendly one.

Glancing at the casket, I wondered if Gene's soul had already departed to heaven. The thought he might be here with us zipping along the highway in a brand-new Cadillac hearse with the radio and refrigerated air blasting was a little much. I shivered, knowing that as a pilot in the Air Force, I too could be coming home in a hearse someday. Being a soldier was a dangerous occupation.

When I'd been stationed up in Alaska, it got so cold we could only work on the airplane engines in the big hangers for fifteen minutes at a time before they had to warm us up again. I dreaded to think what would happen if I got stuck outside somewhere in the bad weather. Even in my cold weather gear it could be fatal.

"Uncle," Marion said, jostling me from my thoughts, "tell Rayne what happened the other day that was so funny. You know what I'm talking about."

"Oh, yeah. I think I know what you're referring to . . ." Uncle Norris let out a little chuckle before beginning his tale. "Let me see. I don't know where to begin." He let out another laugh. "So, I was sitting up front in the passenger seat of our hearse here, and the new guy, Bernie, was driving. It was his first time driving in a funeral procession, and he's asking me questions. 'Is this the right speed? Am I going too fast?' Anyway, this was a really big funeral, and the line of cars behind us was long and winding, so Bernie's understandably nervous. And just as he is starting to relax, we hear little sputtering sounds coming from the hearse's engine. Then much to our surprise, the hearse glides to an abrupt halt. Bernie could hardly steer it to the side of the road, it lost power so fast. Well, the driver behind us slammed on his brakes so he wouldn't hit us. Then he doesn't know what to do, so he pulls around in front of us. And the car behind him pulls over to the side of us.

"I look back, and by now, the whole procession is in the process of stopping behind us. People are getting out to come help. Well . . . I couldn't think what could be wrong with our almost new hearse. Bernie's panicked. So I get out to open the hood . . ."

Uncle Norris let out another little snort of laughter. I could tell he was leading up to a big finish by the way he was trying to compose himself. I watched in the rearview mirror as his face flushed and he took out a handkerchief to wipe his brow. "I glanced back," he continued, "and the long line of cars are all pulled over to the side of the road, waiting for us to do something. Someone suggested the pallbearers carry the casket on to the gravesite. However, we weren't close enough. Anyways, the sun was beating down on us in our Sunday suits, and sweat was just rolling down our faces. We really were perplexed. So Bernie starts to pray. 'Lord Jesus, help us get this dead body to the cemetery.' And lo and behold, a guy gets out of his truck that he has idling in line with the other mourners and says to me that he's a mechanic. Says if he can't get the hearse started right away, we can put the casket in the back of his pickup truck and continue on to the cemetery."

"Oh, no." I chuckled at Uncle Norris's tale. "Don't tell me that's what you did?" There wasn't much room in the small jump seat, and it was hard to sit still and laugh at the same time. I hugged my shoulders, trying to make myself as small as possible.

"No, no sir." Uncle Norris looked back at me while he was driving. "You're not going to believe what happened next. The mechanic looked under the hood, then got behind the wheel. In a moment, he went back to his truck and came back with a five-gallon gas can. Filled her up, started the engine, and we were on our way."

"I bet the family was furious," Marion said. "Did they say anything to you?"

"Oh, yeah!" Uncle Norris said. "Turns out the guy who'd died was something of a jokester, and his family and friends thought he'd planned the whole thing. But I had to tell them he didn't, that it was my fault for not filling the tank when I took the hearse to be washed the day before. Which it was really Bernie who had taken the hearse to be washed, but I didn't want to point fingers."

"So you didn't fire Bernie?" I asked.

"No, son. I didn't even chastise Bernie. He felt bad enough." Uncle Norris stared at the road ahead. "All I told Bernie is that we all make mistakes." His voice took on a serious tone. "That's how we learn. And I'll bet Bernie never runs out of gas again."

I knew what he meant. I had learned the hard way more than once myself. I took a deep breath. The scent of lilies lingering in the back of the hearse made me slightly heady.

"Rayne," Marion's voice broke through my thoughts, "do you want us to let you off at your father's shoe store or your home?"

My house just outside of town on Dog Town Road was out of their way. In fact, the shoe store was, too.

"Just let me off at the funeral home. I'll call someone to come get me."

Uncle Norris twisted around in his seat again. "No, I insist on dropping you at your home. A few more minutes isn't going to hurt anyone. I'm sure your folks are anxious to see you."

"Thank you, sir," I said. I really did want to go straight home. As I looked out the windshield over Marion's shoulder, I was relieved Uncle Norris had turned his attention back to driving. How he managed to stay in his lane while looking backward, talking to me, I'd never know. If I'd been at the wheel, we'd probably all have been in a ditch by this point.

Marion moved forward and turned up the radio. I gazed out the side window at terrain I'd seen a thousand times before. Swiftly we passed fields of winter wheat and cotton. Other fields lying fallow held only grasses gently swaying in the late afternoon breeze. Soon the sun would set, and the heat wouldn't be so oppressive.

———

The hearse pulled up to our modest frame house. I saw my mother through the kitchen window screen as she washed dishes. In two seconds, she was pulling off her apron. In three more, she was out the front door and rushing down the walkway toward the hearse. Her light gray eyes shone with fear. I saw it from where I sat in the backseat of the hearse. I realized what must be going through her mind—her boy coming home in a hearse. Immediately, I threw open the back passenger door and stepped out to put her mind at ease.

"Rayne," she cried when she saw me appear. Her worried look disappeared faster than a rabbit being chased by a hawk.

"Mama." I went to hug her. "Remember my friend Marion from school?"

Marion waved from his rolled down window. Smoothing his bright blond hair into place, he shot her a million-dollar smile.

"And this is Marion's Uncle Norris."

Uncle Norris flashed us a big grin and waved from the driver's seat. At that moment, it registered how much the two looked alike.

"They picked me up on the highway, Mama. Gave me a lift all the way home. If not for them, I'd probably still be out there with my thumb stuck in the air."

Recovering from the shock of having a hearse roll up to her front yard, my mother brushed back her wavy shoulder-length hair. "Thank you so much for bringing my boy home. We've missed him so. He's been gone too long." She hugged me again and chimed, "Thank you. Thank you. Thank you." This time she managed a smile as she spoke, but I saw the tears in her eyes.

"You're welcome." Uncle Norris leaned toward Marion's rolled down window. "Now if you'll excuse us, we must be on our way." He waved once more, and Marion rolled up the window.

Looking down at Mama, I noticed streaks of gray framing her face.

"Rayne," my daddy's voice called out from behind the screen door. The light behind him outlined his tall, thin frame. As always, his thick hair was cut in a military-style flattop. "Rayne," he called out louder, "what are you doing home? Your letter said to expect you next week."

"Daddy, you know how things go with my work. I don't ever know when I'll be coming and going. Besides, I wanted to surprise Mama." I said as I moved forward to give her another big hug.

"Yes, indeed, you did surprise me. Almost gave me a heart attack." There was laughter in her voice. "Come on inside. I'm about finished cooking supper."

Even as she said the words, I caught the scent of fried pork chops wafting through the screen door. The familiar scent made my mouth salivate and my stomach rumble. Not only did it remind me of the many happy meals I'd had with my parents, brother and sisters, but it also reminded me that no one cooks like my mama. Especially the cooks at the commissary. They did their best, but I knew now just how good I'd had it growing up when it came to flavorful food. I'd never take another home-cooked meal for granted again.

"Where is everyone?" I asked as I took my place at the Formica table. I had gifts for each of my siblings, and I anticipated the surprise on their faces when they walked in the door and saw me. "Oh, Michael's at ball practice. The girls, they're at after-school activities right now. But they'll all be home soon. In fact, they're due any minute now." My mother made a plate for me and my father. "Now, you two go ahead . . . eat while it's still warm. The others will be along directly."

My father put his hand on my shoulder and gave it a gentle squeeze before he took his seat at the head of the table.

"I heard about that girl of yours leaving you for your best friend," he said.

His direct words made me wince inside. My heart ached every time I thought about Jennifer and Carl. I should never have told Uncle Mick about the betrayal when I called him the other day.

Even though I didn't look my father in the eye, I knew he was looking at me.

"Let your loss be your lesson, son." He patted my shoulder again.

I nodded that I would, but I couldn't talk about it. Not just yet. Changing the subject, I said, "Daddy, the man who was doing background checks for my new job, did he talk to both you and Mama?"

"Yes, he did. And he talked to Arnold Smith, too."

"That doesn't surprise me. They asked me to also list a few people who have known me for years. Arnold Smith has known me my whole life. I wrote and told him they might interview him about my new career."

"Good thing you told him. Because otherwise he'd have been taken by surprise. The man who interviewed us was a bit intense in Arnold's eyes. As Arnold said, I wouldn't want to have to go through that again."

"Oh, no. I hope the interviews went well with you and Mama."

"They did, it's just, Rayne . . . I don't know how to say this except putting it out there plainly. As your parents, we're concerned about you working for this place. It's so secret. They told us not to tell a soul who you were working for. You know, it's scary because we don't really understand everything you'll be doing and everywhere you'll be going." He put his calloused hand over mine. "I mean the Air Force is something we understand. This other is a whole different ballgame, if you know what I mean."

"Rayne, I've got lemon chess pie for dessert." Mama was an expert at changing the subject when things got too tense. "Your favorite. Must have had an intuition that you'd make it home early."

"That sounds great, Mama," I said as the front screen door banged open, racket followed by a clamor in the front hallway. I could hear both the girls' and Michael's voices as they all piled through, one after another. My father's eyes twinkled as he held a finger up to his mouth in the universal "hush" sign. Mama wadded up her apron in her hands, anticipating the surprise.

Michael came in first, and I swear he almost started crying as he ran to my side, pulling me up for a hug. Joan and little Mae heard him say, "When did you get home?" and they began to scream even before they rounded the kitchen corner.

"Rayne, Rayne," they yelled in unison as they wrapped their arms around me. Then they, too, started to cry, which made me start to tear up. I wiped my eyes on the back of my hand, trying to regain my composure. I'd been gone far too long. Joan no longer looked like a little girl. She had a sophisticated hairstyle and was even wearing makeup. Little Mae was . . . well, no longer little.

"Why didn't you tell us you were coming home?" Joan cried out. "We'd have planned a big, big homecoming party." She was at that age when parties were important. "We still can. Everyone in town will want to see you. You've been away too long. I'd say at least two years. And the last time you visited was way too short. Why, it seemed you left as soon as you got here."

"No, no, Joan, I can't do a party. I'm only stopping by on my way through. Couldn't get this close and not see my family." I took Mama's hand and pulled her close to where Joan and Mae huddled around me. "I'm sorry our time together is so short. But on a happier note, I've got presents for everyone. Mama, where'd you put my AWOL bag?"

"Did you go AWOL?" Mama's voice cracked.

"No, that's a term we use for our bag when we go on a short leave."

Little Mae tugged at Mama's sleeve. "Go get his AWOL bag, Mama. I can't wait to see what he got me. I bet it is something good. Rayne always gives the best presents."

———

Later that night I was sitting on the front porch rocking chair when my brother Michael came outside with a couple of Stokes cigars. Since Mama didn't let us smoke in the house, we usually went down to the creek where she couldn't smell it.

Without a word, I got up and silently acknowledged him. Together we made our way around to the back of the house toward the creek, careful so as not to wake our parents as we passed by their open window where curtains flapped lightly in the breeze. We knew Daddy would be getting up at the rooster's first crow to take care of the cows before he went to work. He needed all the rest he could get as he didn't seem his usual chipper self the last few times we talked on the phone.

Silvery moonlight lit our way down the well-worn path to the creek. In the distance, a lone owl hooted. And, of course, cicadas sang their eternal song as they always did on warm southern nights, a sound I missed when I was away up north.

After about ten minutes, we arrived at our destination—two big rocks near the creek. But before I could sit down, Michael said, "You know what would taste good with this cigar? A big ol' cantaloupe."

I nodded and said, "I'll go get it."

Michael was right. Nothing tasted quite as good with a cigar as a stolen cantaloupe from old Mr. Jeffers's garden. I'd be lucky if I could sneak in and get one before his dog Jinx started barking. Jinx wasn't a mean dog, so I wasn't scared, but he was a loud dog, and I wasn't particularly fond of the idea of waking up the neighbors.

Sprinting back up the creek bed, I made good time to the garden. Coming out of the tree line, I stole up to the area where the cantaloupes were growing. If the old man had been awake, I'd have asked if I could have one. But seeing as it was nearing midnight, I decided it would be best to just take it.

Behind me, I heard the owl hoot again. It was close, possibly in the tree overhead. The sound of it broke my concentration. I tripped on a small branch and let out an "ouch" before I could help myself. Up near the Jeffers house, I heard Jinx let out a bark, which turned into a growl and then an outright howl. I squatted down near a cantaloupe and remained stone still.

"What is it?" I heard Mrs. Jeffers ask her husband.

"I don't know. Can't see anything," he answered. The light on the porch silhouetted his form. He had a rifle in his hand.

"Think it's one of those coyotes again?" Even though she whispered, the night was so still I could hear it across the field. "I saw one the other day stealing a cantaloupe."

After a few minutes, Mr. Jeffers said, "Yeah, it's probably a coyote. Let's go back inside."

I waited until their door squeaked close and the porch light went out. Then I grabbed a couple of cantaloupes off the vine. A medium-sized one for me. A a larger one for Michael. As I neared the creek bed, I saw a flash of silver in the moonlight. It was Michael getting out his knife. Silently, I handed him the larger melon, and watched as he expertly cut it into sections. Then I sat down on the rock beside him and got out my knife, preparing to do the same.

"This is one juicy melon," said Michael, his voice barely a whisper.

"Yeah, I gave you the good one. Figured might as well treat you right as I'm not going to be seeing you for a while."

"Do you know where you're going next?"

Jokingly, I replied, "If I told you I'd have to kill you."

"Then I don't want to know," Michael said as he finished a bite of cantaloupe.

We ate in silence for a few minutes before my brother threw his pieces of rind out in the bushes. Coming back to the rock, he pulled out a cigar and lit it. I could see his face in the flash of fire from the lighter. He looked older than his sixteen years.

"You're getting a beard," I said matter-of-factly.

He rubbed the dark growth on his cheek in appreciation of my comment before adding, "And a mustache. The principal told me to shave the other day. Coach too."

Michael and I were natural athletes. The one saving grace we both had. That and, for me, the fact that I was good at math. Michael not so much, but he had charisma. And he was a handsome sort with his dark wavy hair and his gray eyes that reminded me of our mama's. People liked him, and I knew he'd do okay in life. Reaching into my pocket, I pulled out the Peace Silver Dollar I'd brought especially for him. His face broke into a wide grin as I handed it to him.

Michael liked a good coin. He'd been collecting them since he was ten.

"Now don't you let little Mae get ahold of that," I said. "She wouldn't understand its significance, and she'd spend it in town on movies, popcorn and soda."

"Mae's like a baby raccoon, isn't she? If you don't lock it down, she'll snatch it up and take it off to her nest. Every so often I have to go in her room and see what she's got hid of mine."

I knew he spoke the truth about Mae. She was a good kid, but she often helped herself to whatever she wanted. Especially if it was shiny and bright.

We smoked without talking in that comfortable way people do when they know each other well. I was leaning back looking up at the moon when some creature came out of the bushes and nabbed one of the half-eaten cantaloupe rinds Michael had thrown nearby. I almost fell over backwards the noise startled me so, but I recovered in time to see the coyote.

Michael started to laugh, but not for long.

Because just then another coyote jumped out of the bushes and took the rest of the rind.

It didn't take us long to realize we were surrounded in a semi-circle by four or five pairs of bright shining eyes.

Michael picked up a nearby tree limb and lit its dead leaves with his lighter. As he waved it in their direction, I shouted and kicked at the dirt, "Go on. Git. Go on."

Thankfully, they turned tail and fled. But not without taking what they'd come for—the last piece of cantaloupe.

Michael put out the burning tree limb by covering it in dirt and stomping on it. We were careful to make certain it was totally out before leaving.

Overhead, the full moon shone brightly, lighting our path back home.

In the distance the coyotes began to howl. Jinx barked at the racket before joining in with a blood-curdling howl himself.

Mr. Jeffers rattled his back door open once again. "Dad-burned coyotes!" he exclaimed to the still night air.

———

Morning came early. Real early. If not for the sun blasting through the thin drapes by my cot, I could have slept another few hours. Apparently, it hadn't taken long for Michael to take over our bedroom after I left for the Air Force. The first thing he did was put my twin bed out in the shed. No reason for me to get mad about it. It was way too short for me anyway, and I didn't like sleeping with my feet hanging off the end. So, I guess he did me a favor if you want to look at it that way.

"Oh, oh, oh," I said as I sat up on my cot stretching the aching muscles in my back.

Looking over at Michael's new full-size bed, I noticed no one was in it. It dawned on me he was probably out helping Dad with the chickens. As I grabbed the jeans I had worn the night before, I guessed I'd go out and help, too. But first, a cup of coffee and one of those biscuits I smelled baking. Seems all my memories of home involved Mama's cooking in one way or another. I really missed her cooking when I was on the road. Heck, I really missed her. At least I could count on one female in my life to always be honest and true. I knew she loved me through and through.

Walking down the hallway, I glanced in to see my two sisters still asleep. They seemed so young and innocent. I had missed them, too. Their laughter and silliness. I could always look to them for a really bad joke or stupid story, and both girls were chock full of crazy songs. To be perfectly honest, I think they usually made them up as they went along. Still, they were pretty funny.

I lingered a moment longer, watching them slumber.

Mae had loved the lucky rabbit key chain I brought home for her, and Joan had seemed to like the silver thimble. She was getting old enough to sew. Maybe she'd actually find it useful. I was happy I could get them trinkets because they didn't get a lot of things. Especially gifts just for fun.

As I made my way to the kitchen table, I heard the rumble of a big engine. Glancing outside, I saw what appeared to be two longhorn steer horns. I looked again. Yes, that's what I was seeing. Two longhorn steer horns on the hood of a white Cadillac convertible. And inside the

Cadillac was none other than the famous, or should I say infamous, Cowboy Larson.

Tall, tan and fit with a head full of thick sandy-blond hair just starting to gray at the temples. I swear, if it weren't for his clothes, he would've looked like a sophisticated businessman. His western shirt complete with rhinestones and fringe was pretty hard to look at this early in the morning with its loud shade of dark purple and lavender paisley insets. Maybe this is why my mother always said Cowboy has such a colorful personality when she talked about his high jinxs.

All in all, I admit it was hard not to like him. And my spirits lifted as I realized he'd come for a visit. Cowboy had an easy way about him when it came to making people feel good.

My mother was taking biscuits out of the oven when she heard Cowboy pull up, and she dropped them down on top of the stove. She went to greet him, scurrying faster than a chicken on a June bug. Mama had known Cowboy Larson forever, it seemed. When they were growing up, he was very close to her and her sister Margaret. In fact, he was the music partner of Margaret's husband, Mick McLaren.

"Cowboy," she shrieked. "Cowboy, what brings you to this part of the country? I swear, haven't seen you 'round these parts in a month of Sundays."

As he opened his arms to give her a bearhug, Cowboy said, "Samantha, I've come to chauffeur your boy to Dallas. Mick asked me to stop and pick him up on my way down from Oklahoma."

My ears perked up. I'd called Uncle Mick the week before to tell him I was coming through town earlier than planned, but I hadn't expected this. Usually, I slipped around hitchhiking or riding buses. It'd be nice to ride in style all the way to the big city. If only Cowboy's many adoring music fans didn't slow us down along the way. I put butter on a biscuit and let it melt before putting the biscuit in my mouth. As I savored the taste, I took a deep breath and relaxed. Today was already going better than expected, and it was hardly thirty minutes past sunrise.

Then I caught a glimpse of my mama's disappointed face, and my heart seized. I'd told her I was only passing through on my way to another mission, but I knew she'd hoped for more time. In truth, so had I.

"Mama, maybe I could stay and ride the bus into downtown Dallas tomorrow?"

"No." she gripped her apron. "You go with Cowboy. You'll have more fun, and his Caddy is a way more comfortable ride than an old rickety bus."

———

So here I was riding in an open convertible with Cowboy Larson, or just Cowboy, as family and friends called him—a true music legend. Even heard him called a national treasure on the radio a few times. As we flew down the highway, more than a few people shouted and whooped it up as we passed them at lightning speed. Cowboy always gave them a wave and a smile. I just sat and looked straight ahead not wanting to draw too much attention to myself.

The wind in my hair felt good. And the morning sun was out just enough to keep us warm and toasty. I pushed up my aviator sunglasses and enjoyed the ride.

Just outside Dallas, we pulled into a filling station to get gas. As the teenage attendant came outside to check our oil and pump our gas, we both went inside the station where an older man stood behind the cash register. He had on a white short-sleeved shirt and black tie. A red embroidered patch on his pocket let us know his name was Gavin.

"Good morning." Gavin's eyes flashed recognition as he looked up to see Cowboy Larson. "What can I do for you?"

"Oh, we two are just getting some snacks for the road . . . and I need to use your restroom please, sir." Cowboy kept his recognizable voice low out of habit.

As I perused the snack aisle, I caught sight of Cowboy getting the key to the men's room from the cashier.

"It's on the left side of the station," the older man called out.

My back was turned to the station door, but I heard the little bell on the door tinkle as Cowboy went out. Looking up and down the overloaded racks of chips, crackers, cookies and more, I finally found what

I was looking for—pistachios, my favorite. Next, I got an icy cold bottled drink and went up front to pay. No sooner had I gone out the door than I heard a commotion. A group of fans had Cowboy pinned up against the cinderblock side of the station. They wanted his autograph.

"Folks," he said calmly, "let me go to the bathroom first, then I promise I will sign an autograph for all of you." With that he took the station bathroom key with its big square tag attached and opened the locked restroom door. Before he slipped inside, he turned back to the crowd and said, "I promise I'll wash my hands."

The fans, mostly females, giggled. But they settled down and politely waited over by a few parked cars. I thought I should get Cowboy a soda and maybe some chips or something. He'd probably be starved by the time he finished signing autographs. The last thing he'd want to do was go back inside the station.

So, I went in search of something to sustain him. When I returned with extra snacks for him, he was already working the crowd with his irrepressible personality so I got in the car to wait for him. True to his word, he was signing an autograph for everyone. All twenty of them. I munched on my pistachios as I waited in the Cadillac, careful not to get any hulls on the floorboard.

The young attendant finished checking the oil and hurried around the car to clean the dirty windshield, all while gasoline pumped into the tank of the Caddy. Carefully, he made sure not to impale himself on the longhorn steer horns as he worked at the front of the automobile. When he'd finished, he lingered nearby and watched the show with me.

"Man, oh man, I wish I could play the guitar like Cowboy Larson," he said as he stared in amazement at the chaos going on just feet away. "Do you think he needs some help getting away from those autograph seekers?" He turned and addressed me. "Should I go run them off?"

"No," I said, "he seems to be enjoying the attention."

The attendant watched for a few more minutes, then without looking back at me said, "I bet it gets old."

"What?" I said.

"The fans. The constant attention. Being in the limelight."

I had actually asked Cowboy's musical partner, my Uncle Mick, this very question a few years back. He told me it never gets old because the crowds electrify him from the inside out. I didn't share this with the attendant. Instead, I searched the glove compartment for a piece of paper. I noticed he already had a pen tucked neatly in his plastic pocket protector.

"Here," I said, handing him the paper I managed to find, "go get yourself an autograph, too."

In two skips of a secondhand, the awestruck attendant was in line behind the last girl, who was crying as she moved closer and closer to Cowboy. Occasionally, she'd wipe her tears away with the sleeve of her white cotton shirt, making her bouncy brunette ponytail swing. I wished I had a camera to capture the moment. For myself more than Cowboy because he probably already had more than a few photos of just such a scene.

Standing by the Cadillac's gas tank, I waited for the pump to indicate the tank was full. Finally, I heard the click and let the lock off the handle. Carefully, I held the handle away from me so I wouldn't get drops of gasoline on my pants. Last thing I wanted was to smell like gasoline all day.

Glancing back at the small crowd of fans, I saw that a couple more people had joined the fray. Which meant I'd probably have time to clean the windshield again while I waited. The attendant had missed a couple of spots, but I'd been too polite to point it out. "Oh boy," I muttered to myself. At this pace, we were never going to get to Dallas in time for me to go to the drive-in movies as I'd hoped. Or maybe we would. Cowboy was as fast a driver as he was a talker.

Then a thought hit me. I got behind the seat of the big car. The keys were still in the ignition. Firing it up, I drove slowly around to the side of the station.

"Mr. Larson," I said in my most professional-sounding bodyguard voice, "are you about ready to go? Don't want to miss your big meeting."

Cowboy looked up smiling and gave me a wink.

"Just give me a minute to get everyone in line." Quickly he dashed off signatures as he made his way toward the car. No more gabbing with every single fan making them feel as if they were the only person on the face of God's green earth. Cowboy handed off the restroom key to the attendant who was smiling big as he looked at the autograph he'd just gotten.

When Cowboy got to the passenger side seat, he hopped in, and we took off.

Nodding at the drink and chips in the sack at his feet, I said, "Got you something to tide you over."

As we drove along, he didn't ask to return to the driver's seat. And I didn't offer. Silently, I watched the passing scenery lost in my thoughts. As always, they returned to Jennifer. A pain seared through me when I thought of how I'd found them in each other's arms. How she'd come to find me later that night as I was making my way back to the barracks. I remembered what her face had looked like as she cried, trying to get me back. How I'd cried and almost accepted her back. Because I didn't want it to end. I wanted it to last, but I just couldn't pretend . . .

"Hey," Cowboy gave me a little jab in my right arm. "Rayne . . . I know you love her. And I'm not going to lie to you . . . it's going to hurt for a little while . . . but you need to let it go."

"How did you know what I was thinking about?" My throat choked on the words, and I had to fight to keep my emotions in check.

"You had that 'someone's stabbing me in the heart' look just now." Cowboy stopped talking and crunched a chip. "Like someone was killing you from the inside out kind of pain."

Looking down, I noticed my hands were clenched in fists of rage. Every muscle in my body was tense. It embarrassed me that he'd read me so easily. Uncle Mick must've told Cowboy, too. I was going to have to give him heck about having diarrhea of the mouth.

Cowboy stared off across an open field as we drove along. "It hurts a lot, don't it?" His voice grew softer. "But I swear, you're going to get over her. I promise you will."

"I ain't ever going to get over it." My voice was sharper than I meant for it to be.

"You will," he said. "It's just going to take a little time."

I gave him a weak smile before turning my attention back to the wheel.

He held out a chip in my direction. I took it without taking my eyes off the road.

"Trust me," he said, "I know about these things. I write love songs for a living."

I bit down hard on the chip. Indeed, he did. And I was probably providing him with enough fodder for a whole new album today.

CHAPTER 2

ARLA

When I got the job as Mick and Cowboy's assistant, I was over the moon! I wasn't used to having spectacular things happen to me. I could hardly breathe when I first found out. Now I'd been working with them and their music company for over a year. And it never ceased to amaze me how they made me feel more like a family member than an employee. Because of their loyalty to me, I made sure to work hard for them around the clock, often putting in extra hours I didn't get paid for. No one had to tell me twice that I was darn lucky to have this job. Shoot, people would kill to get this job. And I'm not sure I don't mean those words literally by the way some of Mick and Cowboy's fans treated me on the road. Anyway, being their assistant was about the best thing that'd ever happened to me. I woke up every morning just raring to go to work.

Today I was patiently waiting at the McLaren mansion for Cowboy to get here. He was bringing a load of new vinyl records to be distributed. Sure hoped they'd be okay in the heat of his car trunk because that was the way he was transporting them. Maybe they'd be okay. If they weren't, I don't know what I'd do. All the country music radio stations were waiting to hear their new song "Delta County Blues." Perfect, since Cowboy had got his start singing and playing the Delta blues.

Tapping my new patent leather shoe, I decided to head to the kitchen for a swig of water. Swinging open the door to the galley, I discovered Mick's wife, Margaret, sitting at the table reading a romance novel. Her chestnut brown hair was pulled back in a ponytail, making her look sixteen instead of thirty-six. Beside her was a bowl with leftover cake frosting. I watched as she stopped reading so she could run her index finger around the inside of the bowl before putting it in her mouth. Afterwards, she used a clean tea towel to wipe her hand dry. Then back to her story. She didn't even seem to notice I'd walked into the room.

Quietly, I moved to the refrigerator behind her and looked inside for a pitcher of ice water. The cake she'd just made was resting under a glass cover on the nearby counter. Without looking up, she said, "Don't touch the cake, Darla. It's for Rayne's birthday. You can have one of the cupcakes I made with the leftover batter. They're sitting out on top of the oven."

I watched as she flipped another page and continued reading.

"How did you know I was in here?" I said as I took one of the fluffy white cupcakes.

"Eyes in the back of my head. That's what happens when you have three kids. You get eyes in the back of your head." She turned a page as she said the words.

As I walked to the backdoor window, I gazed out at Margaret's flower garden. The last blooms of summer were parading their beauty.

It was then that we heard what sounded like a cow in the front drive.

"MOOOOOO!" The obnoxious sound came again.

Howling and yelping, the dogs barked up a storm. By the sound of it, you'd think the world was gonna end. In short, the early morning stillness was completely destroyed by the colossal uproar out front.

Margaret bolted upright and ran toward the front door. I clambered close behind.

"Cowboy," she shouted through the open window screen as she ran, "you're early! And oh Lawdy, look who is with you. Rayne!"

As we went out onto the front drive, Cowboy leaned over from the passenger seat and blew his Caddy's horn one more time.

"MOOOOOO!" the big horn on the Cadillac blared.

I almost peed my pants, it was so loud.

But it didn't seem to faze Margaret. She made her way around the longhorn steer hood ornament bolted to the front of the hood and saddled up beside the driver seat. "Rayne," she said as she put her hands on either side of his face, "how's my favorite nephew? Mick's told me all about you and Jennifer. And I have to tell you, son, we never liked her anyway. Prissy little sass. She wasn't good enough for you. She wasn't nearly as pretty as she thought she was. Can't believe what she did to you. If I ever see her, I'm going to slap her silly. Even if it's in church. I'll slap her hard. Right in front of God and everyone."

So, this is the sweet little nephew Margaret talked about incessantly. He wasn't little. In fact, he was rather tall. And his face was way too handsome. Why in the world would some girl break his heart? She must have had good reason. And with his pretty-boy good looks, he may have given her more than one. Experience had made me wary of pretty boys.

A noise from behind me broke my reverie.

Cowboy had already climbed out of the convertible and was searching in the trunk for his records and luggage. "Remind me not to get on Margaret's bad side," he said, smiling as he turned in my direction to hand over an overstuffed briefcase.

Then he looked at Rayne, and his face broke out in a big grin. "No one in this family is ever going to forgive Jennifer for what she's done to you, Rayne. You better never try to get back with her. Might as well find someone new because none of us will ever get over it."

"What's all this? What did this horrible Jennifer do?" I asked as I grabbed the handle of Cowboy's guitar case in the back seat with my free hand.

"She broke Rayne's heart," Margaret said, hands on her hips.

"Oh, yeah?" I looked over at Rayne still sitting in the driver's seat. "He doesn't look too broken up to me."

Rayne flashed a smile in my direction.

I swear my heart melted at the sight. But my brain instantly put a stop to my foolish swooning, flashing a warning not to get mixed up with a pretty boy. Besides, he'd probably think he was too good for a common country girl like me.

Margaret's favorite nephew got out of the car, leisurely stretching as he did so.

He was one of those guys who had huge biceps and thigh muscles. You know the type, the kind of guy with bulging muscles that make his pants and shirts fit a little too tight. I watched as he took off his aviator sunglasses. His thick dark hair was slicked back in the latest look. Elvis hair. But not as long as Elvis's because he was in the Air Force. Or so I'd heard.

I swear that Jennifer must be looney for letting this one go. Because honestly, he was just all-over gorgeous. But I wasn't going to get involved. There must be something wrong with him. I had found this to be the case for most men. So, I decided not to judge his ex-girl too harshly. Anyway, my music career was my focus. My one and only focus. I did not need to know more about this Rayne. Or his girlfriend troubles.

Putting on my proper business assistant's voice, I said, "Cowboy, I intend to distribute these new vinyl records you brought this morning. I've called and lined up meetings at the local stations all over Dallas and Fort Worth."

"Good," Cowboy said. "Don't forget to let Mick listen to a demo before you leave. You know how picky he is about the quality."

At that moment a small boy came out from behind a large shrub. Cowboy bent down and gently picked him up. "Jamison, Jamison! I've missed you, boy."

Mick and Margaret's youngest boy put his arms around Cowboy's neck and buried his head in the musician's shirt.

"What about me?" Cowboy whispered in the boy's ear. "Did you miss me?" The little boy giggled as Cowboy's breath tickled him.

"Yes, sir, I did," the boy said as he shyly pulled at a rhinestone button near Cowboy's chest.

The dogs finally settled down once all the honking had stopped. They walked beside us as we made our way back to the house, loaded down with luggage, records and guitars. Even Jamison carried an armful of concert flyers. But I had the biggest load. Thank goodness Margaret rushed forward to take Cowboy's briefcase off my shoulder. How did she know it was so heavy it was killing me? Turning sideways to hand it off to her, I looked back at the guardhouse situated near the front of the property. The armed guard inside waved to me from his small booth. Behind him the closed metal gates loomed large, with two guitar emblems and two big letter M's for Mick McLaren. Guards weren't usually stationed at the guardhouse this early in the day. But since the recent threats on Cowboy's and Mick's lives, especially Mick's, Margaret had insisted on a guard around the clock.

A few weeks back when the first threat was made, I had asked Mick if he was afraid for his life. "Not for myself, but for my family," he'd said.

Still, I cautioned him, he should add extra bodyguards on his upcoming tour. Maybe even hire one to follow him everywhere.

"No, Darla," he'd said, laughing, "I'm not going to walk around with a bodyguard." Then he said in a reassuring voice, "You know I'm not going to die one minute before my time."

However, I couldn't help but notice he was a little more careful about his comings and goings—his meetings with fans.

Cowboy, on the other hand, acted like it was all a hoax. "I'm not going to let fear dictate my life," he'd said.

I wish I could be so bold. I found myself looking over my shoulder constantly these days.

———

Back in the office section of the main house, Mick was looking over the record label after he'd listened to their new demo. I couldn't get a read on whether he was happy with the sound or not. Cowboy sat in an overstuffed chair in the corner, one long leg thrown over the arm and the other sprawled out and bootless.

"You hurt your foot, Cowboy?" I asked.

Mick replied, still looking at the label, "Naw, he's just too lazy to take the other boot off."

Cowboy chuckled under his breath. Those two had been playing music together so long they knew each other inside and out.

I waited for Mick's final decision on the demo. He always made the final decision on everything, so I was surprised when Cowboy spoke up and reminded Mick I needed to get on the road if I was going to get the records distributed to all the stations before sundown.

Mick called out, "Rayne!"

He yelled again louder.

I tapped my foot. What in the world? Why would Mick value that muscle-bound guy's opinion over mine and Cowboy's? I tapped my foot again with impatience, but I knew better than to cross words with the boss.

Two seconds later, Rayne pushed open the office door. He'd rolled his sleeves up high on his muscular arms and combed his hair. Lawdy, as Margaret would say, I swear he was even better looking than he was an hour ago. To my left, I heard Mick rustling paper as he bent over a cardboard box stacked to the brim with records.

"Hey, Rayne. Will you take this box out to the car for Darla?"

I watched as he handed it over to Rayne, adding, "Watch it, now. It's heavy and those records are fragile."

I blushed red-hot. Not because I was embarrassed, but because I was mad. Why would Mick think I couldn't carry a box of records? Pushing past Rayne, I tried to take the box. "I can get it myself," I said with a huff.

"No," Mick moved the box back securely into Rayne's strong arms. "I want Rayne to drive you to the stations. A couple of them are in bad areas of town."

I murmured a curse as Rayne removed the box from my grasp. But before I could get myself in further trouble, Cowboy stood up and took his keys out of his pocket.

"Here," he said, handing the keys to Rayne, "use my Caddy."

The thought of riding around in Cowboy's convertible made my heart soar.

"Give me those keys," I said to Rayne. "I'm driving."

I held the front door open for the big hulk.

"Thank you, Darla." He smiled as he squeezed past me.

I don't know why, but it irked me that he seemed to be getting so much attention from Mick, Margaret, Cowboy and even little Jamison. Maybe it was because it was his birthday. It certainly wasn't his charming personality. I don't think I'd heard him put two words together at lunch earlier. I did hear him thank his Aunt Margaret for making the cake. So maybe he had some manners, but he had no life to him. He hardly acknowledged me. And he only answered questions when spoken to. Of course, Margaret had more than enough questions for him about her sister, who was his mother. I don't know, he was probably brooding about his ex-girlfriend Jennifer. Whatever the case, Mick and Margaret were certainly making on over him.

And myself, well, I knew I got on both of their nerves at least once a day. Mick said that's why he'd hired me—for my aggressive attitude. He said I needed to be tough to make it in the music industry. Wasn't enough just to sing well. And Margaret, sweet Margaret, never said anything negative, no matter how much I messed up. She forgave my every blunder, of which there were many.

Once outside, Rayne put the box of records on the back seat. "Do you think they'll melt in the Texas heat?"

"No, I plan to drive fast," I said as I took a red headscarf out of my purse. "We can take them inside at each of the stations just to be sure. I think they'll hold up better in the back seat than in the trunk."

Next, I took a list of radio stations and addresses out of my purse. I'd intentionally listed them in order of distance so I wouldn't have to backtrack. As I mentioned this fact out loud, Rayne turned to me and said in his nicest voice, "Darla, I don't care what they say about you— you're a lot smarter than you look."

"Hush up the sweet talk, Romeo," I said as I applied lipstick in the rearview mirror. "We've got work to do."

———

The first station was on the outskirts of downtown Dallas. This was one of the shadier areas of the city Mick had been referring to when he asked Rayne to go with me. I hated to admit it, but I was glad he was with me. Especially since we were driving a fancy longhorn steer convertible.

As I pulled through to the parking lot, I observed a couple of winos sitting near a drainage ditch, clutching their open bottles in brown paper sacks. One of them was eating an orange he'd peeled and broken into sections.

He slowly approached me and asked, "Would you like a piece?"

"No," I replied hastily. Then I realized by the look in his kind eyes that I'd hurt him.

"No, thank you. I'm on a diet." He put a piece of orange in his mouth and said, "You don't need to be on a diet." It was true—I was rail thin—but I had to watch my weight to keep it that way.

I looked back at the Caddy to see Rayne closing the passenger door while balancing the box of records in his other hand. He smiled at me and the man.

He walked up beside us. "Hey, aren't you Ernie Koster?"

The man smiled. "How'd you recognize me?" As he said the words, his voice became stronger, and he stood a little straighter.

"My father took me to see you one time when you played in Oklahoma City."

"Haven't played in Oklahoma City or anywhere for that matter in a long while. Not since my hand was injured."

The door to the station opened, and a well-dressed receptionist stuck her head out. "C'mon in, folks! We've been waiting for you."

Rayne and I turned toward the door. The man shuffled back to his group of friends.

"See ya around," he said with a little wave as he turned his back to us.

———

The receptionist informed us the disc jockey wanted us to come back to the area where he worked. This wasn't unusual as Mick and Cowboy were well-liked and people in the music industry went out of their way to accommodate anyone who worked for them. And that included me.

"Walk this way," the receptionist said as she moved down a dark paneled hallway toward a closed door. Quietly she opened the office door, but not before putting her perfectly polished index finger to her lips, warning us to hush.

Without a word, we walked inside the dimly lit room. I took the lone chair across from the man spinning records, and Rayne stood in the background near the door. As the DJ put another record on to play, I quickly took in his overall persona. Tall, thin, middle-aged, dark eyes and hair. Good looking, but a bit of a sloppy dresser. Cigarette hanging out of his mouth. Another one burning itself out in an overfilled glass ashtray on his desk. It was obvious the man loved what he did for a living, even if he did appear to be overworked.

In a few seconds, he took a short break and turned his attention my way. Quickly, I handed him Mick and Cowboy's latest record. He maneuvered a microphone on a stand in front of him and started to speak just as the record he was playing ended.

"Ladies and gentlemen," he took the cigarette from his mouth, "today we have a new song from Mick and Cowboy." He looked down at the label and said, "It's called 'Delta County Blues.'" With that he turned and put the record on to spin. "I bet it is going to be a good one," he said, dragging out the word "good" over the hissing sound of the vinyl before the music started.

I sat back in my chair across from him and breathed a sigh of relief as the blues guitar riffs filled the room. Looking down at my shoes, I made a mental note to get some new rubber tips for my high heels. They had worn down to a nub. I'd do it when I got my next paycheck. Not a penny was left from the last one.

All too soon the song ended, and the DJ pulled his microphone up again to speak. I wasn't worried. I could tell by his body language he liked the new music, even if it wasn't Mick and Cowboy's usual sound. I relaxed as he began his spiel to his thousands of listeners.

"What did you think about that? Great new song, huh? Don't forget you heard it here first. The first in country music." He flicked ashes in the overflowing ash tray and put the glowing cigarette back in his mouth without missing a beat. "Cowboy and Mick sure know how to write 'em, don't they? Always something new and unexpected with those two. And speaking of unexpected . . . guess who Mick and Cowboy sent us to sing live today?"

I looked around the room. Rayne was standing near the door in the shadows. I made a face at him and pointed as I mouthed the word "You?" He shook his head no.

Then, as if in a dream, I heard the words "here, little lady" broadcast over the airwaves as the DJ took the mic out of its stand and gestured toward me.

"Just a second. Our lady diva is getting into position," he said before handing it over to me.

At these words, my heart stopped. My brain froze.

Horror rose from my gut in a single wave. *Think. Think. Think. What will I sing?*

With legs made of jelly, I rose to take the microphone.

Then I took a quick glance at the DJ before starting to sing "How Great Thou Art," a gospel song I'd sung a cappella many times in church choir practice. So many times, in fact, I didn't even have to think about what I was doing.

Please, God let my voice stop quivering.

Closing my eyes, my voice became stronger and stronger.

Somewhere outside of me I heard myself hitting all the notes crystal clear. Filling the room with music from somewhere deep down in my soul.

Needless to say, I sang my heart out.

Because I knew this was a once-in-a-lifetime opportunity. An opportunity I had waited for. An opportunity I'd never asked for from Mick and Cowboy.

When I finished, I searched Rayne's face for his reaction.

He radiated pride as our eyes met. An electric jolt shot right through my heart—a moment, a feeling I'd never forget. Not even if I lived to be a hundred and four.

The DJ took the microphone from my hand. "Well, folks, I don't know what to say. I'm near swept up with emotion. No wonder Mick and Cowboy recommended her. What's your name, honey?"

"Darla . . . Darla Darling."

I bent down closer to his microphone.

"And, yes, that's my real name."

PART 2

THINKING TOO HARD

CHAPTER 3

The McLaren Mansion
Dallas, Texas
Friday Late Afternoon
September 19, 1958

ARGARET

"How in the tarnation are you two going to go on tour with the IRS breathing down your neck?"

It was a harsh question, but someone had to ask it. Over the years, I'd learned my husband Mick and his business partner, Cowboy, were great at making music, but lousy at doing anything involving money. Maybe that's why Mick married me, because when it came to our finances, I seemed to be the only voice of reason. But I gave him credit. His musical talents earned him an incredible income over the last twenty or so years. Maybe not so much lately, but I'd have to say we were definitely blessed.

Taking off my apron, I looked across the kitchen table at both Mick and Cowboy. Cowboy wouldn't look me in the eye. He kept his head lowered and concentrated on the plate of food in front of him. He used his fork to push around some peas as he stared at the chicken fried steak. Mick looked me in the eye once before turning away and standing. Slowly, he moved to the screen door and watched our two youngest children playing near the fountain.

Finally, he spoke.

"Actually, we're going on tour because we need to make money to pay the IRS. Seems our accountants weren't exactly on the up and up and we owe . . ."

"How much?" I could hear a croak in my voice.

Cowboy looked up and said, "A whole bunch. Add to that, our last album didn't sell so well."

I went and stood in front of the big box fan to cool off. We'd already turned off the air conditioning units in the mansion the first week of September. We usually don't do that until early November, sometimes even later, if the weather is still warm. But this year we were trying to cut back on expenses. And refrigerated air seemed like another extravagance.

"There's something else I think you should know," Cowboy said more to his chicken fried steak than to either of us. "Mick has a fan stalking him in addition to the death threats we've both been getting."

"Yes," I said, "I know a female fan is following him. He told me all about it."

Cowboy pushed back his padded steel chair from the table. This time he looked me in the eye when he spoke. "Margaret, the situation has gotten dangerous. Last time she snuck into our dressing room, she had a gun. It was all Mick could do to get it away from her."

"Oh my gosh," I gasped as I stepped back to brace myself on the counter. "Mick, you told me she was harmless. Just wrote a bunch of love letters and followed you around . . . like a yelping pup you said . . . crying for attention."

Cowboy didn't give Mick time to answer. "Margaret, I'm thinking about hiring security. Darla's right, Mick needs a personal bodyguard."

Mick turned toward Cowboy with eyes flashing. "Now, Cowboy, I don't think we . . ."

Cowboy interrupted, "Yes, you do, Mick."

"No!" Mick yelled. "We can't afford security. We can't even afford a decent hotel. Not with almost all the money from this tour going to pay the IRS back taxes. Back taxes, I might add, for money our agents stole from us. Cowboy, we need to stop trusting people! We need to buck up and start doing everything ourselves. Just like when we started out. And not let anyone, and I mean not even a deranged fan, get anything over on us. It's time for us to remember who we are . . . what we're made of. We didn't get to the top by cowering under a little pressure."

Cowboy sat quietly staring at his iced tea. Slowly, he stirred more sugar into the almost overflowing glass.

"What are you thinking?" I said to Cowboy. "It's clear you're cooking up something in that brain of yours."

But he didn't answer. He just continued staring at the whirling glass of tea and ice as his spoon blended in the granulated sugar.

Mick plopped down in his chair and calmed himself down. Without a word, he buttered a biscuit and took a bite. "This is good Margaret. Real good." I could tell he was trying to diffuse the situation.

Finally, Cowboy looked up from his glass. "I have a plan." He set his spoon down.

I pulled up a chair at the table. Mick leaned in closer to Cowboy. We waited while he took a sip of tea and cleared his throat.

Outside, I could hear the airbrakes of a school bus as it pulled up and stopped outside of our mansion's front gate. Seconds later, giggles and shouts drifted through the open window as Jamison and Debra ran to greet their older brother Thomas. The bus from the high school always got here after the middle school and elementary buses, but today it was running later than usual.

The clock on the wall ticked loudly as we waited in silence for Cowboy to speak.

As I waited, I pondered the fact that Mick had insisted on having our children go to public school. Mentally, I made a note to ask our guard to drive them every day from now on. It might embarrass them in front of their classmates to have a driver, but I didn't care.

Cowboy watched us watch him.

Finally, Mick spoke. "Are you going to share your plan with us?"

"Nope. Not yet."

With that, Cowboy picked up his fork and took a bite of chicken fried steak.

Mick studied me as if I had something to do with Cowboy's odd behavior. But I had no more control over Cowboy than his wife had had when he decided to start wearing rhinestone cowboy shirts with swinging fringe in real life instead of just on stage.

Getting up from the table, I went to get the half-eaten cake I'd made for Rayne's birthday. "Would you two like to have another piece of leftover birthday cake? I forgot Rayne doesn't eat much sugar."

As I got it out of the Tupperware container, I heard a soft female voice just outside the kitchen door.

"I'd like a piece, Margaret."

It was Katherine, Mick's sister. Earlier I'd asked her to eat with us, but she had declined, saying her foot was giving her trouble. Bless her heart, she'd suffered polio as a child and now had a great deal of trouble walking. In fact, she used metal crutches most of the time, as she did today. On her better days, she carried a cane.

Mick's face immediately brightened.

Cowboy stood up and said, "Hola, Bonita!"

Katherine tossed her dark curls, and her bright blue eyes held a mischievous spark. "You're looking pretty dapper in that purple shirt. I like it. Is it new?"

"Why, *yes* it is!" Cowboy shimmied like a showgirl making the fringe move back and forth. Which, of course, brought a big smile to Katherine's face.

I couldn't help but notice how much she looked like Mick when she was happy. Although Mick had auburn hair while hers was dark, they still had the same bright smile that lit up their entire faces.

The bond between brother and sister was strong. It always amazed me how they supported each other in good times and bad. I guessed

Mick might have told her about the stalker before me, but maybe not. He wouldn't want to worry her. Still, she must've had a reason for deciding to come down to be with us that afternoon. Earlier, when I'd invited her, she'd sounded like she was in a lot of pain.

Mick hopped up from the kitchen table, distracting my train of thought as he gave Katherine a quick kiss.

"I'm going to go see if the kids want some cake," he said, heading out of the kitchen. "Hope there is enough to go around."

"I have Moon Pies if there's not," Cowboy piped up.

"Oh, yeah!" Mick called back. "I'll have a Moon Pie and RC Cola. Let the kids eat cake!"

CHAPTER 4

R AYNE

The drive-in theater was overflowing. Everywhere I looked people were packed into cars with their windows rolled down. Others were sitting on tailgates or on blankets spread out picnic-style on the grassy lawn in front of the stage and large picture screen.

Speaker boxes on poles beside each car crackled and popped to life as the announcer tested his microphone. Cowboy was right when he told Darla this place would be a good venue for her to be seen and heard. It was packed to the gills with teens and young adults. I just wish the two of us had a little time to ourselves before I had to take off. I liked her, and she was starting to take my mind off Jennifer.

Distributing the records around town to the DJs this afternoon had been a lot of fun. I don't know about her feelings, but I'd felt a spark between us. Maybe it was best not to follow up on it as my heart was still hurting a good deal. And I had to leave out soon . . . as in later tonight soon. *How am I ever going to find love if I can't stay in one place long enough?* I truly felt that one of the reasons I lost my last girlfriend was because I couldn't be with her in person. Couldn't give her the attention she needed—the attention she deserved.

I hadn't been a very good boyfriend to Jennifer, and in truth, I hadn't even been a very good friend to Carl either. So, I don't know why I'm so uptight about the situation. It's not like I was perfect. I should've done better by both of them.

Still, it surprised me how much it hurt to be done wrong. And it surprised me how much I missed Jennifer.

Enough beating myself up. Tonight, I'd enjoy myself while I could.

Up ahead on the wooden makeshift stage, the musicians started to set up. The stage was right under the big screen where the feature films were shown. The new movie Cat on a Hot Tin Roof was showing—but first local musicians got to strut their stuff. It was here the singers and performers rallied the young folks to get them in the mood for a good time. I guess you could call it an opening act of sorts for the actual movie as the musicians would take the stage right up until the time the feature film rolled. Or that's the way it had been in the past. It'd been some time since I'd been to a drive-in movie. Actually, it had been some time since I'd seen any movie.

Walking toward the food stand, I felt for my wallet in my back pocket. I couldn't decide if I wanted popcorn or a pickle-on-a-stick. As I drew closer to the vendors, I saw they had those chocolate ice cream bon-bon things. Behind me, I heard a guitarist tuning his instrument. Then a drummer testing his set. The crowd grew louder as people anticipated the singer's approach. I knew Darla was supposed to be first as she had built up a small following of fans in this area. Glancing back at the stage, I saw someone bring out a microphone and adjust it. I forgot about the food and moved back toward the stage. After all, I'd never forgive myself if I missed Darla's act.

"Ladies and gentlemen," a man's booming voice announced over the microphone, "give it up for Dallas's own Miss Darla Darling."

Cheers erupted.

Darla pranced toward center stage.

But she didn't make it.

Instead, she tripped and tumbled over a cord making the micro-phone squelch and squeal as her foot pulled it off the stand. My heart leapt in my chest as I saw her all sprawled out in a prone position on the stage. Rushing forward to help her up, the announcer leaned down and took her arm while we all waited to see if she was okay. Motioning for the music to stop, he took control of the situation while the crowd looked on in horror.

I couldn't imagine how Darla must be feeling. All gussied up for her big performance and then falling flat on her face so to speak before she even got started.

The announcer and another woman who'd come out of the back were bending over Darla, obscuring her from our sight. Then suddenly the microphone made another squelching sound, and a confident female voice said—"I'm okay, I'm okay"—over the loudspeakers.

The announcer and the woman moved back. Darla took her place front and center. The crowd went crazy as she coyly said, "I did that on purpose" before letting out a small laugh. Then she smiled her big infectious smile as someone in the crowd shouted, "No, you didn't Darla." She laughed out loud again before pointing to the person hassling her.

"That's my little brother, Dale Darling. And, as you can guess, he's anything but darling."

She kicked off her high heels. "If you guys don't mind . . . I'm going to sing barefoot, okay? I spent a pretty penny dying these high heels to match my dress, but as you can see, they're dangerous."

My heart melted as she put the microphone in the stand in front of her before deciding to take it back out again. The crowd clapped and cheered while she straightened her dress and regained her composure. I stood amazed at how calm she was, standing up there talking to the rowdy crowd as if each and every one of them were her best friend. Honestly, some of them probably were. She seemed to know everyone in Dallas.

Darla motioned for the musicians to start.

She sang a song that belonged to that new boy from Memphis, Tennessee—"I'm All Shook Up." The crowd went wild with approval. Girls and guys alike screamed their lungs out. People all around me started jumping up and down. Some even jumped off tailgates and out of their cars, running closer to the stage.

Sashaying her hips to make the ruffles on her dress shake in time to the music, Darla raised her hands in the air as she sang her heart out. Clearly, she hadn't hurt herself when she fell. Her dancing was spot on. And when she got to the song's line "my hands are shaky, and my knees are weak," the crowd took over and sang with her, "I can't seem to stand on my own two feet."

It was a night to remember. The warm air and the smell of popcorn, hot dogs and candy wafting from the food stands made me feel slightly heady. I sure wish I didn't have to disappear tonight. I sure wish I didn't have to leave without telling her the full truth about where I was going and why.

This is why I'll never find love. This is why love will never find me. This is why what little love I've had in life failed. My dedication to my career, my higher purpose. But then again, Darla had a career calling her, too. I had no doubt soon she'd be doing singing gigs all over the place. Heck, she'd probably be traveling with Mick and Cowboy as it is . . . working as their assistant. Maybe even opening their shows at times.

It appeared the stars weren't lining up for us to be lovers. Add to that my heart still winced from my last emotional train wreck.

No, I'm not going to think bad thoughts tonight.

I picked up my camera and positioned it on Darla Darling.

A flash erupted, capturing her unique personality . . . her special beauty that held the crowd—and me—spellbound.

For one brief moment I allowed love to fill my heart. God, how I wished I could stay with Darla instead of getting on that plane tonight.

CHAPTER 5

COWBOY LARSON

It had only been a day since I'd come into town to visit Mick and Margaret, but I could tell there was something wrong between the two of them. Not that they were fighting or anything like that. Just not talking together in that easy way I was used to observing. Take today, for instance. Mick was in one of his moods. He was probably worried about his stalker, but I knew him, and I knew he wasn't up to talking about it just yet.

So, I got out my guitar.

As I began to strum, he started to tell me what was on his mind.

"Rayne came up with a plan to flush the stalker out," Mick said as he stood ramrod straight, gazing out the office window. "Rayne thinks I should go out to the country where he comes from—to a small, isolated cabin he knows of deep in the East Texas woods. A place that'll be hard to find if you're not from those parts. Then if my worrisome fan shows up, there'll be no place to hide."

"And what would you do then?"

"I don't know. Maybe tie her up and call the law. At least I could address the situation so my family wouldn't be in danger of a lunatic lurking about."

"Why don't I go with you? We could get some writing done." I watched his face perk up as he turned to face me.

"We do need an excuse to get out of town," he said. "Let's go buy an old truck so no one will suspect it's us. Not that I don't love our fans, but we need privacy right now."

"What about my longhorn Cadillac? Should I let Rayne babysit it?"

"No, Cowboy. Rayne had to leave last night. In the middle of the night." Mick stared off into the distance before continuing. "I worry about that boy's new job. It's got him doing all kinds of secretive things. Hard for him to be a part of the family. Hard for him to have a life outside of work."

I didn't say anything else. I knew he didn't expect an answer. He only wanted to vent his worry about his nephew. Mick had always had a soft spot for Rayne. I think it was because he saw so much of himself in the young man. They both were wanderers in life. Couldn't sit still in one place for very long.

Taking my guitar in hand, I went out on the balcony. Margaret had put out a lot of large pot plants so we could sit behind them, unde-tected. That's one thing about Margaret. She was always thinking of ways to make everyone more comfortable. Her every little action was thoughtful. I could stand to learn from her.

Out on the porch I listened to the breeze rustle through the tree boughs. Soon autumn would be in full color, but right now the green grass was still growing, and birds were splashing about in the fountain below. I heard a lawnmower's engine softly roar to life.

"So much for getting some songwriting done," Mick said as he ventured out beside me. Pulling out a cigarette, he lit it and exhaled before lowering himself into one of the metal rocking chairs. "Where's my pillow? Margaret's always taking my pillow back inside so it won't get wet."

"I don't know where your pillow is . . . why don't you get off your skinny butt and go find it?" I had a smile on my face when I said it, thinking he'd rather sit on the hard chair than go root around for it. But that was not the case. He got up and went inside. Down below, I watched the gardener having a grand time testing out the brand-new ride-on lawn-mower. Mick told me he had purchased it just the other day. One more of the latest gadgets he had to have. As Margaret was fond of saying, "Mick has a little spending problem—he can't stop." Oh well, I reckoned . . . sure we were hurting financially, but what was a little more fuel to the fire if we were going down anyway? Might as well have a nice lawnmower.

Just then, the door to the balcony opened, and Mick came out with a big fluffy towel. "It's not my pillow, but it'll do."

Yes, we'd both gotten a little soft. It would do us good to get back to the country and rough it a bit. Maybe even stay in a tent instead of a cabin. No, a cabin would work better. I wasn't up for that much roughing it.

"Where'd you get that towel?" I asked. "I'd like to get one for my butt, too."

No sooner had I said than Margaret appeared at the balcony door. She was holding a pillow. Without a word, she handed it to me.

"Thank you, ma'am."

She nodded as she moved past me to the railing.

Down below, I watched as the groundskeeper stopped mowing and went back to his shed. A bird cawed as it flew overhead, and the children below called out to each other as they ran about. Those two boys of Mick's were always in constant motion. One of them had red hair like Mick and the other a golden brown hair like Margaret. Both were unusually intelligent, but it was the older boy Thomas, the redhead, who was the athlete. A little bit on the thin side, but he was a fast runner. Thomas was a good singer, but not as good a guitar player as he was a piano player.

Margaret stood quietly at the railing, observing her universe.

Mick and I both watched her as she scanned the horizon, looking for who knows what. I knew not to pose too many questions. She was in one of her mental storms. As Mick would say, "Just let her work it out."

Instead of talking, I picked up my guitar and began to play. Quietly so as not to disturb anyone. Not even the bees buzzing near the honey-suckle vines below.

Margaret tuned in and was listening. Still, something weighed heavy on her mind.

Without turning, she said, "Remember Bonnie? Remember how she painted her nails and kept her appearance so neat?"

I knew Margaret wasn't expecting an answer, but still I said, "Yes, I do."

Mick chimed in before I could finish. "Bonnie didn't seem like an outlaw on the run. I believe she just got caught up in something that was bigger than her when she fell for Clyde."

"Still, it was a big adventure for her."

Neither of us said anything.

Margaret walked to the other end of the balcony and leaned over it to look at her children playing. "Thomas, stop acting ugly to Jamison!" She stamped her foot. "I mean it. Stop bullying your brother!"

Thomas's answer floated back up to the balcony.

"I'm not bullying Jamison, Mom!"

"Yes, you are. Sitting on someone who weighs 50 pounds less than you is bullying. Now go on, get up and apologize to him. You'll both be glad you have each other someday. You need to be friends. You need to be kind to each other."

"Remember riding the rails on those boxcars across Texas?" Mick asked. "Now that was a big adventure."

"Yeah," I said as I continued to play, "we had ourselves a grand adventure. I wouldn't trade it for the world, even though there were a few times we almost didn't make it."

"Just think," Margaret said, "if we hadn't been riding those rails, we wouldn't have met each other and gotten to know each other so well."

"The universe has a way of pushing a person in a direction, doesn't it?" Even as I said the words, I knew she wasn't listening. When I finished the song I was playing, I went straight into another one.

"Margaret," Mick said from the other end of the balcony. He'd been so silent, I'd almost forgotten he was there. "Margaret," Mick said again, "I hired a bodyguard for you and the kids. Someone to watch after y'all. I figure you'll need it, especially since the new bodyguard that Cowboy hired will be on tour with us. What was his name again?"

"Clarence." I said. "I reckon you'll remember it one day as I've already told you fifty times."

"He just doesn't look like a Clarence to me. He's so big, he looks more like a Gus."

Margaret was lost in her own world. I continued to play my guitar softly while Mick's groundskeeper's new lawnmower hummed back to life. There was really no reason for any of us to speak. It seemed we were all talked out. Instead, we just enjoyed the pleasant day. I sure was glad Margaret had brought that plush pillow for my butt. Man, I was getting old.

CHAPTER 6

ARLA

Daddy had warned me that smiling faces don't always tell the truth, but I had never seen it in action until today.

The new girl came by Mick's office in the house to drop off a musical royalty report from the studios. Tall and stately, her classic good looks stayed true to her name . . . Angel Valetta. All she needed was a harp and a pair of wings. Her smooth ivory skin must have never suffered from the teenage acne the rest of us dealt with in some form or fashion, for it was flawless. Just like her makeup. Yes, she was wearing the latest shade of lipstick that I had read about being all the rage in Margaret's fashion magazine. It was called "Apple on a Stick". Margaret had pointed the article out to me saying I'd look good in that hue when I went on stage. Now here was this super sexy peroxide-blonde sitting in the same room with me wearing "Apple On A Stick" as if the shade was made just for her. No, I could never match her glamour no matter what I smeared across my lips. Some people were just born with a glow about them.

But that wasn't the real reason I was angry. The reason I wanted to pop her one is she had just pointed out to Mick, Margaret and Cowboy that she'd heard me sing on the radio the other day.

"Seems like Darla's more interested in making sure her own star ascends than she is in promoting your records to the DJs who play them," she said snidely with a quick side glance in my direction. "Of course, I'm just kidding dear. You could never match the musical magic of these two legends." Then she cast a dazzling smile at Mick— her pearly whites made even more so by her rich red lips.

Out of the corner of my eye, I caught Margaret motioning to Angel that she had something on her front teeth. I knew nothing was on her teeth, but I swear I heard Margaret mouth to her she had lipstick on them. I watched as Angel put her index finger to her front teeth and rubbed. Then she showed Margaret her teeth to let her know if she'd successfully removed the mark. Margaret shook her head no. Finally, Angel got up and excused herself to go look in a hallway mirror.

I watched Cowboy wink at Mick. Mick chuckled and said, "Don't drag me into this cat fight. I already know who is going to win."

Cowboy looked over at me and said, "Don't ever underestimate Margaret's ability to fight back. She learned at an early age how to hold her own against anyone. Isn't that right, Margaret?"

I smiled at Margaret, and she smiled back.

"Darla," she whispered softly in my ear as she moved past me toward the office door, "see her for what she is, your competition."

A doorbell clanged to life, making me jump.

However, Margaret was already on her way down the hallway to answer it.

"Never mind, Clarence," we heard her call out to Mick's newly hired bodyguard. "I've got it. It's Miss Katherine."

Mick must've read my mind. "No, Margaret's not psychic. She saw my sister's car pull past the gatehouse."

"Still," Cowboy said, "she shouldn't answer the door with your stalker on the loose. That's why we pay Clarence."

I caught Clarence's large frame gliding down the hallway. His dark hair slicked back from his handsome face accented large brown eyes and high cheekbones. I wondered how he managed to move so silently

. . . almost like a shadow. I guess he learned it at bodyguard school, if such a thing existed.

"Miss Katherine," I heard him say over two soft female voices. "Miss Katherine, we've missed you here at the mansion."

"She's only been gone three days," I heard Margaret say with a girlish laugh. Then much to my dismay, I heard Angel's strong, confident voice mix with the others out in the hallway.

"Clarence," she said, "would you be available to help me move some boxes of records from the foyer to the office. I really need someone with muscle to help."

"Yes, of course." Clarence's voice echoed down the hallway as he followed Angel.

I imagined her swinging her hips as she walked. Swaying from side to side as her expensive high heels clicked on the marble tiles. I could hear her sultry voice directing him "right this way" and "it's so nice to have a strong man around" and "ick, ick, ick." Who knows what else she was saying as their voices became muffled in the distance.

Cowboy broke the silence in the office. "Darla, did you distribute all those records the other day?"

"Yes, all but one. I didn't get in to see Jay Callon in Fort Worth."

"You and Angel want to take my car again and go do it tomorrow. We need as much airplay as we can get." Then he stopped for a moment and pulled a matchstick out of his front pocket. Thoughtfully he put it in the corner of his mouth as we'd all seen him do a thousand times before. "Margaret," he called out as she walked back down the hallway. Stopping, she peeped her head in the office doorway with an inquiring look. "Margaret, we're going to need to go on tour. And I know you asked us not to just yet. But we need to do it soon."

Margaret didn't say a word. She just walked to the window and stared in the distance.

Turning his attention back to me, Cowboy handed me his keys to the Caddy and said, "Tell Jay Callon that this new song 'Delta County Blues' is real important to me. Tell him it is a new sound for us, and I'd appreciate it if he'd give it plenty of air play."

I nodded. Picking up my purse, I tried to slip out without Angel in tow.

But no such luck.

She stood by the front door, Clarence beside her holding a box of records. She smiled sweetly as I approached. "This is going to be so much fun," she said more to Clarence than me. "I haven't driven a Cadillac before."

In the background, Cowboy yelled, "Darla, why don't you drive since you know where you're going."

"Yessir!" I yelled back.

Outside on the porch, I felt the heat of the afternoon wash over me. The sun was beating down. And it seemed like all the birds in the city were trying to take a bath at once in the fountain in the front. I watched for a few moments as a blue jay splashed about, cawing at the others to keep their distance.

Clarence saw him, too. "Must be my lucky day. That's the second blue jay I've seen today."

"Are blue jays lucky?" Angel asked as she coyly played with a strand of her hair.

"Yes." Clarence didn't seem to notice her flirtations. "They are a sign of safety and protection."

"Well, you are in the business of protection, so you should know," I said as I opened the Caddy's spacious trunk for him.

With almost no effort, he hoisted the heavy box inside.

"You know what?" Angel said. "It's so hot. We should ride with the top up and the air conditioner on. Clarence, would you mind moving the box to the back seat?"

She was right, but I wasn't going to acknowledge it.

Opening the driver's side door, I got inside.

Clarence motioned for me to roll the window down.

"Darla, what time do you think you'll be back? Katherine wanted to know if you'll be able to go to the dance with us."

"Dance," said Angel, "what dance? I'd love to go, too."

CHAPTER 7

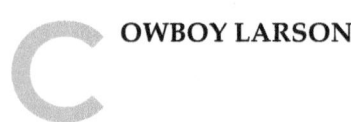OWBOY LARSON

"Any idea of who'd want to stalk you?" I asked as I tuned my guitar.

Mick didn't answer.

"Do you think they want you dead? Or do you think they just want your attention?"

Mick shook his head and put his hands up in the air as if to say, "How do I know?"

"Well, it'll make a difference as to how my plan plays out."

"You mean the plan you're keeping to yourself?"

Since I wasn't getting the information I wanted from Mick, I decided to pour us a couple of stiff drinks instead of arguing with him. Putting my guitar back in its open case, I made my way to the bar in Mick's office. He'd shut the heavy velvet drapes against the looming darkness from outside. Something he had never done before when I was here.

This conversation wasn't getting either one of us anywhere, so I decided to change the subject. It was time to reveal my plan to him. A plan I'd been hatching for some time, even before the stalker got involved in our lives.

"Mick, I've been thinking . . ."

"Oh, no!" he said. "Is your brain hurting?"

Ignoring his latest insult, I continued. "I've been thinking about our going to this little cabin out in the woods. You know, the place Rayne told you about. The one we were talking about the other night. The same one Rayne's father told me about when I stopped by to visit a few days ago. Sounds pretty magical. Apparently, it doesn't have any real roads, either dirt or paved, leading up to it. It's just a little stone and wood cabin that's stood the test of time. The person who owns the property keeps it up. Still has a working well . . . little stream runs nearby for fishing."

Mick swirled the liquid in his glass. However, he didn't respond.

"Like I said earlier, we could get some writing done. Think about which direction to take our music. Get back to our roots."

I walked over to a floor lamp and turned it on.

Mick turned his face from the light.

"Chances are your stalker will follow us." I took a sip of my drink before continuing. "We could hatch a plan to catch the stalker and talk. Not call the law or tie them up. Just try to talk things through. Find out what's going through their head."

"What?" Mick was incredulous.

"Yes, be nice to them. Make them see you for your real self. Not a country music star. Just plain old Mick. Believe me, once they get to know you, they'll realize they were chasing a fantasy. Mick, it's time for you to face your stalker . . . and your fears."

"This is your big plan?"

"Yep."

"Well, it's not a very good one."

CHAPTER 8

ARLA

The meeting in Fort Worth with Jay Callon went well. He immediately played "Delta County Blues" for his listeners. People started calling in before the end of the song to say how much they liked it and all. Mick and Cowboy's new sound that is. I knew this information would be important to both of them. Though they didn't talk about it much, I could tell they were worried their fans were starting to leave them. Mick was very experimental, and he was always trying new things musically. It didn't always go over well. Sometimes Cowboy would get mad. More than once I'd heard him tell Mick to shape up and help him write something that would sell.

Their success was hard on both of them. Each new hit song had made it harder for them to top themselves. Cowboy sometimes worried new music wouldn't come. Mick never worried. Or at least, he didn't show it.

"It'll come," he'd tell Cowboy. "Just relax." Then, as he liked to say,

"He'd let it come to him and through him." His songs weren't always hits, but I thought they were all good. Really good.

It was getting close to three o'clock, and I hadn't yet discussed going to the dance with Katherine. It was so thoughtful of her to invite me. Deep down inside, I couldn't help but wonder if she was a little afraid to go with Clarence by herself. By making it a group thing, she might feel more relaxed.

I admired her brains and beauty. But mostly I admired the fact that she didn't let her disability get her down. She never complained about having difficulty walking due to her childhood bout with polio. She often used her cane. A cane that her father, Lucky McLaren, had specially made for her. It was hand carved with roses and polished to perfection. A work of art. Perfect for Katherine, who had such a creative flair about her.

Mick had made one of the downstairs rooms into an office/bedroom for Katherine to use when she was in town. She didn't always live in the mansion. She spent about half her time in Houston near her parents. At thirty-something years old, she was a fierce businesswoman when it came to handling music tours for a handful of famous musicians. Her brother, Mick, and Cowboy being among the most famous. It didn't hurt that they were family, but still she was a force to be reckoned with on her own. I'd heard that when she was younger, she had one serious relationship with a man who'd played around on her. Since that time, she'd thrown herself into her work.

But it was clear to me there were sparks flying between her and the new bodyguard, Clarence. I'd been with her when she met him, and it had been an almost immediate mutual attraction. She'd been sitting at the kitchen table when he came in to get one of Margaret's homemade cupcakes. His eyes had lit up when he saw her pouring over the newspaper. She didn't look up, and he took advantage of the moment to really look her over.

Time seemed to slow down in the room. I'm not kidding, it seemed like a scene from that television soap opera Margaret watches. Clarence all so lovestruck. Then Katherine finally looked up to see him looking at her, and I could tell her heart jumped a little. She even seemed to have trouble breathing. Glancing away, only to look back. Of course, Clarence was so handsome and well-built he'd make most females sit up and pay attention. I know I definitely noticed him, but he didn't seem to think of me as anything more than a fellow employee.

When he'd asked for a cupcake, I remember I'd started to get up to get it. However, Katherine surprised me by insisting that she do it. I watched as she reached for her cane from the chair next to her. Slowly and carefully she rose, walking to the kitchen counter as her right leg dragged a bit. For just a split second, shock registered across Clarence's face. Then he recovered. Admiration still shone in his eyes. Maybe even more so. Then when she put the still warm cupcake on a napkin, he moved toward the counter so she wouldn't have to come to him. She blushed and shyly pushed her hair behind her ear as he moved up behind her.

"What is your name, lovely lady," he asked as he took it from her.

"Katherine," she said in a soft tone I'd never expected to come from her. "Katherine McLaren. Mick is my brother. I work for him and Cowboy."

"So do I," Clarence said. "I'm their new bodyguard."

At that, I slipped out of the room. Neither one noticed.

When I walked back by the kitchen door a few minutes later, they were sitting at the table, talking like they'd known each other for years. Occasionally, they'd laugh at something the other said. Clearly, they were in their own little world.

And things had continued this way for the past few weeks. Truly, romance was blossoming. I hoped against hope Angel wouldn't steal Clarence away.

Why, oh why had she invited herself to the dance tonight?

———

The night air was balmy and breezy in the open pavilion, making the colorful party atmosphere even more festive. Twinkling lights hanging from tree to tree illuminated the darkness, making a most romantic backdrop. Yes, I'd say the evening was going better than anyone could've planned. Clarence had driven Katherine, Angel and me in his

1956 Chevy truck. It had been a tight fit with all four of us, but Katherine didn't seem to mind being squished in tight beside Clarence. I was impressed with how naturally he took her cane from her and put it behind the seat after she got inside. Then, when we arrived, he helped her out on his side before retrieving it. But he didn't give it to her. Instead he gave her his arm to lean on while he carried the cane.

As a result, no one at the dance had any idea her leg was weak. She looked like the queen arriving on the arm of her handsome prince. Even Angel had not been able to steal the spotlight from her as we sat down at one of the front tables.

I swear I could feel people stop and turn to look at Katherine in her tailored powder blue party dress. The perfect color to enhance her sparkling eyes. Never had I seen her look so pretty and alive. And it was all due to Clarence's attention. Love was most certainly in the air.

My thoughts turned to Rayne. Oh, how I wished he hadn't had to leave. His abrupt departure had left me feeling down, though I don't know why. We hadn't spent more than a few days together really. And we never had a real kiss. Perhaps he didn't like me. If you were comparing looks, most people probably wouldn't consider me on the same scale as Rayne. But deep inside I'd felt a connection. And my mind refused to let him go. Even tonight, as a slow dance started and the partygoers began to twirl, I fantasized about what it might be like to be in Rayne's arms.

Looking down at the soda Clarence had bought me, I used the striped party straw to stir the ice in the cup. It was melting in the heat, watering down the carbonation, but the drink still hit the spot. Katherine sipped hers slowly as she observed the dancers. I wondered if she too was dreaming of being in a lover's arms.

Glancing sideways, I watched Angel finishing her drink in a few out-of-character unladylike gulps. Then she reached in her purse for her lipstick. She applied the new fashion color without a mirror. And she did it perfectly.

"Shall we dance?" Clarence's words broke my reverie. But he wasn't talking to me, he was holding out his hand to Katherine. I watched her confused expression.

Then, to my dismay, Angel blurted out what we'd all been thinking.

"Clarence," she said loudly so others could hear, "Katherine can't dance, she's crippled."

Katherine's face went white. Tears clouded her eyes. Tonight's happiness marred in a way that I was sure she may never recover from.

Clarence ignored Angel. He continued to gaze lovingly at Katherine.

"Shall we dance?" he repeated.

Though she didn't answer, he bent forward and pulled her to her feet, holding her close to his chest. Like a child, he swept her up in his arms and carried her to the dance floor before lightly sitting her on her feet again. She gently reached her arms up across his chest and broad shoulders. Their eyes locked on each other as they gently swayed back and forth.

"I'm dancing," I heard her whisper from the almost empty dance floor.

"No, we're dancing," Clarence said as he bowed his head to touch his lips to hers.

This time it was my eyes that held tears.

Katherine so deserved this night.

Again, my thoughts turned to Rayne. Where was he? What was he doing right now? And was he thinking of me?

PART 3

WILD BLUE YONDER

CHAPTER 9

Pacific Ocean Bordering South Vietnam
Wednesday Morning
October 1, 1958

AYNE

This is about as close to God as a man gets. Flying through whispers of clouds. Surrounded by silence. Azure water below. Blue-gray sky overhead. No one. Not one person in the world below knows I'm up here slicing through the air at 70,000 feet. Too high for any other aircraft to detect me above them. . . way up in the stratosphere, taking high-resolution photos over the villages below.

Surveillance and reconnaissance.

Who'd have believed I'd be doing this for a living? I mean, essentially, the Air Force plucked me out of a cotton field and taught me how to fly. Then, two months ago, "the agency" recruited me for its

Utility-2, or U-2, training at Watertown Strip, Nevada. Said I was perfect for the rigor of flying the new U-2. Said I was athletic, fit for the job. Their endless tests proved I wasn't claustrophobic. Perfect for flying in a tight cockpit. Perfect for fitting into the "cocoon," the pressurized suit U-2 pilots wear to keep from boiling. But most importantly, I fit into "the agency's" program—good camaraderie would keep morale high—possibly keep us alive.

All I know is, I've got it a lot better than most. And I'm thankful for each opportunity that comes my way. I am already a veteran of covert aerial reconnaissance missions, but it never gets old.

No two are ever the same. Today's mission over South Vietnam hasn't been as dangerous as others. However, the weather's bad, and I'm worried about the drop I have to make to the ship below. Yes, I said ship. Unlike most missions, I wasn't dropping to another plane or a net, I was aiming for a ship. A ship full of people who probably couldn't even see me flying over. It was all about timing—perfect timing.

And a little luck, I guess.

Alright, now. Focus. Keep your mind on the task at hand.

The men below were counting on me to be on time. And on mark.

Below and just to my right, I spied the naval ship. A small yellow dinghy filled with three men floating nearby. The waves were dangerously turbulent. The men bobbed perilously in the small yellow dinghy. Their lives at risk to retrieve my precious cargo.

Moving into position, I prayed for accuracy. Didn't want to hit the ship. Didn't want to hit the men in the dinghy. Also, didn't want to drop the film too far away from them. Otherwise, they'd have to fight the heavy rains and raging sea to get to it before it sank.

Breathe in. Breathe out.

Help me, God.

Breathe in. Breathe out.

One . . . two . . . three. Bull's-eye!

From the corner of my eye, I saw the men in the dinghy paddling furiously to retrieve the film. Soundlessly, my U-2 rose as I turned back to Alaska.

"The mission is complete." My own voice startled me as I spoke aloud.

"Roger, LoneWolf100T," the radio crackled back at me.

I can only pray the footage I captured will save lives somewhere. Even one life would be enough.

Fighting for the freedom of people everywhere. I truly believe in it. And would highly recommend it to anyone looking for a path in life to follow. Not that I would ever tell anyone what to do. It's the kind of decision you have to make for yourself. If it's right, you know.

―――――

Eielson Air Force Base
Just Southeast of Moose Creek, Alaska
Wednesday Afternoon
October 1, 1958

Later that afternoon, I tossed and turned on my hard cot, blankets thrown back as I struggled with the heat of the barracks. When the arms of Morpheus finally welcomed me, it was an uneasy sleep. Just on the edge of consciousness, I drifted in and out of a nightmare.

Anna's beautiful face before me. Laughing. Smiling. Beckoning me.

Then flames everywhere.

But I was trapped behind bars, unable to save her. Officers pulled me back. Telling me why I wouldn't want a girl like her . . . a prostitute . . . a whore.

Suddenly, I snapped awake. My first thoughts.

I could've saved her. I should've saved her. My Anna.

Looking around at the concrete floor and bare walls of the barracks, I realized the sun was setting. Gold stripes of light seeped through the nearby window, painting everything a mesmerizing shade. Soon other soldiers would be coming back.

I shook off my emotions, got up, and headed toward the shower.

Plagued by guilt. Overcome by grief. I sought the comfort of the warm stream of water flowing down over me, washing away the past. At times like these, I knew it would do no good to go down this road of thinking. Jennifer was not the only one who'd cheated in our relationship. I had, too, with Anna. Only I was the only one who knew it. No one else.

Well, except God. And perhaps Satan.

I put my arm up into the steady cascade of hot water and let it wash over my back. It was soothing not to think. To be alone in the shower. A soldier isn't afforded many luxuries. Certainly not the right to wallow in his own self-pity. "No good would come from it," I said out loud.

I heard the door open and feet shuffling into the barracks.

"Hurry up in there, pretty boy!"

It was my buddy, Pete.

"Let's go eat!" He shouted.

I reached up and turned the shower knobs to the off position.

I wasn't hungry, but I would eat.

Wrapping a towel around my waist, I walked out to my bunk where Pete waited. Another buddy, Sol, stood beside him. They were looking at the recent photos I'd developed of Darla singing on stage.

"Wow-wee!" Pete said. "She is one hot tamale."

"Yeah, they sure make 'em pretty in Texas," Sol added at a much lower volume. "I bet you're missing her."

I took the photo from Pete's hand and tossed it back in my locker.

"How come you get all the pretty girls?" Pete asked. "I'm better lookin' than you. And ol' Sol here is smarter."

I grabbed my clothes and went back to the privacy of the showers.

"What are they serving tonight?" I yelled as I tucked my shirttail into my pants. Reaching into the pocket, I pulled out the silver coin I always carried. Most people thought it was for good luck. But I knew its true purpose—the poison pin concealed within its ill-fitting sheath made it the perfect instrument of death should I ever be captured and tortured. We had a choice whether to carry one or not—"the agency" said it was up to us. I had opted for one just in case I ever needed it.

"What are they serving?" I repeated louder.

"Food!" Pete bellowed. "Come on, pretty boy. Get your hair combed. And let's get to the chow hall."

When I came back out, Sol held up the photo of Darla.

"If you have any extra prints, I'd like to have one," Sol said sincerely. "It's a real nice photo even though I don't know her name."

"Her name is Darla . . . Darla Darling." I said it slowly, knowing Pete was going to have a field day with that one.

To my surprise, he didn't take the bait for making a joke. He just stood there watching Sol admire the photo.

· "I'll make you a print from the negative next time I'm developing photos."

"I'd like that." Sol carefully placed the photo down on the pillow of my cot.

In my mind, I hoped I'd be able to come through with the photo for Sol, but honestly, I doubted it. Soon, I'd be totally and completely on "the agency" missions. And I'd be known by a different name. Instead of Rayne David Weston, I would now go by Rayne D. Wesley. A new ID would identify me as a civilian employee of the Department of the Air Force. I'd still be a soldier in essence, but a secret soldier, a soldier out of uniform.

Basically, my life was going to be a whole web of secrets. Oh, Lord! What had I signed up for? How would I ever find love and settle down? Heck, even Sol and Pete didn't know I'd been secretly training on the U-2 for the past few months. But then again, they had their secret missions, too. Maybe they'd joined "the agency" as well. Many of the best pilots had.

Flying was what I lived for . . . what I was born to do. I reminded myself, joining "the agency" meant a long flying career.

But it also meant sacrifices would have to be made.

CHAPTER 10

The McLaren Mansion
Dallas, Texas
Thursday Late Afternoon
October 2, 1958

ARGARET

The kids were creating a ruckus in the living room. It was all I could do to keep from hollering at them. Why must they blare the TV at such a high volume? Everything was getting on my last nerve since Cowboy had confirmed he and Mick were going out to the country cabin to write more songs before they went on tour. Under normal circumstances, it wouldn't have bothered me too much. I always missed Mick when he was gone on tour, and he was always gone too long. But I had known what I signed on for when I married him. But with Mick's stalker on the loose, I felt uneasy about them going to a remote cabin.

Instead of yelling at the kids, I took our dog and went upstairs to sit out on our bedroom balcony. Honeysuckle wafted up from below. Somewhere in the distance, I heard the laughter of people having a party. I was pretty sure it was our neighbors down the street. They were different from us because they were born into money, and even though we were polite to each other, no relationship developed.

Oh yes, I think they were impressed by Mick's and Cowboy's fame, but at the same time a little angry at all the fans driving down our street, wanting to stop and take photos outside the gate.

Mick had wanted to move farther out of downtown. But I'd wanted the grand mansion. I absolutely loved it. So, I guess if the neighbors didn't like the fans, then they could just stew in their own frustration or move. What did they expect when they moved in next door to a flashy musician whose bandmate drove a Cadillac with steer horns on the hood? They should've recognized trouble coming.

Swaying slowly back and forth in my wicker rocker, I repositioned the soft rose-colored seat cushion. Its floral pattern was so pretty. Pretty described my life. I had never even dreamed of a life like this when I was a little girl.

I sipped my tea and leaned back. A cool breeze lifted my hair. Fall was on its way— it'd be here in a few more weeks. Soon the leaves would turn. But tonight, in early October, summer's green lawns still prevailed.

Closing my eyes, I began to hum.

Then I began to sing. A song my French grandmother had taught me as a girl.

Softly I sang the tune until I remembered it fully. Then I lifted my voice to the skies.

Somewhere in the distance, the party noises stopped momentarily.

Still, I continued pouring the words from my soul in a language I didn't completely understand. Yes, I felt the emotion deep in my heart. When I stopped singing, silence surrounded me. Not even a chirp from a cicada.

And, then to my surprise, I heard clapping and yelling.

"Magnifique!"

"Belle, madame!"

My heart swelled with emotion. Eyes brimmed with tears. I put my hand to my mouth as I tried to regain my composure. Oh, how I missed singing for an audience. The overwhelming love, the electricity of performing live. Looking out across the freshly mowed lawn, I couldn't help but wonder, what if?

I sensed movement behind me, and I turned to look back.

Mick stepped forward from the balcony French doors.

"Margaret, you should've sung with us. You still can," he said as he wrapped his arms around me.

"That ship has sailed," I told him simply. "Someone had to stay home with the kids, and I wanted children. We both did. They are my life."

"They're my life, too."

"No, Mick. Music is your life. I'm not even sure you had a choice in the matter. It's just who you are. Same with Cowboy."

Mick stood silent, as though my words had nailed his shoes to the balcony. He knew my words were true.

Changing the subject, I said, "How's Cowboy doing now that Saint has been dead for over two years? Does he ever mention her name?"

"No," Mick answered as he held me close, swaying back and forth. "Still hasn't cried yet either."

I breathed in the honeysuckle and let his words sink in. Surely it was a fearsome thing to love so deeply. Cowboy was a survivor. Still . . . by not feeling his grief, he wasn't feeling any other emotions. In time, the sadness would come out in one way or another. Or perhaps not.

It was his decision if he chose to live without a wounded heart.

Each to their own, my mother used to say. At any given time, deep down, we all know what is best for us. However, in my case, I wasn't exactly sure what was troubling my heart as of late. But something deep down inside of me was searching for an answer.

CHAPTER 11

COWBOY LARSON

Taking Clarence's Chevy truck was a superior idea. Fans would think I was still sequestered inside the mansion with Mick. Another brilliant insight from Clarence was to let him pack it up with our camping gear. In the cover of darkness the night before, he'd put our two favorite guitars behind the seat. Out of view from interested parties. Not even the guard at the gate knew what we were up to with our little getaway.

Looking up from polishing my Caddy, I saw Mick walking out the back door of the mansion. Earlier I'd seen him talking to Margaret on the balcony after she'd sung a beautiful song in French. I wasn't even aware that she was fluent in French. Maybe she had the words to the song memorized. I wondered what their conversation had been about. They both looked so serious. I imagined she was worried about us going to the cabin.

As Mick neared the garage, he passed right by me and went inside the wooden structure. This wasn't just a one-car building/workshop. It could hold up to five cars and a boat. Another building was Mick's workshop, and another building of equal size was for the gardeners. Or should I say gardener? Mick used to have multiple workmen for the lawn and house, but he'd cut back to just one gardener. And he would hire a handyman when he needed a job done that he couldn't do himself. Said it would be a good time to teach his sons how to repair a few things. Margaret also had this mindset. In addition to teaching her daughter how to sew and cook, she also taught the boys. They'd surprised me the other night when they had whipped up a cake for dessert. It was a little lopsided, but very tasty.

Now what in the world was Mick doing rattling around in the garage?

"Hey, come help me!" Mick called from inside.

Taking my time, I maneuvered around my Caddy and headed in the direction of his voice. It took a moment or so for my eyes to adjust to the dark interior. A solitary light bulb swung from the middle of the ceiling, illuminating just enough for me to see Mick's legs dangling through an attic opening. He was just hanging there, half in and half out, as his ladder had fallen away. Quickly, I ran to pick it up and adjust it underneath his feet.

"Thanks for taking your time, buddy." Mick's voice held a sarcastic tone but no animosity.

With a solid grip on both railings, I held the ladder as he started to back down. In one hand, he clutched a couple of bows and arrows. When he reached the bottom rung, he handed them over to me and said, "Go put these in the fishing boat over there."

Without a word, I did as he said. No surprise, the fishing boat already held everything an experienced fisherman could want.

Mick grabbed a tarp from the front of the boat and started to lash it down with ties. "Hey, do you still have the directions Rayne gave you to the cabin? Didn't he tell you we'd have to take a canoe up the creek to the cabin on the last leg of the journey?"

"Yes, he did say that. And, yes, I do have his handwritten directions. And I'm also embarrassed to say I hadn't thought things through. It never occurred to me we'd need a boat. Glad you have this one."

"Well," Mick stepped back after he'd finished tying off the tarp, "let's hope it's not too big or too heavy for the creek. Water should be up with the heavy rains we've had in the last few weeks." Then he turned toward the doorway. A lone figure entered and stopped just inside. It was Clarence, Mick's new security guy.

I watched as he gawked all around at the shelves of nails, screws and assorted tools. Cans of this and that stacked everywhere. A motor to something in the corner in a cardboard box. Pieces of wood stacked according to size.

"Wow. Just wow," Clarence said. "Even though I checked this garage out when I was setting up security, I don't think I'll ever get used to how incredible it is. It's got everything a man could ever want."

Mick beamed with pride as he walked over to stand by Clarence. "You do have a hitch on the back of your truck, right?" he asked.

Still overcome by the magnificence of the garage, Clarence didn't speak. He just nodded in the affirmative.

CHAPTER 12

ARLA

I watched Clarence, Cowboy and Mick from the upstairs hallway window. They were standing just inside the garage entryway. The way they were talking and laughing reminded me of three teenagers cutting up. Finally, they came outside. The bright light from the sun gave away their real ages. Still, there was a youthfulness to Mick and Cowboy that made them seem timeless. They were great musicians. And great bosses. How in the world did I find myself working for them? It was the only thing in my life that has ever gone right. They had my back, and I had theirs.

Angel came clicking her high heels behind me. Her perfume entered the room before she did. Unlike her, it was sweet. Some kind of floral concoction. Everything about her was feminine. I just hoped she didn't sway Clarence's gaze away from Katherine. It was obvious to me she was working overtime to get his attention. I'd even noticed her being coy with Mick. No doubt trying to get him to help her singing career.

"What are you looking at?" Angel's voice was bright and cheerful.

"Just looking at the last of the summer roses."

"No, you're not, sweetie. You're looking at Clarence. And so am I." I turned to look at her in disbelief, but she didn't seem to notice. She kept right on talking. "Just look at those rippling muscles. I bet he's a hot lover."

I didn't know how to answer. Honestly, I don't think she expected an answer as she was more or less going for shock value.

"What are you two talking about?" Katherine had silently come up behind us. She had one hand on her hip and the other holding her cane.

Angel's eyes opened wide in surprise, but she recovered quickly.

"Old Darla here was just saying how she bet Clarence was one hot lover."

Before I could protest, the little tart turned and swept past Katherine as if she were Queen Elizabeth II of the Commonwealth.

Stammering, I managed to get out, "I did not say that!"

Katherine smiled mischievously.

"I know. I was standing behind you the whole time. I've got Angel's number. Just don't want her to know that I know what's she's up to. Better to let the enemy think they're not being watched."

Katherine moved beside me, and we both stood watching from the window. After a few moments, Katherine said, "Did you hear Margaret singing on the balcony earlier?"

I nodded. "She's really got a voice, that one does. Wonder why she didn't team up with Mick and Cowboy?"

"She still can," Katherine responded, staring out at the lawn below where Mick, Cowboy and Clarence were loading the truck. "Or better yet, she could go out on her own. The kids are old enough now to do without her sometimes."

"Did she tell you that?"

"No." Katherine still gazed through the open window. "She didn't have to."

CHAPTER 13

Somewhere Between Alaska & California
Thursday Afternoon
October 2, 1958

AYNE

Luck was with me. I had an assignment in Texas. Close enough to be able to visit Darla and my family. I dared not tell a soul until it became a reality. I was superstitious that way.

Sol and the guys were a good lot. I'd had more than my fair share of fun in Alaska camping, hunting and going into town. But memories of Jennifer and Anna wouldn't leave my head. And it was making me a little crazy.

No matter, it was time for me to move forward.

I relaxed in the pilot's seat and reached for the half-empty sea rations box Sol had given me. He'd gotten it when he worked on the flight lines the night before. Filled with pound cake, canned peaches and canned fruit cocktail, it was a real treat. Instead of keeping it for himself, he'd given it to me as a parting gift. "That Sol is a true friend," I thought as I savored a bite of the pound cake.

Readjusting my headphones, I listened to their crackle as the wind roared outside. In the distance, I heard thunder as lightning flashed ahead.

It was going to be a long flight home. With several stops in between.

To while away the time, as usual my mind turned to thoughts of the last few months. It was surreal the way I had been recruited into "the agency," but the thought of being a reconnaissance pilot for the CIA seemed like a dream come true. I'd never envisioned myself as a spy, but helping our country seemed like a good way to spend one's life.

The offer had come out of the blue. On a day not unlike any other, I was simply asked to go to a major's office in our headquarters wing to discuss a possible new career move. As far as I knew, the Air Force wasn't in the business of lining up work for people. So to say the least, it was weird.

Imagine my surprise when they sent me to interview at a motel off base, after hours. All they told me was that they were interviewing pilots to work with a new secret government organization, and I had been recommended. I have to admit, I was more than impressed when they told me they were from the Central Intelligence Agency. I knew little about this agency other than it was new, it was super-secret and it was usually referred to by its initials CIA. During the interview they said they could tell me little about the work I'd be doing except it was patriotic, good for the country. And then came the clincher—the pay was outstanding. Much higher than what I was making at the time.

The contract would be for eighteen months overseas. Adding when the eighteen-month contract was over, I could return to the Air Force if I wanted to with no time or pay grade lost.

I remember the little stab at my heart when they had told me plans could be made to keep my girlfriend or wife satisfied with my whereabouts while I was working. No problems there. No girlfriend. No wife.

I remember looking around the wood-paneled motel room at the two men, each in suit, tie and black horn-rimmed glasses. As sketchy as everything was that they were telling me—it definitely appealed to my sense of adventure.

Immediately, I had told them they could count me in.

They told me to think about it overnight.

The next day, I told them I had not changed my mind—I wanted in.

The following week, routine Air Force orders had been issued directing me to report for several days' temporary duty. These orders covered my absence from the base. No one would ever suspect a thing as I transitioned from one organization to the other. As for my mother and father, they would be given a separate cover story. They would receive just enough information about my new career with the CIA to satisfy their worries while impressing upon them the importance of secrecy.

And so, my life as a reconnaissance pilot commenced.

When I had told Mr. Collins I was proud to be part of the CIA, his face winced as he said, "Call it 'the agency' from now on."

He didn't have to tell me twice. I never made that mistake again.

A few weeks later, after being given my official identification for my fake name Rayne D. Wesley, I found myself taking a cab to the Du Pont Plaza in Washington, D.C. Once safely inside my room, I had waited for a telephone call. And when the call came, the voice on the other end asked me to meet him in another room. I mean what did I expect? This was real-life spy stuff.

Of course, I had gone down to the room as requested. Looking down a long hallway, I found the room number and knocked twice.

A shiver had run down my spine as a businessman with thick black horned-rimmed glasses opened the door, motioning me inside. It was the same Mr. Collins. Behind him another man in a dark suit was walking around checking behind pictures, underneath beds and around desks for microphones. It seemed a little like overkill to me, but apparently not to the agency people. I, too, would soon believe the walls have ears and eyes. I, too, would learn to always be careful about what I said and where I said it.

Things were moving quickly, and I wasn't even through training at that point. Every day I reminded myself that I could quit after the initial contract. If I wanted to. If I needed to. If I should ever fall in love and want to stay grounded, so to speak. In the meantime, I was just glad that I was being assigned near Dallas for a while before my overseas contract started. At least I would get to spend some time getting to know Darla better. Who knows, with her wanting to be a singing star, maybe she would want a guy who didn't mind that she was on the road too.

Rearranging myself in my seat, I brought my mind back to the present as I glanced at my plane's controls. The weather outside had cleared a bit. It was smooth sailing now. So much easier to fly than the U-2, even in the thunderstorm I'd just flown through.

I'd been training so hard on the U-2 that flying a regular plane was a piece of cake. A relaxing ride with not much more to do than sit back and enjoy. So easy, in fact that I allowed myself to daydream more about what I'd been through in the last few months as I trained to become a spy-plane pilot.

Flying a U-2 was a whole different ballgame.

For starters, I always made sure I went to sleep early the night before flying a reconnaissance mission. Because without a doubt, a U-2 pilot's body is stressed to its limit. And that's saying a lot because most of the pilots were athletes used to pushing themselves to the top of their abilities. I don't know about the others, but in my case, the U-2 training pushed my body and mind to a whole new level. My body performed in ways I never imagined it would or could. And, of that, I was pretty proud.

Usually before a training mission, I'd get up early in the morning to prepare. I'm talking around 5:00 a.m. Immediately after eating breakfast I would report to pre-breathing to "get on the hose"—a denitrogenation process during which pilots were given pure oxygen, under slight pressure, so they wouldn't get the bends. Pressurization breathing was reversed from what was normal for most humans.

Inhaling was automatic, while exhaling was an effort. I literally had to learn to breathe backwards.

Next came the suiting up process. Which by the way required quite a bit of assistance because the suit was so bulky and tight. I was told it was a partial-pressure suit designed for high-altitude flight. And trust me it was airtight. Made of stiff rubberized fabric that fit snuggly around the body. Translation: one-could-hardly-bend-an-arm-or-turn-a-knee snug.

A hermetic seal at the neck fastened my helmet into place.

On long flights, counting prep time, we pilots were expected to remain in this getup for up to twelve hours. No wonder they tested us in advance for claustrophobia.

And guess what? We couldn't eat in this contraption because it was dangerous to unfasten the suit. A sudden loss of oxygen could mean trouble. So, we went without food and drink. All the while sweating our butts off. To say a pilot was dehydrated at the end of a flight was an understatement. Plus, because the suits had no ventilation, there was no way for the skin to breathe. Or for perspiration to evaporate. Which meant if you did wear long johns under the suit, you ended up wringing the water out of them at the end of the flight.

Add to all this the constant monitoring of the flights while fulfilling the photo requirements of a reconnaissance mission. All in a very tight cockpit. If you weren't checking the RPM, the EGT, the compass, the fire warning lights or the artificial horizon, you were watching your ever-critical air speed. It was a constant flipping of switches as you homed in on your target. Often, we didn't even know what we were photographing—just that we needed to photograph that exact spot. And, oh boy, you better hope you got it right. Otherwise, all would have been for naught.

Everything took such a toll on a piolot's mental and physical faculties that after landing we wouldn't be able to fly again for two days. Believe you me, it did take two days to recover. Still, the thrill of it all kept me on a constant high.

Imagine being one of the lucky ones to fly at over 70,000 feet in the air.

How I wish I could talk about my missions to someone. But I couldn't. Not even to the other reconnaissance pilots.

CHAPTER 14

COWBOY LARSON

My spirits lifted as Clarence parked his Chevy truck in the small blacktop parking lot near the Sulphur River. It truly was shaping up to be a great getaway for Mick and me. Clarence too. The smell of rotting fish floated up from a nearby trash bin, but even the stench couldn't impede upon my good mood.

We needed some time to write new songs. Rethink our image. Make sure we were keeping things fresh.

Deep down, I was thankful country music fans liked old musicians as well as new ones. It would be hard on my soul to get tossed by the wayside just because we weren't some young kids. I mean, at least we could explore Mick's need to move beyond what we've been doing creatively without totally destroying our fan base.

Our managers were starting to get antsy about Mick's creative visions. Visions they didn't want mucking up the tour they were planning. I understood their concerns. They had some big money backers who expected a return on their investment. But enough of those thoughts. The warm sun was bringing me unexpected joy. I was thankful to be healthy and fit, no real problems to speak of. In fact, this was the first time since my wife's death two years ago that I felt pretty good all over. And I wasn't going to let dark thoughts slip in on such a sunny day.

Mick and I were incognito in floppy fishing hats and vests. We looked like just any ordinary old fishermen. Heck, we were ordinary old fishermen. I'd been fishing since I was three. My daddy used to take my brothers and me fly fishing all the time up at his brother's in Missouri. In fact, a lot of my fishing lures and gear were gifts from my uncle.

I looked down at a skunk tail lure hanging on my vest pocket and smiled, remembering how my brothers and I had laughed at the name when my uncle gave it to me. My father had told me to hang on to it. It was a good lure, no matter how comical it sounded.

"Do you think we dare risk going in that little store over there named Birdie's Bait Shop? Surely no one will recognize us." Mick motioned toward a worn-down shack that had once been painted lemon yellow. Only now it was more of a weathered grayish-clay color with a hint of its former lemon-yellow self shining through. A rickety bench leaned to the left outside the fingerprinted glass door. The only redeeming thing about it was a freshly painted white sign near a big metal bin that read "Live Bait" in big red letters. Whoever had lettered it had some art skills.

"What you thinking about?" Mick poked at my arm.

"Going in that store and getting a cold Dr Pepper and a Moon Pie."

"Let's test out your disguises," Clarence said, listening nearby. "I think it'll be okay. I don't even recognize you two myself. However, you should both keep your traps shut so no one will recognize your voices. Especially you, Mick. No one sounds like you."

"What about me? Aren't I special?"

Clarence ignored me as he carefully untied the tarp covering the back of the boat and swung the metal minnow pail out. With a shake, he dusted cobwebs off its dirty exterior so it'd be good to go. So much for my fancy lures.

When we stepped inside the little bait shop, it took me by surprise.

Once my eyes adjusted to the darkened interior, I could see the place was clean and overflowing with rack after rack of taste-tempting pies and cakes alongside the usual chips, drinks and snacks you'd expect to find.

Behind the clerk's register was a full wall of cigarettes, cigars and chews. A young crewcut kid asked to buy two packages of cigarettes. One for his mother, and the other for his grandmother. The well-tanned cashier put down the cigarette she was smoking in a small red ashtray before giving her bleached blonde hair a flip. Patiently, I watched as she perused the wall behind her for the brand he asked for.

"Now you sure these are for your folks and not yourself?" The blonde flipped her hair again without listening for his answer. She laid two packages on the counter in front of him.

However, the youngster did answer with a sincere, "Yes, ma'am. They are for my folks." Without a doubt, I knew he was telling the truth. Because in my day, I'd be buying them for my teenaged self, and I would have been a little miffed at the cashier for calling me out. But this kid was different. No arrogance. No attitude. He appeared to be as clean on the inside as he looked on the outside.

"Excuse me, mister," the well-mannered boy said, turning and pushing past me toward the door.

Forgetting I was supposed to stay silent, I answered, "No, excuse me, son."

The blonde at the counter straightened up. Her whole demeanor changed. But if she recognized me, she didn't let it show. Nevertheless, I was sorry I'd opened my big mouth. Because in a small town like this, news travels fast. If word got around, fans might find us at the cabin. Or maybe if they did, it'd be a good thing. Especially if Mick's stalker got wind of it. It'd flush her out, so to speak. That way we wouldn't be dealing with an unknown.

Clarence went up to the cashier to pay for our selections. "I also need a pail full of minnows." He put the items near the old-fashioned register. "How's the fishing?"

"Ohhh . . ." the cashier pulled out the word as she stretched forward in a seductive manner, "I'd say fair-to-middlin'. But the weather is nice. Not too hot. Not too windy."

"You mind if we leave my truck in the lot for a few days?"

"Not my lot, but lots of people leave their rides there when they're fishing. I don't think you'll have any trouble leaving it." Her voice was as smoky as her cigarette. She took a long drag as she looked Clarence over from head to toe. Obviously, his good looks were not lost on her. I felt a little twinge of jealousy. Usually, I was the one getting all the attention. Or maybe it was my purple fringed cowboy shirts that Mick had convinced me to leave at home.

———

In three shakes of a lamb's tail, the three of us were boating down the South Sulphur. Even though it was mid-afternoon, the heavy tree-lined shore made for a shadowy ride. And the cottonwood floated down all around us, stuffing up my sinuses. Across the murky water, tiny ripples appeared here and there while insects dipped in and around us, gently luring me into a trance with their buzzing hum. Bullfrogs joined the chorus, and as my late wife Saint used to say, "all was well with the world."

"Hey, did I tell you guys I got a letter from Rayne?" Mick asked.

"Oh yeah?" I said. "What did he have to say?" I knew how much Mick cared for his nephew, and I knew he worried about him being away. "Good news or bad?"

"Good." Mick turned to me and smiled. "He's coming home. Can you believe it? He's been transferred to Texas for a short while." Just as he said the words, a great white Egret dipped straight down from the sky to the water. In seconds, the majestic bird emerged with a splash and a fish in its beak. Seconds later, it took off again.

We three turned just in time to see the miraculous sight. I felt deep in my soul it was an omen of good things to come. This was turning out to be quite a good fishing trip.

And no one had even cast a line.

———

After about an hour or so, Clarence and Mick started to confer on where to dock our boat for the walk to the cabin. Rayne had given landmarks on the hand-drawn map he'd given to Mick a few weeks back.

Clarence turned the map this way and that before saying, "We've already passed the big live oak and the rock outcropping. We should be coming up on the wooden dock and metal pole where we can leave our boat."

"But first we need to pass by the field where we can see the last remains of an old railroad trestle still standing," Mick added.

"I think we already did," I said.

"No, we haven't." Mick was adamant. "I've been watching."

"Watching the wrong direction," I countered. "'Cause I saw the remains of an old railroad bridge a few miles back."

"Okay," Clarence said, "I think Cowboy may be right because that looks like a small wooden dock up ahead on the left."

Sure enough, just as we rounded a curve in the river, I could see some boards sticking up out of the water. Not really a dock so much as a few wooden piers poking up just above water level with a couple of boards tacked to them.

Clarence steered us toward the little pile of wooden mess. Just then, a big raindrop plopped on Mick's head. I watched as he reached up to touch his wet hair. He looked skyward, squinted his eyes.

Then I felt a drop of water. Then another.

It didn't take long for the shower to get stronger. Luckily, Clarence was already tying our boat off to a metal pole positioned just along the shoreline. The water wasn't deep, and he waded through it as he pulled up as close to shore as he could get. Mick was already out and running up under a clump of trees. I grabbed the tarp we'd used to cover our belongings up with in the truck and spread it over our gear in the boat. Good thing I didn't wear one of my expensive cowboy shirts or hats because it was going to be a gully washer.

Clarence gave me a hand, and I got out of the boat, wading to shore. I'm embarrassed to say I was so out of shape, I had trouble getting up the steep rocky shoreline. Almost fell on my butt. To his credit, Clarence remained silent. Just kept a grip on my hand, pulling and tugging me up. Once ashore, I took a moment to compose myself before we joined Mick under the trees.

Clarence walked at a regular pace, only stopping once to push his wet hair out of his eyes. As he did, he looked upward and shook his hair back. Just another small obstacle in Clarence's day to be overcome. I swear the guy had nerves of steel. Absolutely nothing rattled him. Mentally and physically, he was one of the strongest people I'd ever met. No wonder Mick had hired him to be his bodyguard. He certainly had moxie.

"You know what they say about the weather in Texas," Mick said to no one in particular. "If you don't like it—give it five minutes and it will change."

Just then, a large clap of thunder hit a tree in the distance.

I swear I felt a charge in my feet as we stood under the big oak.

"Gentlemen," I said, "shall we move onward to the cabin?"

"I'm ready," Mick said. "This tree isn't providing much cover. Why don't we go to the house and dry out, then come back for the stuff in the boat? The tarp should keep it dry. At least more dry than we could keep it if we carried it in this downpour."

"Let me get the guns." Clarence turned and started toward the boat.

"We brought guns?" I asked.

"Yeah," Mick answered.

"Why do we need guns? I thought we were going fishing."

"Well, you know, we might need to shoot a snake or a wild animal."

As he got closer to our boat, Clarence turned around and added loudly. "Or a disgruntled fan!"

Things got real for me real fast as it occurred to me that Mick's stalker might actually come this far out in the boonies. I mean, I had said the stalker might follow us to get him to come away and focus on writing, but I didn't think they'd actually do it. But Clarence was taking his job as bodyguard very seriously. I guess that's what Mick was paying him for.

I watched as Clarence waded around in thigh-high water to the boat, pulling a metal box used to hold crackers out of the back of it. He put it under his arm and started making his way toward the slippery shoreline. He made it up without a hitch.

As he got closer to us, I wiped the rain from my eyes and slicked back my hair.

"Well," I said, gesturing at the saltine cracker tin, "weren't you going to get the guns?"

"I did." He held up the cracker tin. "Don't worry. They're both wrapped in plastic. As well as the bullets."

"And I've got extra ammunition in my guitar case," Mick said as he turned and scanned the horizon to our right. "According to Rayne's directions, the cabin is about a hundred yards southwest along this trail. Maybe hidden up in that tree line."

We walked along the beaten area. I twisted my foot a bit on the rocky path.

"Ouch," I said.

No one asked what my problem was because they were too intent on walking.

A chill ran down my spine as I glanced at the metal cracker tin under Clarence's arm. The cold rain soaked me through and through. Onward I slushed behind my friends, through the long, wet grass and slippery mud until, in my annoyance, I finally exclaimed, "Mick, are you sure this is a trail?"

"No." He continued trudging determinedly.

Clarence straightened his collar against the gusting wind with his free hand as he followed closely behind Mick. I got in line. Drudging behind the two of them. Surely we'd end up somewhere.

Somehow.

PART 4

CHASING A DOLLAR

CHAPTER 15

Just Outside of Fort Worth, Texas
Thursday Morning
October 9, 1958

AYNE

Hitchhiking in the wee hours of the early morning was always a pleasant experience. The golden pink horizon got prettier and prettier as the sun rose. Plus, the heat was still bearable even if the wind wasn't blowing. Lucky for me, it was gusting today with just a hint of rain in the air. I carefully readjusted my small suitcase using only three fingers instead of four to keep its cheap plastic handle from cutting into my hand. I'd bought the case because it was lightweight, but here out on the road it was proving to be a nuisance. I made a mental note to stay with a satchel in the future.

The smell of airplane fuel from the nearby airfield I'd just left mixed with the aroma of baking biscuits from inside the small roadside café up ahead. After pondering whether I should stop and eat breakfast or forge on ahead, I opted for the former. Experience had taught me I better eat when I could. Hopping across a bar ditch, I walked diagonally across a nearby field to get to the café. It was a much shorter walk than following the road. As my boots crunched over rocks and dirt, I watched a small snake slither away. I slowed my pace to make certain he had plenty of time to escape. Didn't feel like tangling with a copperhead in October. My grandfather always warned me they had trouble seeing in October because they were shedding their skin, and it made them blind. Was it a true fact? I didn't know, but I didn't want to test it.

As I approached the café, a puppy came toward me, wagging its tail in a friendly manner. I knew when I saw it someone had probably dumped the poor pooch here. It was a little too skinny and dirty to be someone's pet. Looking closer, I judged it to be part terrier and part border collie—Heinz 57-variety mix, my buddy Sol would say.

As I attempted to open the glass café door, the little dog tried to enter.

"Go on. Git!" I stamped my foot. But he wouldn't be deterred.

Pushing and shoving, he hopped over my dusty boot and ran inside.

Chaos ensued as he ran around, knocking over a stand of magazines and a display of candy. Nothing was broken, but nothing was left in the place it should be.

"That your dog, mister?"

I looked up to see one of the biggest human beings I'd ever seen. Dressed in jeans, a white T-shirt and a white apron, he wore a paper hat on his bald head. Huge muscles bulged as he gathered up the pup in his heavy arms.

"No," I answered, "pretty sure he's a stray. Tried to keep him out, but he got around me."

The man looked at me and blinked.

I took a deep breath.

"Here, let me take him outside and I'll help you clean up this mess." Most of the customers and waitstaff had already started the process, but there was still a ways to go to getting things back to the way they were.

I reached out to take the puppy from him, but the big man kept the little mutt close to his chest.

Then, he took me by surprise as he softly said, "If he's not yours, do you think it'll be alright if I keep him?"

Just then a tiny woman stepped out from around the big man. "Bill," she pleaded with her hands on her hips, "we don't need another dog. We already have three."

The big man moved around me and opened the café door. Positioning his body half in and half out, he turned back to the woman and said, "Just look at that cute little face."

I moved to the right of the woman and began picking up what was left of the magazines, making sure not to wrinkle them.

"He's a pest. Look at all the mess he made in here," the woman exclaimed.

The man held the little dog closer to his chest, and the dog strained to kiss his face.

"Oh, sweet mother of pearl!" The woman said. "Go put him in the office, and I'll take him home when we've finished with the breakfast crowd."

Big guy Bill's face brightened as a big smile broke out over his face. He held the dog closer and kissed it back.

"Here," the woman screeched, "give me the dog and go wash your hands. Those eggs ain't going to cook themselves. Johnny's back there frying bacon and it's going to get cold before he can plate it up."

Not knowing what to do with myself, I went up to the bar and took a seat on one of the vinyl-covered swirling stools. It creaked when I sat and made little screeching sounds when I moved. So, I tried to sit still and blend in with the usual crowd—workers in overalls, airmen in uniforms and a few salesmen. I assumed they were salesmen because they had cases full of something and they were dressed in suits with ties. Their hair was carefully combed and they ate with their ties flipped back over their shoulders so as to keep themselves spotlessly clean. Which wasn't that easy in a place like this, where grease seemed to cover everything. Even the floor was a little slick. This seemed to be particularly pleasing to the young ones who were sliding around behind me at the bar. Every so often, one of their mothers would chastise them and tell them to hold it down. But really it didn't matter. The whole place vibrated with sounds from the kitchen, occasional roars from the nearby airport and a rollicking tune on the jukebox.

Of course, my scrambled eggs smothered in ketchup were some of the best I'd ever had.

———

Back out on the open highway, I raised my thumb and tried to look pleasant and trustworthy. Before long, a car pulled over with one of the salesmen from the diner. Same salesman who'd been giving kids quarters to put in the jukebox back at the café. He seemed like a nice guy in spite of his perfect hair.

"Hey," I yelled, "going to Dallas?"

"Yes," he yelled back, motioning for me to get in the passenger seat.

Once I got in, he waited for me to close the door before he accelerated back into the stream of traffic.

"Boy, this new interstate sure is something, isn't it? Going to be real nice when they've finished it." His entire face lit up in a smile, and he extended his hand. "Buddy Gilmore," he said.

"Rayne Wesley," I said, shaking his hand. "Thanks for picking me up."

"Would have given you a ride from the diner if I knew you needed one."

He turned up the radio.

Then he turned it down again.

"Say, do you like music?"

"Yes."

"Do you like it loud? Because I like it loud."

"Loud is good."

And just like that he turned up the volume and we didn't speak again for twenty minutes. Which was just fine by me because I don't like to jabber a lot unless I have something important to say.

As we moved along the highway, the silhouette of Fort Worth's downtown fell away, replaced mostly by open fields. Both our car windows were rolled down so we could get maximum air through our hair. His suit coat flopped from a hanger in the back. And for a little while I saw him as the young man he was, out having fun instead of making a living. Even his perfect hair flew free and wild. This guy definitely loved his music, turned up so loud I imagined more than a few cars got an earful as we flew past.

As we blew into the east part of downtown Dallas, I motioned for him to let me out. Without a word he exited the interstate and pulled over to the side of the road. As I gathered my few things, I asked him what he did for a living. "I sell and repair jukeboxes," he said. "Let me know if you're ever in need of one." He handed me a business card.

"Thank you, sir," I said, knowing he was very near my age. "Much obliged for the ride to Dallas. I sure do appreciate it."

With a smile and a wave of his hand he was off again. That guy, Buddy Gilmore, he sure liked his job. I could probably take a lesson or two from him about the way he lived his life.

The sun pulled up overhead, and the brick road under my feet burned through my boots. So, I decided to go into the nearby barber shop and ask if I could use the phone. The little shop was busy for a Thursday. Picking up a magazine, I sat down on a hardback chair positioned near the wall. Didn't want to disturb the barber while he was finishing his customer. Looking around I saw at least five other men waiting their turn. The smell of Old Spice and other scents circulated around as the cooler in the back window blew icy air up front. I must admit, it did its job well for a window unit. Finally, the barber whipped off the black cape he had snapped around the man's neck with a dramatic flair as he said, "Volia! Herman, you're a new man."

Looking at the next customer in line, he motioned for him to take the barber chair.

"Sir," I interrupted.

"What can I do for you, son?"

"May I use your phone to call someone to pick me up?"

"Sure, the phone's over yonder." He pointed back toward a small hallway that led to a bathroom. "You're not calling long distance, are you?"

"No, sir, it's local."

"Just don't stay on it too long because it's a party line."

At that point one of the customers piped up and added, "And don't say anything you wouldn't say out loud in church because Old Lady Simpson is always listening."

The other men laughed, and one of them said, "Oh, don't you know that's the truth."

Another echoed from the corner, "I thought Old Lady Simpson was dead?"

"No," the barber said as he cut his customer's hair, "she just has one foot in the grave . . . and the other foot on a banana peel."

I left them to their jokes and stories that only old men know how to tell. Right at that moment, I wanted to get to the McLaren mansion and have a glass of iced tea with my Aunt Margaret. But what I really was hoping in my heart was that Darla would be working at the mansion today. Because she was all I'd been thinking about on the trip back. I thought of the letter she'd written me. While it didn't say anything romantic, it did have a big lipstick print on the envelope in the shape of a kiss.

Picking up the receiver, I could hardly hear the dial rotating for all the chuckling in the background. The phone only rang once when an unfamiliar voice answered. "Hello, McLaren residence. This is Angel speaking."

I was pretty sure I heard Old Lady Simpson gasping.

"Yes, this is Rayne. I'm Mick's nephew. Would you please tell my Aunt Margaret I need a ride in from the barbershop on Fifth and Main?"

"I can pick you up. I'll be right there," Angel said just before hanging up.

Now how in blue blazes was I going to know what Angel looked like? Was she someone new working for Mick and Cowboy? I guessed I'd fine out soon.

"You get yourself a ride?" the barber asked, looking up from his work.

"Yes, sir. Said she'd be right up to get me."

"Well, have yourself a seat where it's cool to wait. Get yourself a soda if you're thirsty."

As I went to get the soda, the barber continued with his story. "I'm telling you," he said, "that woman could start a fight in an empty house." The men all laughed. Truth be told, I did too. I think the barber had missed his calling as a comedian.

Suddenly, the room quieted with the squeal of fast wheels turning into a screeching brake. Everyone gawked out the front window. I recognized Cowboy Larson's convertible Caddy with longhorns on the front. The woman inside got out and adjusted her skirt. Carefully she put on her high heels before ascending the concrete steps to the barber shop. I heard the tinkling bell as she opened the door and stepped inside. What could I say? She looked like an angel.

The barber struggled to gain his composure. The only sound in the shop was the swishing sound of the Carrier window unit blowing hard.

Looking from face to face, the woman stopped when her eyes landed on me.

"You must be Rayne," she said smiling brightly. "Darla told me you were terribly good-looking."

My heart jumped at her words.

At that she took the soda I'd just opened from my hand and took a big swig.

"You ready to go? Your Aunt Margaret and the kids can't wait to see you."

I nodded and waited for her to hand my soda back.

She didn't.

She just turned and sashayed to the glass door as she drained down the rest of my drink. As she opened the door, she turned back and said to the men in the room, "Nice meeting you guys!" Then she motioned to me. "C'mon, Rayne. All the cold air will get out."

"And I ain't paying to air condition the parking lot." Somehow the barber had found his voice, and the room went back to its jolly vibe.

CHAPTER 16

ARLA

"What in the tarnation?" I could hear my mother call from the front room where she was ironing. "Darla," she cried out, loud enough to be heard through the open windows, "there's a blonde floozy in a Cadillac with long-horn steer antlers out front."

"It's my ride, Mama."

Grabbing my purse, I ran toward the door. The last thing I needed was Angel surveying my family's front room with all the laundry spread everywhere while Mama ironed. I hoped Angel hadn't heard Mama call her a floozy. But then again maybe it would do her some good to know what people really thought of her flamboyant-peacock style. Speaking of style, I, myself, could be compared to a little brown hen today. I didn't have a speck of makeup on, and my hair wasn't as fresh as it could be. Darned old oily hair. I could start the day doing okay, but by lunch it would look pretty bad. Well, no time to do anything about it now. Glad I had pulled it back in a ponytail.

The doorbell rang as I slid my sunglasses over my tired-looking eyes.

I pulled the door open to make a fast getaway. My mouth fell to the ground. Angel wasn't standing in front of me. Rayne was.

Of all the people, I didn't expect him. Pushing my dark sunglasses up, I prayed I was at least halfway presentable. When he reached out, I wasn't prepared for the warmth of his touch on my forearm. My pulse raced. My breath caught. Oh, dear Lord! Why didn't I put makeup on today?

Things couldn't get worse.

Oh yes they could.

Mama stood right behind me complete with pink sponge rollers in her hair and a worn-out housedress. To my horror, she invited Rayne inside. And, what's more, Angel had parked the Caddy out front and was preparing to join us. I looked around. Where would we all sit? Mama had insisted on keeping a plastic slipcover over her good couch.

No, no, no! my mind screamed. This is a nightmare. Wake up. Wake up.

Rayne moved past me into the living room. He held out his hand to my mama and said, "Rayne Weston." My mother giggled like a young girl before replying, "Virginia Darling. But most people call me Vergie."

Angel moved forward.

My heart sank as she surveyed the worn furnishings. Suddenly I saw every flaw. Every crack in the wall. Every chip in the paint on the moldings. Every scuff on the floor. Our hardwoods did not gleam. And I was embarrassed we didn't have real curtains. Mama had made curtains, but they weren't up to snuff.

Angel walked over to a shelf on the wall. Her attention was focused on some small figurines my uncle had brought back from overseas. Turning she addressed my mama. "They're absolutely beautiful. So delicate. Each one is a tiny masterpiece. Would you consider selling them to me?"

Mama hesitated. I knew they were her pride and joy.

So, I interrupted. "Oh no, we couldn't sell them. They're priceless to us because they are some of the few things we have to remind us of my uncle. He brought them back to us from his time in the war." As much as my mother irritated me, I couldn't stand the thought of her losing her figurines. Or myself for that matter. How many times had I stared at them as a little girl and imagined myself as a Geisha girl. The heat was growing in my cheeks as I reached up to smooth my greasy hair.

Angel's perfume overpowered the small room—*Shalimar*. A nice enough scent if you don't bathe in it. Her sensuous fumes sickened me as she moved past me and took Rayne's arm. Or maybe it was the fact that they seemed to be together that made me feel ill. I didn't even know they knew each other. When I'd spoken of Rayne, Angel didn't indicate she'd met him. But then she was devilish that way. She never disclosed any information unless it benefitted her. I had to admit she was far smarter than she appeared. Even her dumb blonde persona seemed to be a way for her to manipulate those around her. As my grandpa would say, "She was playing chess while the rest of us were playing checkers."

My heart was beating fast. I felt faint as I searched the pantry for something to feed our guests. There was nothing but potato chips and iced tea.

Mama came up behind me and took me by the arm. Leading me to the kitchen counter, she whispered, "Darla, you need to go put some lipstick on. You look like a pale prune against that girl. As it is, you don't stand much of a chance with a guy like him. He has what they call 'movie star' good looks." She glanced back at Angel and Rayne sitting at the kitchen table. "Go, do something with yourself. I'll take care of our guests." With that she put a new package of Lorna Doone cookies on the counter.

All I could think as I scurried to freshen up in the back room was, "Where was she hiding the Lorna Doones?"

Under the stark light that hung over the bathroom sink, I took in my appearance. Mama's words cut me through and through. She was right. I didn't stand a chance with Rayne. I'd been foolish to think I did. Just look at how perfect he looked with Angel. They were a matched set in the looks department.

Leaning toward the mirror I made an "O" shape with my mouth as

I attempted to apply Mama's red lipstick. But I couldn't bring myself to do it. Instead, the lump in my throat started to close down tight and my eyes and forehead crinkled up as I started to cry. Not just a few tears, but a heart-rending torrent of burning hot tears. I tried to keep the noise down, but my silent sobs and gasps just made me cry harder as I watched the girl in the mirror.

Why, oh why wasn't I ever the special one? Why wasn't love ever for me? I just wasn't going to be able to have someone like Rayne want me the way I wanted him. Stupid, stupid, stupid me. I couldn't go out to face them again. I had no idea what to do except escape through the bathroom window so I could hide in the garage.

My throat was so dry and it hurt so bad. Plus, my nose was swollen and running. I pulled off a few sheets of toilet paper to blow it hard. That's when I looked up and saw Rayne standing in the hallway.

"Darla," he said, sounding concerned, "what's wrong?"

"Rayne, my cat died this morning." I lied in an attempt to explain my outburst of tears.

With that he came into the messy bathroom and pulled me into his arms. His strength ebbed through his muscles as he pulled me closer than anyone had ever held me. My head rested on his beating heart. I tried not to turn my face into his nicely pressed shirt to avoid getting snot on it.

Oh Lawd, please don't let Mother tell him I don't have a cat.

At that moment, I decided to come clean.

"Rayne," I managed to get out, "I don't have a cat."

His face looked perplexed.

Behind him I saw Angel's face stick around the corner. "Of course you don't, honey. Your cat is deader than a doornail . . ."

Rayne looked back at Angel. Apparently, her harsh words had surprised both of us. "I mean," she lowered to a softer tone, "just because Scooter's left his earthly home doesn't mean he won't live on in your heart. Now you get yourself together and come with us. We've got work to do at the McLaren mansion." Angel touched Rayne's arm as she added, "Please give us two women a minute, would ya?"

Rayne stepped out and went down the hallway.

Angel stepped forward and pulled a piece of toilet paper from the fresh roll perched on the back of the fuzzy pink toilet tank cover.

"Blow your nose . . . and let's get going. I know why you're really crying."

"You do?" I asked while getting more toilet paper off the roll.

"Yes. And Rayne and I aren't an item. And furthermore, I'm not after him. Margaret had me pick him up after he called her. She knew I needed to come pick you up as well. Now splash some cold water on your face."

"Angel, why are you being so nice to me?"

"Because I can't be mean to everybody all the time—if I was I wouldn't have any friends. Listen, Darla! If you're going to be a star, you've got to have a thicker skin. Quit being an idgit."

"What's an idgit?"

"A nice word for 'idiot.'"

She gently pulled my arm toward the bathroom door in an attempt to guide me out.

"Just a minute."

I picked up the blue *Avon Here's My Heart* bottle from the mint green tiled sink and gave myself a spritz. The advertisement in the magazine had claimed "it adds to your niceness." I doubted this, but for a moment I contemplated squirting a little on Angel. However, I didn't think I could stand one more heady scent at the moment.

As we went down the hallway and rounded the corner, I heard lots of laughter from the kitchen where Rayne and Mama sat eating Lorna Doones. Maybe today wasn't going to be so bad after all.

"Guess what?" Angel whispered conspiratorially in my ear. "Margaret's come up with a plan for the three of us to cut a record together."

My heart jerked erratically at her words.

And just like that I rode a rollercoaster of emotions right up to the highest high.

CHAPTER 17

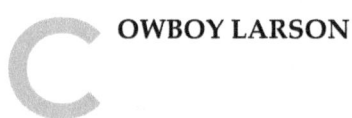C OWBOY LARSON

Trees hid the cabin. Mick and Clarence reached it first as I felt a little under the weather. Dragging behind, I watched as they tried the door —locked. Clarence circled to the back to see if there was another entrance. There wasn't. But he did tell us he saw poison ivy leaves as big as his face in the backyard. I watched as Mick searched for a key.

"Mick quit poking around at stuff sitting on the front porch!" I was more than irritated at the situation. "Get over here and break the window."

"You break the window." He continued to look through planters and pots and pans. There was even a set of dishes sitting outside by an old metal glider. A couple of rocking chairs that had seen better days sat nearby.

Clarence went over by Mick and started feeling the top of the window trim. In less than a minute flat he produced a key. It was rusted, but it was a key.

My heart felt relief when he stuck it in the door lock and it turned with only a little resistance. Next he put his shoulder to the swollen door and pushed hard. Finally it started to move. Not without a lot of creaking. But he got it open. To my surprise, he took a flashlight out of his pocket and went inside. Suddenly, the cabin came to life with light. He'd found and flipped on light switches.

"This cabin has electricity?" I muttered more to myself than anyone else.

"That ain't right." Mick passed me to go inside. "Seems like it should have candles or oil lamps. Something old fashioned. I can't believe they got electricity to it. Rayne's father and uncle must come out here a lot."

With more than a little hesitation, I ventured inside. The door stoop creaked ominously as I passed over it. I worried I might fall through the floorboards. But once inside, I could see that all the decay was deceptively on the outside. The inside was a fisherman's dream. From plush leather couches and an oak table with four matching chairs, it was anything but rustic. In fact, it looked like the kitchen came out of a magazine.

"Well, this is certainly not what I expected." Mick plopped down on the sofa and picked up a wooden box from the coffee table.

"Is that filled with cigars?" I asked.

"Yes." He took one out and looked it over. "The fancy kind."

Clarence came out of one of the bedrooms. "Guys," he said smilingly, "looks like we found ourselves a little bit of heaven on earth. And talk about secure. No one is likely to venture out this far." With that he went to the front door. "I saw a wheelbarrow on the side of the house. I'm fixin' to go get it and head back to the boat. It'll be perfect for getting all our gear up here, now that the rain has slackened up."

Of course, Mick offered to help. Which meant I had to help, too.

I tried to have a good attitude, but really, I just wanted to take a nap. So I had to make an effort to hide my crankiness.

Once outside, I didn't have to fake it anymore. The rain had cleared the air, giving it that uplifting charge that comes after a shower. The birds had begun singing again. Crickets chirped and somewhere in the distance bullfrogs groaned. Yes, this getaway was going to be good for us, I thought as I looked up through a cover of live oak leaves.

Clarence led the way with the wheelbarrow. His stride held a sense of purpose as he got out ahead of us on the trail. I tagged along behind Mick and tried not to breathe heavily. I didn't like being old. Cigarettes and alcohol were doing me in. I made a resolution to myself to try to stop.

But I knew even as I made it, I wouldn't quit.

———

The boat sat just as we'd left it. Still wet from the thunder shower, but the wind hadn't budged the tied down tarp. I watched as Mick maneuvered the wheelbarrow close to the shore. Clarence waded out to the side of the boat. The water lapped at his thighs, leaving his light-colored jeans a shade darker down below. They would dry out in no time in this heat, but still I hated to see Clarence doing the dirty work. But not so much that I got in myself. Instead, I waited up on shore with my arms crossed. Soon, Clarence was hauling our gear up to the wheelbarrow where Mick took it and stacked it in a most orderly way.

"Hey, Clarence," I said, "when you get to our guitars, hand'em here and I'll carry'em. Plus, I think I can carry a couple of those gunny sacks of food."

"I dunno know," Clarence lifted up one of the gunny sacks. "These are pretty heavy. Better stack them on top of the stuff in the wheelbarrow." I watched as he handed the sack of food off to Mick. Then he turned and brought out our guitars. I moved forward and took the handle of my case in my right hand and Mick's case in my left. I immediately felt better. Even though these weren't our most expensive instruments, they were a couple of our favorites. In fact, Mick called this one his "songwriting guitar."

Before too long, we were on our way back to the cabin, which in my mind was more like a plush hideaway. Don't know why I'd expected we'd be roughing it. Guess I just expected everything to be hard because I had been brought up in the Depression era.

I must say this was a far cry from the Dust Bowl.

PART 5

THE PAIN OF LOVING YOU

CHAPTER 18

Garden of the McLaren Mansion, Dallas, TX
Friday Afternoon
October 17, 1958

ARGARET

Standing in the back door of the kitchen, and staring out across the rows of flowering bushes that I'd had planted earlier in the spring, I wished for love. Love was a long, long time ago. Way back when. Life was nice, but something was missing. Sometimes, in the middle of the night, I let myself think of what was going on in the deep recesses of my mind. I believed Mick was infatuated with being a star and all it brought with it. Which was undoubtedly women. And lots of them.

Cowboy would never betray Mick. If Mick was doing something wrong, Cowboy'd just act like it hadn't happened. The only other person in the world who'd know would be Mick himself. And he'd never admit any wrongdoing. Not even to himself.

So, I acted like nothing was wrong. But I knew.

I smoothed the front of my cotton dress, the one I wore when I didn't have errands to run downtown. Moving forward, I walked to the small picket fence that separated our property from our neighbor's. A gate in the fence separated the properties, but I doubt it'd ever been opened. At least not since we moved in years ago. Especially seeing as the fence was in disrepair. White paint curled up, leaving gray wood exposed. I moved to the gate and tried the latch. It opened easily, barely squeaking. I pushed it forward into the overgrown brambles.

A lilac bush overhanging a gazebo beckoned me forward. Inside were wooden Adirondack chairs. And they were somewhat clean. Only the lightest layer of dust. Could it be our neighbors had been using the gazebo and we hadn't even realized it? It certainly was a way from their main house. Maybe the servants kept it clean.

Picking my way across fallen tree limbs, grateful for my sensible leather shoes, I ventured up to the steps of the gazebo. No one would find me here. A chill ran up my spine at the thought of having a secret hideaway. Mick wasn't the only one in need of a getaway. I needed some alone time as well, if only for an hour or so.

On my approach, the scent of lilacs floated past me, making me feel fine.

Nearby, a pair of doves cooed in unison.

My heart soared. Absolute exhilaration filled every fiber of my being. Like a kid finding a secret hideout, I surveyed my surroundings. This would be the perfect place to write songs. Mick and Cowboy weren't the only two musicians in this family. Now that the kids were older, I needed to express myself creatively too.

The wind rustled the few leaves piled up inside the gazebo. I made a mental note to bring a broom with me the next time. I sat down on one of the wooden Adirondack chairs to gather my wits. Leaves of gold, burnt orange and pure yellow rained down around my fairy shelter. Every little whisper of the wind brought a new batch with it. Nearby, a squirrel busied itself digging up a nut before scurrying up a birch tree. Dappled sunlight fell through the intricate gazebo roof in just a few places where patches of shingles had fallen by the wayside. A spider's web glistened high above me.

"Perfect, perfect," I said. And a large black crow answered me with a squawk. His reply reminded me that the spark of life flows through all creatures great and small. We're all part of this world together.

Who built this place? And would our neighbor mind me being on their property? Would they ever know of my trespassing? Chances are I'd hear them coming long before they saw me. Leaning back in the chair, I glanced up at the overhanging tree boughs in the autumn sky. Today the sunshine was surrounded by a light gray cloudless backdrop. It felt good to be here. It felt right. It felt like the universe had meant for me to discover this private little Garden of Eden.

It had been so long since I'd written songs or sang them for an audience. This is what I wanted to do, but somehow, I'd found myself cooking, cleaning and doing the laundry. Day in and day out. The same routine really unless I went to one of the lady luncheons where I can't say I really fit in all that well.

Getting up, I went to the gazebo railing and looked out across the wooded area. A tree had fallen in the recent storm. Its side stripped bare of bark where a heavy limb had crashed to the ground. Even if I'd heard it back at our big house, I don't know if I'd have given it another thought. Not with all I had to do in my safe, secure world.

And then I began to sing—a quiet song I'd loved since I was a girl.

Then I sang louder. A spiritual song I'd learned years ago from a blues singer named Sister Rosetta.

I tried to belt it out like she did, swaying my hips, raising my hands to the air. Then bringing it home in almost a whisper. Sister Rosetta had taught me a lot about working a crowd. I was a much better person because our paths had crossed.

The birds stopped their singing and listened to me. A squirrel stood spellbound with an acorn in its tiny paws. My audience wasn't large, but it was attentive. I couldn't ask for more.

After I finished my song, Mother Nature took back over with all her sounds. Even a murder of crows nearby started hollering. I stood still and listened. Letting the sounds vibrate off my very soul.

Then I moved up on the gazebo steps, and I picked up a big stick to use as my microphone. First, I made sure to thank everyone for coming. Then I told them a story about where the next song came from. It was one I'd written about the day when my mother died.

"Now, you guys are going to have to pipe down a little bit," I said to the trees and abundant wildlife, "because this is a sad song . . . and you're going to have to hush now." And to my amazement, the crows calmed and the wind blew soft. Deep and low, I started singing from the bottom of my heart. It was cathartic to sing the song with every emotion I could muster. My passion came through in every single word as I sang to absolutely no one but the wind and the wildlife. And, of course, to myself.

Trust me, I knew how to be alone. I'd spent so much time alone late at night after the kids had gone to sleep or were engaged in school or their activities. I knew Mick and Cowboy needed to be on the road to make a living, but knowing that didn't make it any easier on me. Not having love on a daily basis was hard. So many people with the same problem having to make peace with their circumstances and gut it up. I would too. I had so much to be thankful for. Even when I was alone.

The wind whispered its secrets to me and the leaves danced down in a light rain of beauty. I wanted so much to turn to Mick and say "Beautiful!" Instead, I said it to myself. Mother Nature was putting on a show. I stood still and watched.

Without warning, the skies started to plop down big fat raindrops. Experience had taught me that I needed to run home or brave it out in the gazebo.

I decided to make a run for it. Hesitating momentarily, I lifted my skirt and ran to our side of the fence, leaving behind my mystical, magical hideaway.

I glanced backward—I knew I'd be back. And I was going to bring a few things with me to fix it up special. No one would know. And if a neighbor did venture out this far, they'd assume one of the kids had done it.

In a few moments, I came up to the back screen door. Swinging it open, I rushed inside the back foyer, pulling off my wet shoes, shaking my damp hair. I'd made it inside just in time before the downpour.

Turning, I watched the rain pour in torrents for a little while before softly closing the back door.

Walking back to the kitchen, I could hear the kids playing in the living room. Most of the time I'd chase them out of this particular part of the house because I wanted to keep it perfect for visitors, but with Mick out of town, there would be no visitors. I had no friends or business acquaintances to entertain. Mick's sister Katherine was my best friend, but she was family. No need to clean up for her.

I needed to fix supper. But I was completely uninspired. So, instead, I went to our bedroom where Mick kept a small upright piano. He said it was for me, but really, he was the one who used it, writing melodies and songs at all hours of the night.

When did I let my creativity go? Could I even write a song anymore? For years now, my life has been all about supporting Mick, taking care of kids, making all our lives run on time. Sure, when they were younger, I'd insist on doing all their care myself. Hardly ever hired a nanny or a sitter. So, I had to admit it was me that had let myself stagnate. Now how to turn it around?

I put one finger down on the key of B. Then I played a little from memory. But not very much. And not very well.

Soon I was digging through some old sheet music at the bottom of the hinged piano seat. The last thing I discovered was a song I'd written as a teen, when I had first returned from being on the road with Mick and Cowboy. The ink was faded. The sheet a bit messy. But the chords and lyrics to my song remained intact. Appropriately enough, I'd titled it "From Long Ago." The words rang true today. Standing straight and tall, I started to sing my forgotten tune. A tune straight from the heart. Sad, lamenting, turning hopeful at the end. It was decent.

And it was enough to make me want to try again.

Going back to the piano, I caught my reflection in the mirror at its top edge. I'd certainly aged since I'd penned that song. Wisps of gray hair now framed my face. My skin looked pale and doughy. Nothing like the spirited young girl Mick had fallen in love with. Perhaps this was why he played around on me. I hadn't admitted that last thought to anyone, not even myself. Until now. But I suspected that the person stalking him was some female fan who had spent a short period of time with him on the road. Now she wanted revenge for him breaking her heart. No need to ask Cowboy. He'd never tell.

But I knew.

I'd heard Mick saying her name in his sleep. Both in a good way and a bad way.

A clattering of feet headed up the stairs. I turned to see my eldest son walk into our room.

"Mama," Thomas said, "it's time to eat and nothing is cooking in the kitchen. Does that mean we're going out to a restaurant?"

"Yes," I smiled, "tell everyone to wash up."

At that, Debra and Jamison appeared, their faces with questioning expressions.

"Hurry, everyone. Go put on some shoes. Wash your hands and face even if you don't think it needs it. We're going uptown. You kids are old enough to appreciate a good meal. Lawd knows I haven't had one in a while." It was true. Mick's stalker had put the kibosh on so many everyday things in our family life. I was tired of having to look over my shoulder, especially when I thought the threat came from a delusional fan who was really only after Mick. In fact, I'd told him, "We don't want or need a bodyguard. You keep Clarence for yourself." I was determined the kids and I were going to live a normal life once again. Or at least as normal a life as we could have with a famous person in our family. It did pain me that the kids would never know the simple life Mick and I had known growing up.

The kids had wanted burgers instead of steak, so we settled on Jack's café just a few miles from our house. Filled with customers of every age, the place was jumping tonight. Someone put one of Mick and Cowboy's most famous tunes on the jukebox when we came in the front door. The name of the song was "Up Near Dallas" and it always reminded me of our time together when we first met and really got to know each other. Maybe tonight I'd tell the kids about how Mick, Cowboy and I had hopped trains to get back home.

Before I could start the story, a man came over to take our orders. He wasn't just a regular waiter anxious to get our order under way. He was the owner. It surprised me that he would go out of his way to come meet us. After all, neither Mick nor Cowboy was with us. Not even the less famous but still recognizable Darla or Angel. No singer or musician among us, yet he still made us feel special.

After he turned our orders in, he came back and sat beside me.

"You don't know me, do you?" He extended his hand. "I'm Jack Donovan, your neighbor."

I blushed. It was true I hadn't recognized him, but I knew his name. We didn't really socialize with any of our neighbors. Mainly because we all lived in big, gated estates set back from the road.

"Jack Donovan." I took his hand. Looking up, I tried not to stare into his beautiful brown eyes, soft as velvet. His white teeth gleamed against his tanned skin. I'd heard our neighbor was a well-known tennis player, but I had never thought much about it until now, seeing him in person. It made perfect sense that he'd own a restaurant like this one, with sports memorabilia everywhere. Sports photographs of all kinds lined the walls.

I turned to the kids and introduced Jack as our neighbor. Then I told him our names.

"Yes, I know. But it's nice to meet everyone in person," he said.

Next thing I knew, a waitress and waiter delivered chocolate milk-shakes all around to the children's delighted squeals. I didn't remember anyone ordering a milkshake, but I wasn't about to send them back. Tonight my kids would celebrate being normal. Even if they didn't know what normal was all about.

Hamburgers and fries came out next. Jack came back to our table to check on us and then told me he had to get back to work.

I blushed again and told him how much I appreciated him stopping by our table to visit.

When he left, I looked down at my hands. I wished I hadn't put off filing and painting my fingernails. I wished I'd worn my blue dress instead of this pink paisley one. I wished I'd taken the time to apply fresh lipstick. It was time to pay attention. Not only to myself, but to my kids' needs. Tonight they were happier than they'd been in a long time. Tonight was about us, instead of Mick and Cowboy. Tonight my way of thinking about life had turned a corner.

———

As the kids and I went out to the restaurant parking lot, an uneasiness rippled through me. But it wasn't until we were almost to our car that my son Thomas pointed to the tires—all four of them were flat.

A slice of sharp fear stabbed in my stomach. No way would all four would go flat at once. As if to confirm my thoughts, Thomas, who'd run up to take a closer look, shouted, "They were cut."

"Let's go back inside the restaurant," I said trying to appear calm. I grabbed the two younger children by the hand. "Thomas, let's go," I called back over my shoulder.

Jack met us at the door, holding one of the kid's sweater. He handed it to me. "I think you forgot this."

I didn't reply, just took the sweater and handed it off to the first kid behind me. "Jack,"—I tried not to sound hysterical, but I could feel my voice rising with each word— "someone has vandalized our car. All four tires have been slit."

Jack's face dropped. "We hardly have any crime in this area of town. Let me take you and the kids home, then I'll call the police and sort it out. Tomorrow I can have someone bring over four new tires."

"Please don't call the police." My voice sounded more pleading than I'd intended. "It will only bring unnecessary attention to Mick and Cowboy. They've been having problems with a fan lately. You may have seen a few stories on the news."

Jack stepped back and spoke privately to one of the waiters. I imagined it had to do with driving us home. The waiter nodded. Then Jack turned back to us.

"Let me get my jacket." He turned to leave, heading in the direction of what I assumed to be his office. A few minutes later, he came out carrying his jacket and a briefcase. He'd also put a hat on his head. Clearly, he was leaving for the night.

"If you won't let me alert the police, will you at least let me drive you home? I can check things out since you told me Mick was out of town. And I can make certain no one follows you."

I didn't know what to say. One side of me did want him to come check out our house. But my good judgment cautioned me to remember he was a stranger, too. All I really knew about him was that he lived on the estate next door.

———

The clock struck midnight, and I still couldn't sleep. Even with Jack on the couch downstairs and Thomas in the room next to mine. The two younger children were sleeping in my room. I picked up the phone to call Mick's agent but thought better of it. I'd do that in the morning. Perhaps he could get someone to run a message out to the remote cabin where Mick and Cowboy were staying. I wondered if they would come back if they knew. But I didn't want to take them away from their songwriting. They needed this getaway on so many levels. Perhaps it would be better not to say anything to anyone.

Both kids were asleep and my mind wouldn't quit racing. Quietly, I opened the bedroom door and went out into the hallway. I moved soundlessly to the grand staircase. Looking down, I could see Jack asleep on the sofa in the den, the room closest to the front door. I swept down the stairs in my bare feet and padded across the marble tiles in the formal living room to make my way to the kitchen.

I often thought of the kitchen as *my* room. I spent so much time there. Not just cooking. This was where I talked on the phone to my friends. Where I ironed and folded laundry. Where I filed my nails and gave myself a manicure. Which I reminded myself once again I needed badly.

The back door had a window in it. It didn't have much of a window covering, just sheer lace curtains. I sat at the table with my face toward it. I tried not to look at the darkness behind the lace. A chill ran over me, making the hair on the back of my neck stand up. I felt like I was being watched. Surely not, my common sense assured me.

A glass of milk would help me sleep.

My body moved mindlessly. First getting out the milk from the refrigerator. Then the glass from the cupboard. My favorite one with the cartoon character on it. Next, I poured, walked over and put the full glass of milk on the table.

I must have put the milk carton back in the refrigerator. It wasn't on the cabinet. I must have. Yes, I had. I clutched the back of a chair.

My nerves were shattered. My thoughts were coming in tattered, haphazard.

Wait. Was the back doorknob being turned?

Oh, dear God, let it be locked.

I clutched the top of my robe.

I watched in horror. Someone started rattling the knob harder, attempting to enter.

"Jack." My voice came out in a hoarse whisper. He'd never hear me. "Jack," I managed to shout. "Jack!" I screamed again louder and louder. I turned, ran from the kitchen door, straight into Jack's arms in the kitchen doorway.

The flash of the camera strobe behind me was blinding. Turning to look in the direction of the kitchen door window, a stalking photographer fired off another photo of the two of us. And then another.

I wasn't prepared for it to be in the next morning's newspapers. But I was prepared for it to be in the trash tabloids.

Who had I been kidding? Thinking my kids and I could ever have a normal life.

CHAPTER 19

COWBOY LARSON

Every time I wrote a new song it was like I was doing it for the first time. No matter that I'd been doing it for over twenty years. As always, I wrote almost every day, writing many songs to get that just right one. Then perfecting it. Yes, divine inspiration did come at times, but more often than not, it was practice and perseverance that got a good song out of me or Mick. And lately, Mick had been veering off our country roots and moving into some other kind of sound. A sound I could appreciate and try to follow, but not so much our agents and producers. Their take was "if it ain't broke, don't fix it" or something of that sort of thinking.

So here we were, way out in the middle of nowhere, trying to get away from all the business meetings and bickering. Just the two of us, like when we were young. Doing music our way without a lot of people putting in their two cents' worth.

Maybe it was time for me to put down my pen and pick up a fishing pole for a while. The sun beat down hotter than blazes, and the heavy lunch we'd eaten made me feel like it was more time for a siesta down near the river shore than songwriting in the cabin. I knew from experience I wasn't going to make the words or the music come. If I was out there trying, in a bit something would show up, maybe a little ripple, or if I was lucky, a big wave. I'd just have to keep committing things on paper and waiting for the big one to come. Lucky for me, I'd brought plenty of yellow legal pads. If they got wet, I'd have another. Days like this, I was happy I didn't have an office job.

"Where's the minnow bucket?" I asked no one in particular.

"Down by where we docked the boat," Mick called back.

I didn't ask him or Clarence to come with me. If they wanted to, they'd come. Truth be told, I wanted to be by myself. Work some things out in my mind without any idle chattering going on in the background.

The fishing poles were still inside the boat. So, I moseyed in that direction with nothing but the beer in my hand. Pulling down the brim of my straw cowboy hat, I felt for the cigarette package in my shirt pocket. As always, it was there along with the matchbook I'd picked up at our last recording. The studio was giving them out free as promotions. I figured Mick and I had paid for them as we'd spent quite a lot that day recording. More than we usually spend. We didn't have our stuff worked out when we arrived. And we'd argue about every detail of the styling. It still irked me that when I'd asked Mick how he liked some chords I was trying to add to one of the new songs he'd written, he'd replied, "That fits like socks on a rooster." I knew what he meant, but it still stung. Mick was funny, but he more often than not used his wit to cut and wound.

Today he was in a piss poor mood.

Walking through the soft grass, I noticed most everything was still fairly green. Some burnt orange, red and golden leaves were starting to flutter down. I imagined the recent spate of thunderstorms and showers were keeping the leaves and grass from turning too fast. Which was good for country folks as grass fires were less likely to start. The meadow I was walking through teemed with the sounds of life even though I couldn't see anything but the occasional bug flitting by my blue jeans that I wore tucked in my cowboy boots. Best in case I encountered a snake. Deadly or not, I didn't want a snake going up my pant leg.

When I got to the shore, I stood and surveyed the area.

The water was still with the occasional bubble. Gnats swarmed nearby where a bird lay dead. I wondered how it had died. Instead of smoking as I'd intended, I pulled a can of chewing tobacco from my back pants pocket and put a pinch in my mouth. Dammit, I left my notepad and pen. Oh well, I'd just fish. Fish and think. Let my mind wander.

I didn't hear him come up on me. I just felt his presence, and I turned around slowly. It was the teenage boy we'd encountered at the store. His short blond crewcut gleamed in the sun, and his tanned skin glistened from sweat. He'd been out running, he said. Trying to make the track team. Said he saw me sitting there and wanted to make sure I didn't need anything from town. He'd be running that way if I wanted him to bring me something back. I told him no, that I was just fishing.

He turned to leave and then came back. I made out his age to be around fifteen or sixteen. Maybe older. It was hard to tell he was so clean-cut.

"Mind if I sit here awhile?" he asked. "I understand if you might not want company. Won't offend me if you need time alone."

"Sit," I said.

And he did. But to my surprise he didn't talk.

He just stretched out his long legs and leaned back on his arms. Gazing across the river, he lifted his hand to block the sun's rays from his eyes. His feet were covered in dust from running on the backroads. I noticed he didn't wear track shoes. I could only imagine how fast he'd travel with the proper footwear. Dressed in a white T-shirt and blue dungarees, he was a typical teenager on the outside. But on the inside, he was different, I could tell. He was a deep-down thinker. Even now his mind was wandering off in its own orbit far away from the both of us.

I let him be. Just as he let me be.

After a while, he asked me if I thought there was an actual heaven and an actual hell.

"I don't know," I said. "Hadn't really thought about it that much.

Maybe it's more of a different place in space. I don't know so much that it is above or below us."

"Uh huh," he said. "Are you going to the big church revival event?"

"Haven't heard anything about it. When and where is it going to be held?"

"It's tonight. Just outside of the town square. In the big park near the covered picnic area. That is, if it don't rain no more. The ground is already soaked. Any more rain and it'll be too boggy to hold a revival." He was silent for a bit. Then he added, "There's going to be singing and such. Gospel music. Do you like any of that?" He looked me directly in the eye even though the sun shining behind me made him squint hard.

"Yes," I said, "I was raised on gospel music."

"Good. Because I'm going to be performing. Pretty much last to go on . . . but I made it on the docket."

I thought back to the first time I'd ever played. It had been at a county fair. Now I knew why this boy had sought me out. He had the music inside him and he had recognized us. And he didn't have a lot of people around him who understood.

"Why don't we walk back up to the cabin?" I said more than asked. "You can meet my friends Mick and Clarence."

I saw excitement flash across his face before he settled back in to his calm demeanor.

"That'd be just great." He said the words low and without any emotion. "But aren't you going to fish first?"

"No," I answered, "I don't feel like fishing anymore today."

"Are you sure Mick will want to meet a local? I mean I saw that you two were disguised the other day at the store. Figured you didn't want anyone bothering you for autographs."

"I didn't think our disguises were fooling anyone," I laughed. "Come meet Mick. We're trying to get some songs written, but so far we've come up dry. Maybe you'll inspire us."

"Okay," he said sincerely, "I'll try."

"What's your name?" I asked as I gathered my fishing gear and put it back in the boat.

"Daniel, but people call me Danny."

"Nice to meet you. My name's Cowboy . . . Cowboy Larson. But seems you might already know that." I shook his hand ,and we turned without speaking to walk back up to the cabin. The silence between us was not uncomfortable. It felt natural. It felt right.

However, he was so quiet, I almost forgot he was beside me when I opened the cabin door.

Mick and Clarence jumped to their feet when they saw the boy enter. I brought him forward and introduced them to him one at a time. Clarence first and Mick second. Danny turned bright red under Mick's gaze. I knew he was in awe, so I took over the conversation.

"This here is Danny," I said. "Met him fishing. He was also at the bait shack we stopped at on our way here."

"Do you live near here?" Clarence asked cautiously. I knew he and Mick didn't want word getting out we were staying in the cabin.

"Yes," said Danny, "just up the way. I live on Dog Town Road with my parents, brothers and sisters."

"Danny offered to get us anything we needed on his way into town." I watched Clarence's shoulders relax, and Mick smiled as he said he would like a cake.

"It's Cowboy's birthday today. We need a cake." He turned to Danny and pulled out some dollars. "How much do you think you'll need?"

I was surprised Mick had remembered. I'd almost forgotten myself. But I can't say I wasn't pleased at the thought of a cake.

That's when Clarence jumped into the conversation. "Let's go out to eat. We can buy the cake on the way back. I saw a catfish restaurant on the way down. You know the place I'm talking about, Danny?"

"Yessir. It's a great place to eat."

Mick put his money back in his wallet. "Let's go. Will we need to take the boat to get back to the bait shop?"

"There is a little faster way to get to the store than by water . . . I usually run down this winding dirt path that goes through these woods," Danny said as he pointed into a heavily wooded area. "Only the locals know about it."

"Do we have to run? Couldn't we just walk real fast?" Mick asked as he got his cowboy hat and sunglasses.

Clarence strapped on his gun before pulling his dark sunglasses out of his shirt pocket.

I looked at the clock on the wall. Straight up noon. The day was starting to shape up.

"When we get our pickup truck from the bait shack parking lot, we can stop in and buy a cake to take with us," Mick said, as if my having a cake on my actual birthday was important. And in a way, I guess it was. The thought of someone acknowledging my birthday on the actual day of my birth was a nice gesture. I appreciated Mick for it. He could be as kind as he was cruel. I'd never get used to his peculiar ways, but I loved him like a brother.

I opened the cabin door and gestured for Danny to go out in front of us.

"Lead the way, Danny Boy!"

Nothing like the start of a new adventure. I felt it in my bones—we were about to go in a direction we'd never gone before. Both figuratively and literally. Mick must've felt it too, because the air around us seemed amped up and charged, in a way I've only experienced when we were about to play to an audience. Yes, Mick and I both were tuned into the situation as we followed the boy outside. The screen door slammed shut behind us. I hoped to all get-out we didn't end up on the ten o'clock news. Or worse yet, the front page of the newspaper.

Mick's stalker had gotten a little too close to us on our last gig. Sure didn't want them to track us out here, even though I knew that was what Clarence and Mick were hoping for.

Looking up, I saw fluffy white clouds parting in the bright blue Texas sky.

Son of a gun! It was my birthday, and I was going to get cake.

CHAPTER 20

ARGARET

"Your voice is soft, like summer rain."

My heart beat fast as he said the words. I pretended not to notice the compliment, instead concentrating on my tennis racket. One of the kids had given it a beating, scraping its top as they used it to twirl around and around on the asphalt-covered court. Most likely one of the younger kids pretending to be a dancer. Who knows why kids do what they do?

"I should get a new racket." I showed him the damage.

He took the racket from my hands, examining it. "It is in bad shape. However, no worries, I'll bring one of mine next time. I've got one you can have that's just right for your size grip."

Nodding my head, I tried to concentrate on the game at hand. I couldn't believe I'd accepted Jack's, offer to come next door and play tennis. The sun beat down on my head, making me lightheaded. Sweat trickled down my back. I was glad I'd pulled my hair up in a ponytail. I could feel it swing every time I swung the racket. Maybe next time I should try a bun, but then again maybe I shouldn't be playing tennis when I had so many chores to do at home.

"Your serve," I pointed my racket at him.

I'd immediately said yes when Jack had called. I guess I desperately needed a little fun in my life. There was still so much to get done around the house, especially when Mick was on the road. I had to do it all. As Cowboy had joked once, I was married, but essentially a single mother.

I'd laughed as he'd said it, but the truth stung. Both Mick and Cowboy knew what family sacrifices had to be made for their career. Cowboy, especially, since he'd lost the love of his life, Saint, a few years back. Said the heartache had made him a better songwriter.

I repositioned my stance and waited for Jack's serve. When the ball did come, I was ready and I smacked hard. But my worthy opponent was also ready.

"Go ahead. Take whatever's bothering you out on me," he said as he returned with a strong swing of his own. His words were punctuated by the solid *thud* of the ball hitting his racket.

As I returned his volley, my heart contracted in pain as I wondered where Mick was and what he might be doing. Why did I even care? Over the course of our marriage, he'd been gone more than he was home. Still, I yearned to know the love we'd shared back in the early days. Before kids, I could travel with him and Cowboy. Even got to go on stage and sing with them some. But those days were long gone.

My thoughts became even darker on this sunny day. I hit the ball hard as I replayed in my mind how these days, I'm just a housewife with not much to look forward to—unless you count doing laundry and dishes as fun. Doing laundry and dishes . . . I'd done so much of it for so long it was automatic . . . just like breathing really.

My opponent took advantage of my wandering mind. I missed the ball, and he scored on me.

He delightedly declared himself the winner.

Yes, he was the winner. Not just of this game we were playing, but of life.

I swear I felt pea green envy at the freedom he had.

I steeled myself before turning around to gather my things.

"Will I see you tomorrow?" Jack sprinted across the court to me.

My first thought was to shake my head no. Then I thought better of it. Slowly, I turned around and smiled coyly, "Yes, you will. I'm tired of being a loser. I'll be back tomorrow to beat the pants off you."

"I look forward to it." His smile made his eyes sparkle in a mischievous way. I couldn't help but smile back. It was nice to have someone interesting in my life. Even if I did feel incredibly guilty about finding him so interesting. But who wouldn't? He was funny, smart, incredibly good-looking. My heart jumped at that last thought. It really wasn't a good idea to encourage him. I shouldn't. And I wouldn't. Next time he called and asked me to play, I'd tell him no . . . at least I thought I would. That is if he ever called again. After all, he was a former pro tennis player, and I, on the other hand, was not even a tennis player. I was . . . I was just a frumpy housewife. Whatever could he find interesting about me. Stop it! Stop it! Stop it! Stop thinking bad thoughts. Just enjoy this day for what it was. Two friends playing tennis. Once again, my mind turned to worry. I wondered if the stalker who'd taken the photo of Jack and me all arm in arm in the kitchen was going to use it for nefarious purposes. Most likely, they were out trying to sell it to a newspaper or magazine right now. But maybe not. It had already been a couple days.

PART 6

TRAVELING SALVATION SHOW

CHAPTER 21

Just Outside of Klondike, Texas
Wednesday Evening
October 22, 1958

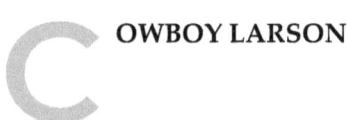 OWBOY LARSON

As we hiked to the bait shop, Mick got the bright idea that we'd all go watch Danny play and sing at the traveling salvation show instead of going to the catfish restaurant. So, in addition to picking my cake up at the little store, we also got a whole bunch of picnic food, including chicken fried steak, mashed taters and green beans. It smelled heavenly.

Now I'd never been to a traveling salvation show so I didn't know what to expect. Suffice it to say, I went into the experience with no preconceived notions. But, just like Mick, I definitely wanted to watch Danny perform.

When we got there, I was surprised to see almost everyone in town had turned out. I do mean absolutely every person in town was there. All the way from old-timers to newborn babies. The atmosphere was charged with excitement. This was going to be some kind of show. Of that I was sure.

The sun was setting low, taking some of its heat with it, but not nearly enough for me. The salvation show was being held in an outdoor auditorium setting, not the air-conditioned church as I'd hoped.

Outside in a park-like area, some girls played with those newfangled hula hoops. Over and over, they'd try to make the hoops swing around their waists in a flowing swirl—not unlike a hula dancer or belly dancer. Not at all appropriate for a church event. But who am I to judge? I hadn't been to church in years. Besides, the girls weren't too great at hula-hooping. Only one could get it going for any length of time.

I sat down at a wooden picnic table to observe. Mick, Clarence and Danny were back at the car getting the food and cake we'd just bought at Birdie's Bait Shop. Didn't think I'd be passing a milestone birthday like this with a cake from Birdie's Bait Shop. But the cake looked good, and it was Coconut Cream, my favorite. The food had smelled fantastic when we bought it. Aromas of chicken fried steak wafted through the gentle breeze making my tastebuds water in anticipation. I wished they'd hurry up. My stomach was growling. I looked around at the people socializing. Pretty nice birthday celebration, I'd say. I guessed a traveling salvation show was kind of like a musical show, but with preaching thrown in the mix.

The microphones on the stage were being checked. Occasionally, a reverberating screeching noise rang out. Loud enough to hurt my ears, but I tried not to show it. Only flinched and gritted my teeth a little. Tried to act like I was readjusting my hat instead of holding my hands over my ears. Mick and I weren't wearing heavy disguises as we had when we originally came to town. The two of us were just wearing sunglasses and hats pulled low. No one seemed to notice us at all. At least if they did, they didn't let on in any way. Or maybe we just weren't as famous as we thought we were. Or maybe the people never expected us to be in this part of the country. One thing for sure—Danny Boy must have tight lips. No one had shown up at our cabin even though he said he'd known it was my voice when he first laid eyes on us at the bait shop. He was a real nice kid. The sort of person you knew instinctively you could trust. It would be fun to see him do his show. I hoped for his sake most people hadn't left before he got on stage.

Then I heard the shriek.

Followed by high-pitched squeals.

And more shrieks.

Yup. Mick had been discovered. That wavy auburn hair did him in every time. He'd probably taken off his ball cap to readjust it or something as simple as that . . . and suddenly he was no longer a stranger in the crowd . . . he was his public persona. I couldn't see him, but I could see the crowd building around him.

Neither of us could complain. We'd worked our tails off for years to achieve fame. Now we needed to have a relaxed mental attitude about all the hubbub surrounding it. I settled down for a smoke on the edge of the picnic bench. It'd be a while before they figured out where I was hiding.

Looking back at the group of fans going wild, I saw Danny emerge with a covered dish and a cake box. He headed my way . . . must've heard my stomach growling. Like I said, he was a good kid.

He walked closer and motioned for me to follow.

Without saying a word, I fell in step beside him. We crossed over the park area onto an asphalt trail. Then into a grove of trees where an overhead wooden platform peeked out from the still mostly green leaves above us. A series of nailed boards went up the side of the tree, like a ladder.

Handing the covered plastic food tray to me, Danny took the cake box and put it on a dumbwaiter of sorts. Then he grabbed the food container from me and nestled it alongside the box.

"I'll go up first." He scurried up the wooden rungs like a squirrel escaping a dog.

Reaching down, I arranged the covered food container more securely on the homemade dumbwaiter. I looked up to see Danny was already on the wooden platform waiting for me to start pulling on the rope. I tried to do it slow and even . . . easy, easy, easy, so my cake wouldn't fall off. In less than a few steady pulls, I had it almost to the platform when it got stuck. I had to swing the rope out wide and then pull to get it off a limb. The cake box wobbled. My heart sank. I realized I really wanted a birthday cake. Just because I was old didn't mean there wasn't a little kid in me.

Finally, Danny pulled the birthday feast to safety.

Slowly, I released the rope, letting the dumbwaiter gently glide back down. I wondered who in tarnation designed the contraption. Some genius, no doubt.

Next, I started up the wooden rungs. Not nearly as fast as Danny. I really was getting old. Even heard the bones in my knee creak. Damn, I was out of breath. I should've quit smoking years ago. Danny helped pull me onto the wooden platform, but once there, I felt secure. Happy. Like a kid again. It was a great place to watch what was happening below. I could see Mick signing autographs for a never-ending line of people. Male. Female. Young. Old. And every age in between.

Mick must've escaped somewhere because the shrieking and screams had subsided almost as soon as they started. I could only hope the commotion of Mick's fans didn't hamper the night's events. I really wanted to see a salvation show. Danny had promised lots of good music.

Before too long, the sun set lower in the sky, making the stage lights glow. As if on cue, everyone took their places in the wooden pews set out in staggered rows that gave most people a good view. Excitement rippled through the crowd. This time I knew it wasn't Mick. I could see a tall dark-haired man striding purposely up the steps to the pulpit on stage. He was dressed all in black. His eyes flashed in the evening glow of the lanterns placed on the stage. He was a sight to behold. A figure not even for the devil to reckon with.

The congregation grew quiet. However, the atmosphere became more charged.

The preacher man took the microphone. His voice thundered, "Brothers and sisters, let us pray!"

From my position in the treehouse, I watched as every head bowed.

Only the cicadas sang softly in the background as he began his holy communication with the Lord. His powerful voice punctuated his heartfelt words. His message pounded in my head.

When he was finished, the preacher made several announcements before inviting the musicians and choir to sing. Angelic voices rose in unison. The hair on my arms stood up. Totally captivating was the only way to describe the singing.

Where was Mick? I hoped he'd taken it all in so we could somehow, someway incorporate the sound into our music. I looked behind me to see Danny's reaction. He was nowhere to be seen.

Out in the audience people raised their hands to clap along with the choir.

Turning back to the stage, I saw Danny among the choir members. Of course, he'd told me he'd be playing tonight. I didn't realize he'd be singing in the choir, too. I don't know why it surprised me to see him there. Guess it was because he had gotten on stage so fast after making certain I was safely hidden up in the treehouse with our food. I needed to exercise more. It wasn't that long ago that I could move as fast and as flexibly as Danny did. Today was my birthday and I felt like an old man. Just lucky to make it this far in life, I guess.

I reached over to the long plastic tray of food Danny had set down beside me and took a few bites before settling my long, lanky frame across the wooden deck I was perched upon. Not the most comfortable accommodations but, all in all, not bad either. At least I had a bird's-eye view of the entire place. And with all the glowing lanterns on poles, I could see both the faces of the preacher and most of the congregation.

No wonder the whole town had turned out. So much more than I'd expected musically.

Talk about making a beautiful noise unto the Lord.

Now Danny moved forward out of the crowd. Taking off his choir robe, he stood in his blue jeans and white T-shirt. Someone handed him his electric guitar. For a moment, he held it up, making certain it was in tune. Then he put it up against his body and became one with it as he played song after song.

The gospel beat pounded out over the crowd, engulfing people in its power. He didn't sing the words to the songs—but the people did. And their voices rose above his solo riffs. Sometimes drowning him out. Other times their voices were a soft murmur. More of a hum, really.

Then all too soon it ended. Danny left the stage. And the preacher man returned.

His voice started off low as he brought forth his message of hope.

Then his voice reverberated like a small earthquake.

He talked about helping your fellow man, about letting God help you, how when you struggle you become closer to God. And I was totally engrossed. Overwhelmed by the power of his message. My throat clenched. Tears edged my eyes. I pulled my cap down lower over my face and thought of my late wife's last request that I find salvation. My heart told me tonight was the night to go down to the stage where so many others already were.

I hardly felt the ladder rungs as I descended the tree and crossed the grassy area below.

At the stage, I knelt and bowed my head.

The crowd gasped in unison when I took off my cap.

Recognition rippled through as I'd heard it do so many times before.

But this night was different.

The preacher knelt beside me and prayed with me as I accepted Christ.

No one invaded my privacy.

This was just between me and God.

And for that I was thankful.

CHAPTER 22

R AYNE

As I slipped into the deep sleep that comes from being completely and totally exhausted, I hadn't been prepared for the vivid dream. So real it would stay with me for days. Punctuating my thoughts. Making me remember. Making me smile.

There are moments in life that define you. This was one for me. And frankly, I was surprised it showed up again in a dream. A dream about Anna. The girl I had cheated on Jennifer with in Alaska. But when I first took up with Anna, I didn't consider it cheating.

She was a prostitute. A young village woman from Alaska who came down from the mountains and decided to make it on her own. On her own she had decided to make money with her looks. And I'm certain she did well because she was one of the most naturally beautiful people I'd ever seen. With glossy dark hair flowing to her waist and soft doe-like brown eyes. Her presence was ethereal.

She wasn't your ordinary prostitute. She was very particular about her clientele. I felt honored when she accepted my proposition. I only felt a tinge of guilt about Jennifer. After all, we weren't married, and Anna would be a short-time thing. Reflecting on it, I see how flawed my double-edged thinking had been. How Jennifer may have ended up straying because I put myself, my desires, my ambitions before her.

The dream was so lifelike—just like the night it had really happened.

Anna had beckoned for me to come aboard a houseboat floating on the frosty lake. It wasn't terribly cold, but there was a chill in the air. A single mattress with cotton sheets and a blanket filled the open deck of the boat.

Our lovemaking was long and slow. Filled with passionate kisses and soft caresses. The very scent of her made me heady with desire. On and on we went as we whet our appetites for each other. I never wanted it to end.

Afterwards, I glanced up at the heavens above as I lay in her arms.

The stars were spectacular. Twinkling, shimmering above.

Desire filled my heart as she ran her soft hand down the muscles of my arm.

Turning, I snuggled closer to her while pulling the blanket up around us as the calm water below rocked us gently. I heard the waves swooshing rhythmically upon the not too distant shoreline, and lapping in response against the sides of the boat. Glancing over the rails of the houseboat, I saw a hazy smoke hovering in the sky above the nearby town rising from chimneys as people slept securely inside their homes. Unaware that we were even here. In our own little private cocoon.

It was that night I realized I was falling for Anna. It was no longer a business transaction for me. I gazed at her as she gazed at the heavens above.

What was she thinking?

I breathed a deep sigh and wrapped her tighter in my arms as I watched a star darting across the night sky's eternal glow. Someone told me once that each star represented an angel. It was easy to believe that night, for I'd never experienced such rich beauty in all my life.

And I don't think I ever will again. Except in my dreams.

Anna was gone. Lost in a fire that I couldn't have done anything about. A fire that raged in the rickety old apartment she'd chosen to live in so she could save money. A fire that extinguished her beautiful spirit long before she should've left this world. I knew she'd plans for a different life in the Lower 48. But when she died, she was simply a call girl.

And the fire wasn't even investigated. Authorities felt their time and resources could be used on more important things. The newspapers reported a fire had burned down an old apartment building and a nameless Alaskan woman had perished.

My heart surged with pain at the direction my thoughts were headed.

Jennifer was gone as well. She'd deserted me for my good friend. Though not as final as death still incredibly painful. My heart hurt each time I heard her name said aloud.

It was time to quit remembering anything but the positive moments and move forward with my life. And I hoped I might do it with Darla. I hoped to be a better man with her. She was unlike anyone I'd ever met. My heart and mind were drawn to her uniqueness. She held her dreams close and aspired in a way that most women don't in this day and age. She seemed to be drawn to me as well. I swear I had felt a gravitational pull the first time we met. But that was my heart talking. In my head I knew it was going to be hard to establish any kind of relationship with me flying missions back and forth overseas for the next eighteen months. That along with her getting her singing career off the ground. She'd already told me she was going on Mick and Cowboy's next cross-country tour. I guessed the best we could do was try.

Right now, I was happy to be home for a while and that she was still in town for a few more months. It would give us a chance to get to know each other more. Taking another deep breath, I rationalized, if a relationship with Darla was supposed to happen, it would happen. The physical distance between us would not be a problem if our minds were as one.

Sitting up on the side of the bed, I looked around the guest room my Aunt Margaret had put me in the day before when I had arrived without any notice. Obviously, she must always be ready for guests in this big mansion of hers and Mick's. Fresh towels sat on a chair near the door. My bed linens smelled of lavender, and she even had a bottle of water and glasses brought in before I went to sleep last night. She was so thoughtful. I could learn a lesson from her. Mostly I just thought of myself. Or at least that's what Jennifer used to say a lot. So maybe I wasn't a great boyfriend.

I shook my head as if to shake off the remnants of the houseboat dream. I hadn't been good to Anna either. Where was I when the fire broke out in the rickety old apartment? I was in jail for drunk and disorderly conduct. I had been out with some of the guys. We had too much to drink and not enough to do, and we got into a fight with some of the locals. Big guys who knew how to fight. So not only was I thrown in jail, sleeping on what felt like a piece of plywood with a sheet covering it, but I was hurting pretty badly as well.

When I had gotten back to the base, they called me into the Big Guy's office. I thought I would get disciplined. Instead, they told me things had been taken care of. Fines paid. Charges dropped. Then the last thing in the world I expected to happen, happened. The Big Guy told me I'd been promoted to sergeant. I was in complete and utter shock. But the joy didn't last too long. Later that day I found out about the fire and Anna's death. I know I was just a client to her. But I believe we both knew it was becoming something more. I grieved her loss deep in my gut before the pain finally settled in my heart. I still felt that pain with each thought of her.

Hitchhiking in the heat the previous day had worn me out. I was plum tuckered, as my grandmother used to say. Every muscle in my body screamed as I got out of the feather bed and walked across the room to my clothes. After a quick sniff, I decided it was time to get a new T-shirt out of my bag. I also had some clean fatigues.

Thank goodness I had showered the night before.

———

At the breakfast table, I found a spot near the end right between the two boys. They both turned and said, "Good morning!" I mumbled a greeting back. They were already eating. In fact, one was almost finished. Looking down at my plate, I saw that my pancakes had been turned into a face complete with blueberry eyes and a dash of U-shaped whipped cream for a mouth. Now whose artistic work was this? Jamison, I suspected.

"Thank you for the hospitality, Aunt Margaret. You're always so good to me."

I could hear the front door opening and the clatter of high heels.

My heart jumped and held high in my throat as I expected Darla to turn the corner into the kitchen. But no, it was Angel. She held several pieces of mail and a newspaper in her hands.

"Where's Darla?" Aunt Margaret said without turning from her work at the stove.

"How did you know it was Angel?" Jamison asked out loud the question everyone was wondering.

"I can tell by the sound of their high heels."

Without missing a beat, Angel did a little tap dance that made everyone laugh. Even I smiled.

"Here," Angel said as she pushed the newspaper at me. "Catch up on what's been happening since you've been gone." Then, putting the mail on the counter near Aunt Margaret, she said, "Darla went out to deliver more records. Seems the new song is getting a lot of airplay. Even stations that aren't country have played it."

Margaret looked up from buttering biscuits. "Won't Cowboy and Mick be pleased when they get back. That is if they ever come back. They must be having fun because they're already a day overdue."

Looking down, I opened the paper and spread out the front page.

"Oh my Lawd!" Aunt Margaret practically screamed.

No one had to ask what was wrong. We all saw it. There on the front page—a big black and white photo of Aunt Margaret in another man's arms. It was obviously taken through one of the kitchen windows.

"Who is that man?" Angel stammered.

"He's our next-door neighbor, Jack," Jamison replied, unconcerned.

"Oh, no!" Aunt Margaret cried. "It isn't what it looks like." She directed this last part toward me and Angel. Neither of us knew what to say. We'd both been a part of Mick's and Cowboy's lives long enough to know that journalists could make a mountain out of a mole-hill. But it did look pretty incriminating. Especially the headline —"Love at First Sight." The photo caption then went on to explain that the famous tennis player, Jack Donovan, had been seen giving Margaret McLaren tennis lessons recently.

I felt certain Aunt Margaret could explain it to us. But could she explain it to the whole world? This photo was probably all over America by now. Or at least it would be in the next couple of days.

Angel rushed over to the stove while grabbing a hot pad to take out the burning biscuits.

Aunt Margaret stood silently sobbing into her apron.

And little Jamison asked if I was through reading the paper so he could read the funnies.

CHAPTER 23

ARGARET

When I first saw the photo in the newspaper, my heart leapt up in my throat and I could hardly breathe. I was sobbing but making no sound. Air wouldn't come in. Air wouldn't go out. I thought surely I'd die from lack of oxygen.

When I finally did come down from the shock of it, I ran right out the back door in my bare feet. The morning dew was cold and chilled me through and through. But I kept running. That is, as fast as I could run with ragged breath.

At last, I reached the sanctuary of the wooden gazebo.

No one would find me here.

Climbing the exterior steps, I finally felt like I could cope. Inside, I picked up a stick I'd put nearby to fight spider webs. There was only one today. It was large and spectacular, and it wasn't near the bench I wanted to sit upon, so I let it be.

Plopping myself down in a most unladylike fashion, I felt for my apron and used it to dry my eyes. After a few moments, I untied the apron from my waist and used it to blow my nose.

I sat for some time, staring out over our land.

Then, I stared at a spider weaving its web.

Then, I watched a squirrel burying a pecan.

"Oh, Lawd, Lawd, Lawd," I said to the spider, "why do all the bad things have to happen to me? Mick does rotten things behind my back on the road, I'm sure. And he never gets caught. Although he does have a stalker. Some hot-blooded groupie, I bet. A one-night stand gone wrong."

I stopped my outburst and listened.

I heard footsteps in the leaves. Someone was coming my way.

I listened intently as a twig broke underfoot.

Who could it be?

I dropped my apron and stood.

It was Jack, holding a tennis racket down by his side as he walked along.

"Margaret, I saw this morning's newspaper," he called out from a few feet away. "I thought I'd find you here."

"How did you know I'd come here?"

"Because this is where you come to be yourself. Although I have to admit, I'd hoped I'd find you singing, not crying."

He stepped inside and gently wrapped an arm around me.

"Don't be upset. The world will forget about it in a day or two. Mick will understand once we tell him how it all came about. The kids will tell him as well. After all, it was his stalker situation that caused us to react so at your tires being slit. No one would have hurt your car under normal circumstances. We haven't had any trouble in our parking lot before or since."

My head hurt. My heart hurt. Even my left foot throbbed. But the panic had passed. I was still and stable. I felt grounded in Jack's arms.

"Yes, you're right. I'll just go home and forget about it. Burn that nasty paper. It'll all blow over in a few days."

Jack suddenly stiffened and turned his head as if to listen.

"I heard it, too." My voice was barely a whisper.

In the next few seconds, we were blinded by a flash. *Pop, pop, pop.* The photographer had been in the nearby bushes, hiding before I even ran out of the house. Waiting for me. Had they been watching me for some time? Knowing this was my secret place? Guessing I'd come here?

This journalist, this photographer, who seemed to be stalking us must indeed be a most hateful man. Check that.

The person who stepped out from the bushes was a female. Sexy. Petite. And dark haired. That's all I could make out as she ran away, her camera bag swinging at her side.

Turning back, I saw Jack with his tennis racket raised as if to strike. Clearly, he was as surprised as I was by our stalker. Our should I say Mick's stalker? Seeing her for myself made it real. I recognized her as one of Mick and Cowboy's many groupies. I had definitely seen her before.

"Oh, Lawd, Lawd, Lawd," I said more to myself than to Jack.

CHAPTER 24

COWBOY LARSON

It was a beautiful day to be sitting outside. Mick had picked out the perfect location for us to do some songwriting. We were perched high on a big rock overlooking the river. Puffy white clouds dotted the true-blue Texas sky even as fall touched the leaves making them all shades of golden brown and deep rust. Some had already started to fall, and whenever a wind rustled them, they danced down upon us and the river. Mother Nature sure knew how to put on a show.

Bringing my tattered notebook out of my knapsack, I stretched out my long legs before sitting cross-legged. I took my newly sharpened pencil out of my shirt pocket. I'd picked one with a good pink eraser on the end because I knew I might need it. Sometimes words and music flowed out at once. Other times they came in fits and bits, as my grandmother used to say. I watched as Mick got his notebook out. We'd been writing independently. Now we were going to share what we had.

"What do you have good?" Mick asked. He'd also brought his guitar to help if a melody popped out in our brainstorming session.

Without hesitation I turned to the last lyrics I'd put down. "I wrote a song about Saint, or rather I wrote a song for Saint."

I sat completely still. My gaze followed the flow of the river.

The bright sun shone down upon us. I could see little black things squiggling in the atmosphere. Overhead a bird squawked. A blue jay, no doubt.

Mick took my notebook from me and started to read my words.

Words about the crushing pain I'd felt when Saint died. She was so young. I thought we'd have more time.

My words relayed the anxiety of missing the one you love the most.

And they told of how I couldn't deceive myself anymore. I'd used my time together with Saint to chase my own ambitions. The lyrics revealed my not really being able to love her the way I should have or could have. Or grieve her the way I wanted. Leaving me emotionally numb. Unable to even cry.

Continuing to gaze past Mick toward the river, I waited for a reaction.

He was just about to say something when I felt the first teardrops brim my eyes before flooding down my face.

I won't lie.

Crying hurts when you haven't cried in a long, long time.

My whole being shook. My whole soul quaked. And my body started to spasm as I silently cried the tears I'd been waiting for. The tears I'd hoped would come but didn't want to feel. I cried hard. And somewhere beside me I felt a hand on my shoulder as my body heaved back and forth.

It was Mick.

He didn't say a word. Good thing because I couldn't talk. It was hard to breathe as my heart seized so hard I thought it would break. So, this is what a broken heart feels like? No wonder my subconscious had put off feeling for so long. But I wasn't just crying for Saint. I was crying for myself, for my family, for all the suffering I'd felt back up in Oklahoma —all those years ago in the dust storms, in the Great Depression. It's a wonder we lived through it at all. Thank goodness my mother had died before it all started. I hadn't really cried for her either back then. Now I was making up for it all at once. And the pain played out long and hard.

Mick sat quietly beside me.

I was so glad to have him as a friend and business partner. He knew me better than a brother.

He put his arm around my shoulder and pulled me close.

We sat staring straight ahead at the river.

Finally, Mick spoke.

"This is a good song. A real good song. What do you think we call it 'Waiting on the Heartache to Come'?" He paused before adding, "Or maybe just 'Saint's Song'?"

Nodding, I wiped my tears on my white cotton shirt sleeve and said, "Life is so damn hard."

Mick took out his handkerchief and handed it to me.

"Thank you," I said as I blew my nose hard. My throat ached. My forehead throbbed. And I didn't need a mirror to know how puffy and red my eyes were.

"Look," Mick pointed up the river, "Clarence is back from his run to the store. I hope he remembered the Moon Pies."

Drying my eyes one more time, I turned toward the boat floating our way. Clarence slowly paddled as he took advantage of the strong current pulling him toward us.

"Hola," he shouted from a few yards away. "I got some ice-cold colas." He paddled again before holding up a plain brown bag. "Burgers and fries for lunch," he shouted again. "And beans and franks for supper."

If Clarence noticed my tearstained face, he didn't say anything. Instead, he just asked if we wanted to eat there on the rock or take the burgers back to the cabin.

"We're hungry. Let's eat here," I said as I watched Clarence tie the boat up on the bank below.

"Been working hard?" Clarence called up at us.

"Yes," Mick answered. "We've got some good stuff. This trip was a great idea for getting our creative juices flowing."

At that point, It occurred to me I hadn't asked Mick if he had anything new.

"You got something?"

"Yes," he replied with a smile, "and it's good, but not as good as yours." He stopped for a moment. "We can go over my new stuff later." He paused again before continuing. "We almost have enough for another album, buddy. Maybe one more good song."

"I've been thinking."

"Oh yeah, does your head hurt?" Mick laughed at his own joke as he always did. And I ignored him as I always did.

"I've been thinking. What if we put in the gospel song Danny played at the traveling salvation show? We could even put Danny on guitar. I could sing. Or maybe we could even get the church choir to back it up?"

Mick looked down at the ground and squished his forehead up as he thought about my suggestion.

"I don't know," he said. "It wouldn't necessarily fit in with the rest of the songs."

Clarence was standing beside us holding his sack of greasy burgers.

"Maybe," Clarence said as he passed out burgers, fries and napkins, "maybe you could do a whole other album of church songs? You know, something different."

"Now that's a good idea," I said.

"I don't know." Mick continued staring downward. "I'm not that good of a Christian. People might start to speculate about it. But I do like the thought of it. Maybe we get Danny and Darla to work on it together. Darla's got the perfect voice for it. And she killed it when she sang "How Great Thou Art" impromptu at the radio station. Also, the other day I heard Margaret, Darla and Angel singing harmony in the kitchen. It was pretty incredible hearing the mix of their voices. They weren't necessarily singing a church song, but some kind of folk song. The kind Margaret used to sing when she was younger."

Clarence handed me a couple of extra napkins.

"You doing all right, Cowboy?" His tone was gentle.

"Yeah," I said, "just got all my sadness that had been building up inside out. I'll be okay." Even as I said the words I could still feel a lump in my throat from my outburst.

"Yes," Clarence said, "being out in nature will do that to you. Bring all your feelings to the surface." He bent down and brought up another sack. Quietly, he felt around inside before bringing out a couple of Moon Pies.

"Clarence, my friend, you are the perfect bodyguard. It's moments like this that make me glad I hired you." Mick took one of the Moon Pies and tore off the wrapper. "Don't mind me. I'm going to eat dessert first."

———

The air was warm and breezy on our walk back to the cabin. Everyone agreed an afternoon siesta was in order. Full stomachs. Good friends. Life was looking up. Better days were coming. I could feel it in my bones. We were heading down the right track musically. In fact, we even had a title for our new album—*Delta County Blues.* A nod to the area we were in right now, and to the Delta blues guitarists who would be on the album.

"What is that on the cabin's front door?" Mick motioned ahead.

Clarence narrowed his eyes and quickened his pace so he could get to the door before us. We watched him pull the fancy pink envelope off the door and open it. His face darkened as he looked up and all around the front porch.

Shoving the note in Mick's hand, he took off surveying all sides of the cabin.

Mick opened the letter. And I looked over his shoulder, craning my neck to see.

It read, "You cannot escape. I will follow you to the ends of the earth."

The smell of a woman's sweet perfume wafted by me on the gentle breeze just as Clarence called back, "I found tracks in the muddy area behind the cabin, and they don't belong to any of us that's for sure."

"What makes you think they aren't any of ours? Do you think they belong to the woman stalker?" My voice carried a worried tone.

"No, I think they belong to a really big man. They had to be a size thirteen or larger. And they were deep. He's a big guy."

CHAPTER 25

ARLA

I'd picked up some new records at the radio station while delivering Mick and Cowboy's latest. And I couldn't wait to take a listen all by myself. Didn't want to hear Angel's opinion. Didn't want to hear Margaret's opinion. Didn't want to hear the kids tell me their thoughts. Just wanted to experience these new songs all by myself. Therefore, I opened the front door as quietly as I could before slipping down the hallway and making a right into the office area where the good record player was kept.

The first song was a slow song. Closing my eyes, I leaned back a little against the desk, crossed my arms to hug myself, and let the music flow over me. Swaying this way and that. That way and this. Whose song was this? I'd never heard of them. Maybe that's why the girl at the front desk was handing out their records for free. As it got to the middle of the song, the music started to crescendo. I leaned my head back and shook my hair as chills ran up and down my body. Truly I was lost in the moment.

That's when I felt it.

A presence in front of me.

Gasping, I opened my eyes to reveal Rayne. Surely not. No one said anything about Rayne coming back.

My mind swirled as he reached out and swept me close. Gently turning, he moved us in time to the music. Breathe, I reminded myself —breathe. He intertwined his fingers with mine. I could feel the rough palm of his hand as he held me close. Heat coursed through my veins each time our bodies touched. Absolutely unbelievable. Rayne was back. And we were dancing.

"I've missed you so," he whispered in my ear. His warm breath slightly blowing over my ear made waves of passion flow over me. All thoughts left my head.

Truly moments like this one were what made life worth living.

And then the music stopped. But our bodies still swayed in rhythm. Hearts beating as one. And time stood still as we looked deep into each other's eyes. Each other's soul.

"Have you missed me?" He bent close to my cheek before lowering his head to kiss my throat. Tiny kisses trailing down toward my shoulder. His soft dark hair brushed lightly against my face as he nestled his head in the crevice of my neck and shoulder, slightly pulling down on my blouse to do so.

I couldn't speak.

"You're all I've thought about since I've been gone," he said between tiny kisses.

Then he pulled away and looked down at me before coming in for a kiss on the lips.

"We're kissing" is all I could think.

Then came more kisses as he pushed me back up against the desk. I fell, or more like floated, backwards on all the many organized piles of paperwork. The song on the record player had ended a few moments ago. The needle made a low hiss as the disc went round and round.

What would Margaret say if she came in and saw us full on making out? I must've said that last part out loud because all of a sudden I heard Angel's voice at the office door saying, "I'm sure she'd be speechless." Then I heard Angel's high heels tap, tap, tap over to the record player. "Do you two lovebirds mind if I flip this record over to the B side?" I couldn't see her because Rayne hovered over me smiling down, but I heard the scratching sound of Angel moving the needle and flipping the record.

Side B was a faster rhythm.

Rayne straightened back up and helped me to follow.

My cheeks flushed even redder than they had when Rayne first walked in the room.

Angel stood tapping her foot and said with a little smirk in her voice, "I'll just listen out in the hallway if you two don't mind. It's a little too hot in here for me." She picked up a few pieces of paper from the desk and fanned herself as she said the words.

But before she could move, Margaret rounded the corner, saying, "Darla, oh good, you're back. I need you to go find Mick and Cowboy out in the country—convince them to come on back."

This took me by surprise. Margaret never sent a request like this out to Mick and Cowboy. She just took their comings and goings as part of their musician lifestyle. She knew it took them time and privacy to write new songs.

Finding my voice, I willed my heart to stop trembling at the shock of all that had happened in the last few moments. Shaking my hair back from my flushed face, I stammered, "I wouldn't know where to find them. Maybe Rayne should go."

"Maybe they both should go," Angel chimed in just when I'd forgotten she was still in the room.

"Yes, of course, both of you go. Together you can convince them they're needed back home. Rayne, I know you just arrived, but you're really the only one of us who can figure out how to get to that remote cabin." Margaret's voice was raspy. Her eyes were swollen and rimmed with red as if she'd been crying.

"Yes, I'll go." I heard myself saying from somewhere outside of my body. It was all I could manage to squeak the words out as I still had not recovered from the most romantic moment of my life. Which, by the way, I never would've imagined could have happened on a workday morning a few minutes before ten o'clock. All I could think was at last I'll have something to write in my diary worth reading.

However, as I looked at Margaret, my thoughts turned cloudy. Why was my friend and mentor looking so blue? It was obvious she was upset in a way I'd never seen her before.

But before I could say anything more, Margaret quipped back, "Good, going to East Texas is a few hours' drive. If you two leave now you should be back before dark."

She took the folded newspaper she was holding and gave it to Rayne. "Please explain this fiasco to Darla . . . and to Mick. Tell him he needs to come home. That his special dark-haired friend paid me a visit this morning. He'll know what I mean."

With that she marched out of the room.

As we drove along the highway, it was hard to talk with the windows rolled down, so I held my hair in place with my hand and pretended to look out the passenger window. Every once in a while I'd sneak a peek at Rayne's profile as he drove looking straight ahead. The radio was blaring, and all was right with the world. Well, at least our world. Mick and Margaret's world was messed up, that's for sure, according to what we'd learned about the morning's happenings. Why did the press feel the need to put photos like that in the paper? I mean, I guess it sells papers, but still, it was not truthful.

I turned from gazing out the window to observe Rayne one more time. Angel had been right when she described him as dreamy. He was dreamy alright, and I couldn't help but wonder why he'd want someone like me. Hadn't my mother said as much after meeting him?

Rayne caught me looking at him and flashed a smile my way before picking up my hand and kissing it. Which resulted in a thousand electrical sparks moving though my heart. I'd been attracted to him since I had first set eyes on him, but I wouldn't even admit it to myself. He was . . . and is way out of my league. I wondered if he truly liked me or if this was just his way of making yet another girl swoon. He certainly was very skilled in the art of seduction. Never in a million years would I have anticipated what had happened earlier. Heck, I didn't even expect him back. It seems that he walks in and out of our lives at random. Who does that?

He gave my hand a gentle squeeze.

Even just holding his hand gave me goosebumps. I decided this was the happiest any person had ever made me in my whole life. And I wasn't going to ruin it by being insecure. I'd just go with the flow, see where it takes me. Everything would be okay as long as I didn't get in over my head. I just needed to play it cool.

Looking down, I saw Margaret's folded newspaper tucked securely in my oversized purse that I used especially for running errands. I felt so bad for her that the photos portrayed her in such a bad light. Especially when it was Mick that might be playing around on her as I suspected he was. Rayne had only taken a few minutes to go over the morning's events with Margaret before we got on the highway, and I didn't catch all of their conversation. I wanted to know more, but the road noise canceled out any further conversation. I guess I didn't really need to know much more than Margaret wanted Mick to come home.

And so it was that we went flying down the highway—content to be in each other's company. No one else in the world around. Just us two.

My conscience bothered me because I was so happy when Margaret's heart was breaking.

Looking out the window I saw a road sign ahead. Rayne slowed his speed before exiting the interstate. He was a careful and safe driver, using his arm out the window to signal whenever he was going to turn. However, I did think he drove a little too fast. Maybe because we were on a special mission or maybe because pilots were used to speed. Either way, I didn't complain. The breezy air felt fine. Fall was one of my favorite times of the year what with the trees starting to turn colors and such. I could smell the smoke from a bonfire as a farmer burned some tree limbs out in his field.

As the car slowed on the main road into town, Rayne turned down the volume of the radio. Then he began to explain we'd have to get a boat at this little bait shop to continue on to the cabin. It's so remote that's the fastest way to get there, he assured me. My sensible side thought it sounded a little bit dangerous, but I was up for the adventure as long as he was by my side.

In spite of its lowered volume, the radio crackled with life, sometimes fading in strong before fading out again. Rayne explained this happened because the town was built on lower ground and the reception could be spotty at times, even though he'd tuned it to the local station. I watched as he fiddled with the radio knobs tuning it as best he could. Finally, somehow, he managed to make it come in loud and clear.

Pulling into the dirt parking lot of the bait shop, I started to comb my hair with my hands.

"Come here." Rayne took a comb out of his back pocket and ran it through my fine straight locks. "What?" he said looking at me.

"Nothing. I'm just not used to being taken care of."

He kissed me on the nose before reaching to turn off the engine.

Then he abruptly stopped.

The radio made an alert siren type sound. Rayne instinctively turned the volume up to listen. The local DJ came over the airwaves stating, "This is a special news alert. Today at 10:00 a.m., well-known musician Mick McLaren shot legendary Delta blues guitarist Ernie Koster in a jealous rage. Apparently the two had been collaborating on new music when the fight broke out. Ernie Koster has been taken to the local hospital where he is listed in serious condition." Then the DJ returned to the regularly scheduled program of country music. I couldn't help but notice he was playing one of Mick and Cowboy's most famous songs hopefully cashing in on the fact that everyone would be talking about this new Mick, Cowboy and Ernie debacle.

Rayne turned the volume of the music down.

We sat and looked at each other in stunned silence.

Finally, I managed to speak. "Isn't Ernie Koster the bum we saw outside of the music station when we were delivering records?"

"Yes, remember I told you he used to be a well-known blues guitarist. When we got back from delivering records to the radio stations, I'd told Uncle Mick that we saw Ernie and described what kind of shape he was in. Uncle Mick had said something about trying to get him work. Maybe working for their record label. But I don't think he meant musical work because Ernie can't play anymore. I think he meant janitorial-type work. In fact, old Ernie's hands were shaking so hard when we saw him, I told Uncle Mick, I didn't think Ernie could even pick up a guitar much less play it. At least not like he used to."

We sat for a few more minutes trying to let this strange turn of events sink in.

Rayne gently picked up my hand again. "I'm starved. Let's go inside and get some lunch. Then," he paused and sighed, "I guess we'll head to the hospital and see what's going on there. I can't imagine Mick and Cowboy are at the cabin if Ernie is in the hospital."

"Rayne, this just doesn't make sense. Mick wouldn't shoot Ernie in a fit of jealous rage. It doesn't make sense."

"Darla, I've found many things in this world don't make sense. C'mon, let's go inside and see if the lady who runs the bait shop knows anything more."

"Why would she know anything?"

Rayne looked at me like I was crazy.

"Darla, this is a small town. And she owns the bait shop. Trust me, she knows everything about everybody."

PART 7

BOTH SIDES OF THE STORY

CHAPTER 26

Clinic Waiting Room, Klondike, Texas
Wednesday Afternoon
October 29, 1958

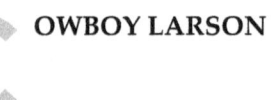OWBOY LARSON

Son of a gun! My head hurt something fierce. Sitting in the waiting room rubbing my temples, I contemplated our situation. Mick had indeed shot Ernie in the butt. And he was in a heap of trouble for it. How were we going to explain to the sheriff why he'd shot Ernie? No way was Mick going to confess that he thought Ernie was his female stalker fan and that he'd feared for his life when Ernie popped up in the woods. All we needed was more bad press about Mick's female stalker. Normally, I tried to let Mick work things out by himself, but things were getting out of control. And it was a fact, no one would believe the truth.

I thought back to all that had happened when Mick shot Ernie.

It was such a blur.

I remembered I could not imagine what in the Sam Hill an intruder was doing hiding in the bushes near our cabin with a hat and a Lone Ranger face mask on. He looked like a common criminal. Although I had to admit, not a female criminal. So, I didn't believe he was Mick's stalker. I thought maybe he was a robber. When Clarence tried to approach him, he ran. When Clarence gave chase, the intruder fell. And when Clarence started to struggle with him, he fought back. Why? Why was he even there? Then all the sudden Mick came up out of the cabin with his gun. Clarence loosened his grip on the person who we didn't know was Ernie at the time.

"Stand up," Mick had commanded the masked stranger.

"Walk to the cabin." Mick's voice was firm.

I had no doubt he'd shoot him.

But apparently Ernie doubted because he took off running lightning fast.

Unfortunately for him, Mick was a crack shot. He aimed for Ernie's right buttock and that's where it hit, knocking Ernie to the ground. Taking his mask off, he screeched, "Mick, don't shoot! Don't shoot! It's me, Ernie Koster."

My heart just about fell through my stomach.

"Put the gun away," I yelled as I ran to Ernie's side.

"Ernie Koster?" Mick had cried in disbelief. "What are you doing creeping around our cabin in a Halloween mask? Surely you aren't out trick or treating."

"Your record label sent me," Ernie shouted over his obvious pain. "Sent me and Harold out here." Ernie held his backside with a white handkerchief that was starting to turn blood red.

"I thought I told them to hire you for handyman work or something . . . maybe as an assistant. I specifically know I didn't say to follow me. How'd you even find the cabin?"

"Harold Wilkins. One of the guys from my old band. He's from 'round these parts."

"Well, where's Harold?" We all looked around as Mick asked the question. I fully expected another ambush from the nearby wooded area.

"Looks like he's done ran off." Ernie winced in pain. "McLaren, why'd you have to shoot me in the butt of all places? I was just trying to help your career. Your manager said last time the news broke about your female stalker your record sales went through the roof. Me and Harold, we were trying to act like we were your stalker. Get you some free publicity. Record label has already called the newspapers about you being stalked again."

As I listened to Ernie speak, I realized the accidental shooting was going to make the headline news. And we needed to put it out there in a more favorable light right fast. But how in the world were we going to explain things? That's when my brain surprised me. It started to conjure up a dozen ways we could spin it. Who knew I could be so devious?

Clarence moved forward and gently examined Ernie. "We need to get you to a hospital," he said as he pressed another clean handker-chief against Ernie's wound. "Cowboy, go get a fresh blanket and let's put Ernie in the wheelbarrow yonder. We need to get him to the boat, then we can drive him to the hospital ourselves. The last thing we need is for this to get out before we can guide the story of how it all went down. Maybe we can make it look like a hunting accident."

"That's exactly what I was thinking," I said.

Hurrying to get a blanket, I heard Ernie asking Mick again.

"McLaren, why'd you go and shoot me in the butt?"

Mick and Clarence helped me get Ernie as comfortable as we could in the wheelbarrow before we headed toward the boat.

"I'm so sorry, Ernie." Mick's eyes were full of tears and fear. His voice choked as he uttered the words.

"I know you are my friend," Ernie said reaching out to pat Mick's arm. "Accidents happen," he said softly. Then he reared back his head and laughed through his pain. "Sweet mother of pearl! This is not how I intended this day to go. Oh, oh, oh. This dad-burned wheelbarrow's a bumpy ride."

CHAPTER 27

AYNE

The glaring lights in the clinic made everything and everyone look slightly green. So, suffice it to say, Ernie Koster wasn't looking that good. Even though his skin was naturally very dark, he still looked greenish to me. However, he seemed to be in good spirits. His face had lit up when Darla and I entered his room.

"Oh, oh. Look who it is." His happy tone belied the pain he must be feeling. "It's Rayne. And who is that with him, but Miss Darla, Mick's assistant. Remember meeting me outside the station?"

Darla moved to his beside and took up his hand.

"Yessir, I sure do." She smiled at him as she arranged his blankets with her other hand. "Cowboy told us what the record company sent you and Harold to do. Well-intentioned but look what has happened. I'm so sorry." Darla plumped the pillow near his head as he groaned and moved to a different position.

Ernie became serious as he glanced over at Cowboy who'd been sitting in the far corner of the room all this time. "I've got to tell you something. And you need to let Mick know when he gets back here. Harold and I planted a few more stalker setups back at the cabin. You guys will probably encounter them, so don't be frightened. We don't want anyone else getting hurt."

Cowboy moved forward, close to Ernie. "We'll be on the lookout. But, Ernie, I have to ask you if we can paint this situation to make it look better for everyone involved. We want to tell the press and the authorities that you were collaborating with us on songwriting. We decided to take a break and go hunting. While out in the woods, Mick accidentally dropped his gun. It discharged and the bullet hit you."

Ernie looked over our small group of three. "Well, you know what my father always said, 'Never let the truth get in the way of a good story.' You can trust me, Cowboy. Hey, where is McLaren anyway?"

Cowboy paused for a moment. "Mick is at the sheriff's office. They took him in for questioning." He waited a moment more before adding, "They want to know if you want to press charges."

Ernie rubbed the stubble on his chin as he considered his situation. "If I press charges, Mick might feel he needs to tell the truth about me and Harold stalking him. Then we'd all be in trouble, wouldn't we? Heck no, I'm not going to press charges. Mick was good to me. Got me a job when no one even cared."

Darla rustled around to Cowboy's side. I saw her hand reach in her oversized purse. "Cowboy, I don't know if this is the right time to bring this up, but there's a reason Rayne and I came to ask you and Mick to come home. I hope the sheriff doesn't keep him long." She pulled a newspaper out as she said the words. Carefully, she opened it to the photos of Margaret and their neighbor Jack.

Both Cowboy and Ernie appeared shocked as she held it before them.

That's when I stepped up and took over the conversation.

"It appears the real stalker is after Margaret back in Dallas. She's been following Margaret, taking photos of her and the neighbor that could be interpreted in the wrong way."

"Are you sure it's not just another photographer from a gossip magazine?" Cowboy took the paper out of Darla's hands and began to read the story that accompanied the photos.

"No," I replied, "Margaret had a run-in with the deranged lady stalker at the gazebo on the back property."

"Rayne, are you sure? How does Margaret even know what Mick's stalker looks like?" Cowboy lowered his voice an octave as he tried to cover for Mick, but it was time to let him know the truth.

"Cowboy," I said, "Margaret knows. She hired a private detective to follow Mick a few months ago when the real stalker first attacked him. She did it with Mick's safety in mind, but she ended up finding out more than she wanted to know. Now the lady stalker has turned on her. And she fears for both herself and the children. She wants you and Mick to come home. She sent Darla and me to tell you."

———

Darla seemed hesitant to enter my parents' house. Maybe I was pushing her too fast, but I didn't have a lot of time to let our romance move at a normal pace. My assignments back and forth to Dallas were over. Soon I'd be flying out to Turkey. And I wanted to see my parents before I left again. Maybe more importantly, I wanted them to meet Darla. And, of course, for her to meet them. Not just my parents but my entire family. I considered it a stroke of luck that our unplanned road trip had sent us so near their house.

Walking up the front walkway, Darla tried to arrange her hair.

"Oh, I should have put on some lipstick."

I assured her she looked beautiful. And I meant it. One of the things that attracted me to her was that she didn't think of herself as overly good-looking. In fact, she acted like she was only average. Which she was anything but. My last girlfriend Jennifer overestimated her attractiveness. Add to that she wasn't smart or talented like Darla.

Darla's hand was shaking as I intertwined my fingers with hers, bringing back memories of earlier that morning. Her passion had surprised me as I expected her to be a little timid in that department. She certainly was something special. Unlike any other girl I'd ever met.

"I just know Mama will love you," I said as we walked up to the house.

It nearly shocked my mama to death when I opened the front

screen door and walked inside her kitchen. At first she thought I was one of the other kids, but then it dawned on her who I was and that I had a girl with me. Her face went from surprise to absolute joy to worry about how she was dressed. Which I could see her point as she was wearing Dad's old overalls that were two sizes too big for her. Apparently, she'd been working in the garden earlier. There was still a smudge of dirt on the side of her face.

"Mama, this is Darla. She works for Mick and Cowboy."

"So nice to meet you." Mama quickly washed her hands at the kitchen sink and dried them on a cup towel.

"Nice to meet you, Darla." Mama extended her clean hand.

"Nice to meet you, too," Darla whispered back as they shook.

"Goodness gracious! What are you doing here, Rayne? Your daddy told me you were going to Turkey with your new job. Said you had taken an eighteen-month contract."

I felt Darla's hand slip from mine. Now she was the one with the surprised look on her face. This isn't how I wanted to tell her. But here it was out in the open now.

"Mama . . . yes, I will be going overseas, but . . ." I hesitated, uncertain how much I could tell or even if I should tell. Finally, I got my bearings. "But you know, I'll be coming back and forth. It won't seem like eighteen months." As I said the words, I picked up Darla's hand and squeezed it before turning to see her reaction. She looked like she was going to start crying.

I turned back to my mama. And she was crying.

"Don't mind me, son," she sniffed. "I'm just so happy to see you . . . all that secret stuff around your new job scares me—makes me think it's dangerous work."

I didn't know what to say because quite simply it was.

———

I felt like the last few hours with my family had gone well. They really seemed to like Darla. But I could tell she was still sad about me heading overseas. Gripping the steering wheel tighter, I watched the single car ahead on the highway. Darla had her window rolled up for the trip back. She said so it wouldn't blow her hair and make it tangle. I left my side down so we wouldn't suffocate in the heat. Turning on the headlights, I watched the sun dip low on the horizon. Soon it would be dark.

Darla said something, but I couldn't really hear her over the whipping wind.

Luckily, we were near a roadside park. A rest stop for travelers, really. When I was in high school, we'd often had impromptu parties there. And, I have to admit, it was a great place for teens to make out.

Pulling into the rest area, I observed we were the only ones there.

I heard Darla crying.

Leaning over to touch her hand, I asked, "What's wrong? Why the tears?"

"I just told you," she answered as she dabbed her eyes with a fresh tissue.

"I'm sorry. I couldn't hear a word you were saying as we were driving. The wind was too much. Will you please tell me again?"

She sobbed. "There's no need to say it again."

"But I want to know what you're thinking."

She took some tissues out of her oversized bag and blew her nose.

"I'm just disappointed. I don't see any way a relationship with you can work out. What with me on tour and you going overseas. I just …" she hesitated, "I just want to be around you, you know? I can't even afford the overseas paper and postage to write you very often." She shook her head and rolled down the passenger side window. I waited for her to say more, but she just stared off toward a row of picnic tables.

"We'll work it out. I know there are a lot of secrets to what I'm doing, but they do allow us to tell our wives and girlfriends a few things. But it is true I can't reveal much about my comings and goings. My contract is only eighteen months. Afterwards, I can go back in the Air Force or start a new job. Maybe I can get on with Mick and Cowboy . . . then I can go on the road with you."

"Yeah?" Her voice and face brightened at my words. "I never thought about anything like that. Or you could get a job doing just about anything. Dallas is a big city."

I leaned over, gently moving her hair back from her face. As I pulled her toward me, I felt a slight hesitation.

"Rayne, we need to get back and tell Margaret about Mick shooting Ernie. I'm sure she's heard some version of the story on the radio by now. I'm sure the whole world has heard. But she needs to know the real story. You know what I mean?"

Fame was a funny thing. It seemed like everyone was always up in Mick's and Cowboy's business. It was a real problem for them. And Darla had a firsthand view of what fame was like for them, yet she was still pursuing it. In my heart, I knew I'd never stop her from chasing her dreams. But in my head, I thought I might ought to try to sway her. However, right then, right there . . . I wanted nothing else but to kiss Darla. And that's what I did.

Aunt Margaret could wait a few more minutes for news of Mick. After all, she'd been waiting on Mick for most of her adult life.

CHAPTER 28

ARLA

Did Rayne just say they allow us to tell wives and girlfriends? Does that mean he thinks of me as his girlfriend? Oh my gosh! That makes my heart sing. And we're kissing again. I'm in heaven and I was just in hell a few minutes ago. What a roller coaster of a day it's been . . . and the sun hasn't even completely set yet. Only one problem. My nose is stopped up from crying and I'm having trouble breathing as we kiss.

Oh, I think I'm going to die, but I mean that in a good way.

CHAPTER 29

McLaren Mansion, Dallas, Texas
Wednesday Evening
October 29, 1958

ARGARET

We were sitting at the piano drinking bottled sodas and working out the song I'd written the day before. Angel didn't have much background in song writing, but she was a very good singer. In fact, she not only had a lovely voice, but she was also a fast study.

"Angel," I said as we worked, "you really have a knack for this songwriting. You're one smart cookie." I took a sip of my soda pop and continued. "I have to admit—when Cowboy first introduced you, I got a totally different impression from how you really are as a person."

"How's that, Margaret?" Angel continued writing and rustling paper.

"When Cowboy told us you were his cousin's daughter, and he wanted to hire you as an assistant, we didn't know what to expect. Excuse me for saying this, but in spite of the fact that you were all gussied up pretty-like, you also had a look on your face like . . ."

"Like what, Margaret?"

"Oh, I don't know. You looked like a bit of a bubblehead," I said it with a smile.

"What?" Angel had just taken a drink, and she almost spit it out, making us both laugh.

"Margaret!" Angel started laughing again.

"Yes, you did. I took one look at your big blue eyes and thought . . . oh, Lawd, that's the kind of girl . . . oh, I don't know, how can I say this? You kinda looked like the type of girl that a thought might startle. But really, you're not like that at all now that I know you."

Angel laughed one more time. And then she sat still, considering my words.

"I didn't mean to hurt your feelings, honey."

"You didn't," Angel said, as she took another swig of her bottled Coke.

I continued. "You're tough, Angel. And you're smart. You definitely have the mindset it takes to make it in this business."

I watched her from the corner of my eye as I worked out a few chords on the piano. I wanted to see her reaction to what I was going to say next.

"Angel, you and Darla need to team up. Your voices harmonize well."

Angel looked shocked.

After a moment, she replied, "I don't think Darla likes me."

"Oh, yeah. What makes you say that?"

"Just the other day she called me a brazen hussy."

"Angel, you are a brazen hussy. And you need to be to succeed in a man's world. Darla would do well to follow your example. Otherwise . . ." my voice trailed off as I continued to softly play the piano.

"Otherwise what, Margaret?"

"You'll end up like me. A frumpy old housewife yelling at the kids. I swear on my tombstone I'm going to have them engrave, 'Here lies

Margaret McLaren. She did more than her fair share of laundry and dishes.' So be brave. Go out there and try your hardest to succeed. Don't end up like me."

Angel laughed.

"Margaret, you've got a good life."

"Yes, I do. But I'd like to have a better life. Especially now that the kids are getting older."

Standing up from the piano bench, I walked to the window and gazed out. An automobile was stopped at the guard gate. Its head-lights shone in my direction. Quickly I stepped back behind the heavy curtains. Peeping around, I watched as a truck pulled forward into the circular drive near our gaslight illuminating Mick, Cowboy and Clarence inside. I waited, thinking Rayne and Darla would follow behind them through the guard gates. But no, they didn't.

Footsteps clattered up the front porch steps. All three men were holding instrument cases and fishing gear. They looked tired, worn out and hungry.

I was glad Angel had stayed late to listen to the new songs I'd been writing. Maybe she'd stay longer to hear what Mick had to say about his female stalker. I sure was dreading hearing his story. I didn't want to face the truth of who she was, or rather who she was to Mick. I knew if I told him everything the private investigator had told me there would be no going back to the way things were, the way things had always been.

CHAPTER 30

RAYNE

After we left the roadside park, we drove for another thirty minutes before I decided to pull into a restaurant so we could get a quick burger and fries. I know I was stalling on getting back to Dallas, but I wanted to spend as much time with Darla as I could. Sitting face to face in a leather-padded booth, I found I couldn't stop staring at her. She wasn't aware of how attractive she was, even with very little makeup. In fact, her windblown hair made her sexier than ever.

I watched as she brought the straw of her chocolate shake up to her lips, and all I could think of was how good it had felt to kiss her. I hoped I wouldn't scare her away by moving too fast. But I needed to move fast if we were going to have any hope of a relationship. Soon I'd have to leave, and I hoped I'd get the chance to say a proper goodbye. I hoped to have hope for a future.

Darla told a funny story, and I have to admit, she was one of my first girlfriends to have a really good sense of humor. Certainly Jennifer didn't. She couldn't even tell a joke without messing up the punchline.

I watched Darla as she continued with her silliness. Waving her hands to accentuate certain words, her animated face glowing as she spoke. Darla was a singer, but I tell you she'd also have made a great comedy actress.

Then, much to my amusement, she got up from our red leather booth and went to the jukebox. With a shiny silver dime in hand, she looked over the list of songs, finally making her selection—"Rumble" by Link Wray. It was one of my new favorites, but the last song I expected her to pick. As the discordant music played, Darla turned and swayed, dancing her way back to our booth like a hoodlum swinging a switchblade in an invitation to a knife fight. Her movements right in time with the music. A mischievous grin on her face. I almost died when she picked up one of my French fries and held it like she was smoking a cigarette before stubbing it out on the table near what was left of my burger. Then she danced directly to me for a few more minutes before sitting down and popping another one of my fries in her mouth. She was definitely a dramatic type.

Her every movement attracted me. I wanted so badly to take her in my arms and do a repeat make-out session like the one we'd had earlier.

Instead, I reached for her hand as I said, "I can't believe you picked 'Rumble' . . . It has such a raunchy sound. Never in a million years would I've thought you even knew about this song."

"I love it. It's such a different sound from anything else on the radio. It's those ominous power chords. Did you know Link Wray discovered them by accident when someone asked him to play a song he didn't know?" Darla looked up at me with soulful eyes as she said the words.

"No, I didn't know that. But I did hear the song was so controversial it was banned from the airwaves. My friends and I only discovered it on the jukebox when some of our other friends told us to look for it. Can you imagine banning a song on the radio for its sound when it doesn't even have lyrics? Like it's really going to encourage juvenile delinquents to have dangerous street fights?"

I thought back to Darla's sultry dance moves and how she had made my pulse pound. Maybe it wasn't street fights that made them ban it. All I could think about while she was dancing was . . . well, the two of us having a little rumble of our own. Bringing my thoughts back to the present, I took a sip of soda and tried to cool down as I watched her from across the table.

She twirled her hair with her finger, then flashed me a flirtatious little smile while sliding her eyes to the side.

"Careful, your rebel side is coming out. It's listening to that devil music," I teased her.

"I don't know about that, but I do know it encouraged me and my music. I want to experiment and do new things that no one else has done. I want to be a musical pioneer."

Darla threw back her head and laughed.

It was the first time I'd seen her totally at ease. And I liked it. Her true self was shining through. Yes, she certainly was a firecracker. Just full of surprises. And I loved every moment of being with her.

We sat for a moment, saying nothing until the song ended.

Glancing up at the clock on the wall, I realized we needed to get on the road. Much more time had passed than I realized. All I could concentrate on was being with Darla right now, right here in this greasy fast-food restaurant somewhere north of Dallas. In spite of its dirty walls, greasy floors and poor overhead fluorescent lighting, I wanted to stay here all night.

Darla glanced up to see what I was looking at. Suddenly seeing the clock, she said, "Oh, oh. We need to go. Margaret is going to be worried about us. Here, help me get this table cleared off and into that trash barrel over there." Apparently, she must have been a waitress at some point in her life because I'd never seen someone clean a table so fast or so efficiently.

I wrapped my arm around her and held her close as we walked to the car. When we got there, I opened her car door first and helped her inside. Jennifer had always complained I didn't know how to treat a woman. I guess she'd gotten through to me. Finally, I was doing all the things she'd wanted me to do. Except, of course, I was doing them for Darla.

CHAPTER 31

COWBOY LARSON

Margaret and Angel were singing together when we first arrived. And their voices harmonized perfectly. Which only made me more convinced than ever that Mick and I should produce an album with Darla, Margaret and Angel. Of course, I wanted to have Danny as part of it, too. Maybe in time I would convince Mick it was a good idea. Right now, he was more concerned with doing some experimental stuff. Maybe more blues than country. Perhaps it wasn't a bad thing Ernie Koster coming back into our lives. I truly do believe everything happens for a reason.

I sat my fishing tackle box down near the front door.

Based on her demeanor, Margaret obviously didn't know anything about what'd happened with Ernie Koster. But that didn't surprise me all that much. Margaret rarely watched television or listened to the radio. She'd probably been cooking and cleaning all afternoon. But still, I'm surprised Angel hadn't gotten word. If she had, she certainly wasn't asking about it. So, I decided to jump right in and get the bad news out of the way first.

"Margaret, has Rayne or Darla told you about what happened with Ernie Koster?"

"No, Rayne and Darla haven't come back yet. But Ernie Koster—that's a name I haven't heard in a while. What happened to him?"

Before I could answer, Mick moved forward in the room.

"I accidentally shot him in the butt. But it's all over the news I did it in a jealous rage."

Margaret audibly gasped.

And Angel tumbled off the piano bench she turned around so fast.

I went over and switched another light on in the darkened room before trying to help Angel.

"Did you hurt yourself?" Margaret asked her.

"No, but I spilt soda on the song we were writing."

Clarence pulled out a handkerchief and blotted at the paper. "It can be saved," he said.

"If it can't," Margaret bent over to help Clarence, "we'll just write it again.

"I don't know, Margaret." Angel's voice was shaky and nervous sounding. "It took a lot of braining to write that song. You think we can do it again?"

Angel was obviously very stressed, but Margaret was cool as a cucumber. "Honey, I've got it memorized. Don't you worry. Everything is going to be okay. I just wish Darla would get back so we could practice singing it together."

It wasn't the right time to speak to Margaret and Angel about the album I wanted to produce. First, I'd need to talk out the details with our record company. I would call them in the morning as I also had one more thing to discuss with them. I'd noticed on the way home the country station I listened to not only kept playing mine and Mick's music, but they also were giving a lot of airplay to Ernie Koster's old songs. It'd be the perfect time for them to re-release some of his old music. Even if he couldn't play anymore, he could finally make money on his earlier stuff. None of us had made what we were worth back then when Ernie was popular. It would be nice if he could have a good retirement.

Maybe even get some play for his sidekick Harold. He'd played on some of Ernie's earlier albums. But so far he hadn't appeared since running off into the woods after the shooting incident. Or as Ernie put it to me this morning, "Old Harold up and disappeared like a fart in the wind, didn't he?" Yet another reminder that Ernie wasn't only a good guitar player, but he also had a most unique way with words. Maybe he still had another song or two in him. At least as far as writing them, his creativity would still be strong.

PART 8

TWO WORLDS—ONE LIFE

CHAPTER 32

Watertown Strip, Nevada
Wednesday Morning
November 5, 1958

R AYNE

Pope John XXIII was inaugurated yesterday. And Soviet Premier
Nikita Khrushchev delivered a speech demanding the Western powers
of the United States, Great Britain and France pull forces out of West
Berlin. Other than that, we haven't gotten much news from the outside
world here at Watertown Strip—or "the ranch," as we were told to call
it. Our secret temporary base out in the southern Nevada desert could
only be described as desolate.

As a training site for the revolutionary new U-2, the remote location
of the ranch made it perfect. As a place to live, the remoteness left it
severely lacking.

In fact, the only convenient way for us to reach the ranch was by plane. We took shuttle flights from a Burbank, California, terminal every Monday and flew out again on Friday. As I mentioned, this was a secret temporary base. During the week we lived four to a trailer. No PX. No club. No privacy. Hard to sleep at night as I could hear every toss and turn of those around me. I liked to get up early so I could shower before the hot water ran out.

But for some reason the mess hall served exceptional cuisine. I mean, I'm talking about great food that would be considered exceptional anywhere—not just out here in nowhere land. But exceptional food only satisfies one of the senses. My others soaked in the remoteness and secrecy of my purpose for being here. It was strange to know that I really didn't know anything about the other pilots. And perhaps even stranger, I couldn't tell them anything real about me.

The weather was cool this morning, the sun bright. Aside from a few light showers, we were good to go ahead with flight training. Training I'd need before my assignment in Turkey.

As I walked around outside, I pondered how I could live in two different worlds at once. There was what I guess you'd call the world of my real life. That which I had with family, friends and Darla back in Texas. And then there was this world. The ranch. It seemed far away and distant. Dreamlike when you consider what we were doing out here.

I really felt like I was helping my country and my fellow Americans. Never in my life had I imagined this would be my calling. But when the opportunity arose, I knew it was what I was destined to do. If only I could find a way to make it work for both Darla and me. A few of the other pilots were married. I'd heard one of them say his wife would be joining him when we got to Turkey. This surprised me because of the secret nature of our missions. As I pondered the situation, I'm certain the wives would be kept at a distance so they wouldn't know what we were flying or where we were going. Which would be hard on a marriage. Stil,l there was hope of having a real life with a real woman.

But today I needed to concentrate on the job at hand. The U-2 was fairly safe, even though there had already been one crash. We all knew the risks of flying an experimental plane, but still it had taken us all by surprise. The pilot who had gone down was one of our best, which meant it was probably something to do with the plane itself. Either way, his death had been a jolt to all of us.

Hopefully, the mechanics had repaired any flukes in the system. However, when a plane takes off, you can tell by the absolute silence that permeates the air that every pilot and ground crew member is holding their breath.

I definitely didn't want my mind wandering while flying.

Moving toward the paved runway, I stood admiring the U-2 parked inside. It was a magnificent sight to behold. Unlike any other aircraft.

Its maker, Kelly Johnson, had eliminated weight wherever he could in its ingenious design. For example, the plane had no ejection seat—a pilot literally had to climb out if there were an emergency. Another economy was the landing gear. Instead of the usual tricycle type with a gear under the nose and another under each wing, the U-2 had a gear under the nose and one under the tail. More like a bicycle. An extension with a small wheel on the end was set in a socket underneath each wing to support the aircraft on the ground. We called them "pogos," and they also kept the wings level while taxiing. But upon takeoff they dropped off. I won't lie, it was tricky to land.

Learning to expertly fly the U-2 had been exhilarating. Standing around in the desert, waiting and wondering when my turn would come next was excruciating. We had a couple of pool tables to while away the time. And, if we weren't shooting pool, we played poker.

And, of course, I daydreamed about Darla. I wondered if she would be just as wonderful as I remembered when I got to see her again. So far, I'd been lucky that I'd been able to go to Dallas for part of my new work. Soon, I'd be overseas. Would she wait for me? If only I could bring her over. The timing sure stunk—finding my dream job, only to have it interfere with finding my dream girl. I kept reminding myself, if it was meant to be, our relationship would stand the test of being apart. What with her singing career and touring, maybe we were perfect for each other. We'd just have to wait and see. I wish I could tell her more about my work.

Soon, the weekend would be here. As usual we would all fly via the shuttle back to Burbank on Friday, only to return en masse on Monday. For a few days we were free to go back to our old lives, using our real names and identification. We also had a card identifying us as employees of Lockheed on loan to the National Advisory Committee for Aeronautic (NACA). Once back at the base, we turned in our real-life identification. Using our cover names while training added an extra layer of security as not all personnel from Watertown would be going overseas with us.

Of course, our real names were close to our fake names in case anyone should ever see us from the other life we led. But as far as the other pilots I was training with, I'd probably never know their true identities. All this secret stuff to contend with. I must admit it bothered me. Did the United States really need a secret agency? I guess we did to keep the country safe. After all, Russia had the KGB.

I picked up a stick and drew my cover name in the sand while I waited.

When flying the U-2, we were instructed to never carry identification. That way, if our mission failed, the enemy wouldn't know who we were or where we were from. Which in my mind was a bit disconcerting, to say the least. Would Darla ever know what happened to me? What would they tell my family? I thought of Mama. She'd never get over it, especially if she didn't know what had happened to me. I hate the thought of those I love aways wondering whatever became of me. But I guess a lot of folks who have soldiers in their family have come up against this situation. I knew why they didn't want us identified, but still it made me feel less than human. As if Rayne the man wasn't important. Only the mission. Which brings me to another thing that bothered me. What would happen if I was ever caught or shot down on one of my reconnaissance missions? Certainly the agency hadn't given us much instruction on how to handle the situation. I'd already asked several times, only to get the nebulous response back that I should handle things the best way I could as any number of scenarios could happen in a real-life mission.

When I pushed the issue with one of our superiors, he said, "Tell them everything you know. Because in truth you know very little about the mission itself other than targets on a map." If that didn't make me feel like a disposable military asset. At least they had given us the coin with the poisoned pin hidden inside. It was one escape if we were being tortured. But not one that I would ever want to take.

Earlier, when I had suggested they include maps of safe exits on the ground for our most dangerous flights, the supervisor didn't even comment. I suppose the powers that be didn't expect the U-2 to ever be shot down as it was too high in the atmosphere to be detected. But in my heart, I suspected they didn't believe a pilot would survive if the U-2 ever crashed to Earth. I sure as hell hoped I'd never have to find out for myself.

CHAPTER 33

McLaren Mansion, Dallas, Texas
Friday Afternoon
November 14, 1958

ARGARET

Tension filled the air.

Mick's booming voice had quit yelling. Now there was only a sad silence.

My stomach twisted upon itself. I didn't like conflict. But there was no escaping this fight with Mick. The two of us had put it off far too long. Years really. The truth had come out. And light turned to darkness in our world. Words were being said that couldn't be unsaid. Truths were making their way to the surface, and there was no way of ignoring the distance between us anymore.

I had built my entire adult life around Mick. And at this moment, I saw him for the selfish entitled child he'd always been. I had a vague memory of being worried about his attitude before we tied the knot. But I had wanted to be with him. Which meant I was willing to over-look any negative signs I may have noticed. Swept negative thoughts aside as I believed he'd grow into the person I wanted him to be, needed him to be. How many times had I assured myself of this? All we needed was our love. And we did have that, which made this breakup even worse. How could we have let it slip away? Why didn't we fight for each other? Why did I let him have his secrets for so long? If I'd brought them out in the open early on, maybe we would still have had a chance.

Mick took a deep breath and turned away from me before going out onto the balcony.

I didn't follow.

Instead, I ran down the stairs, tears flooding my eyes.

The time had come for us to discuss the dark-haired woman. His stalker. His real stalker, not the one the record company sent out. They said sending Ernie Koster to stalk him was to increase the sales of Mick and Cowboy's newest album. Maybe so, but I felt it may have been to cover up the real stalker. If that news got out, it would hurt their latest album sales.

Reaching the last stair, I sat down to catch my breath. Huge sobs made my body shudder. Made my heart hammer. Made our love die.

Oh, the heartbreak.

Where was Cowboy? This would make great material for one of his songs he was always writing.

Life as I knew it was over. I was so frightened by the changes to come. But at the same time, a little exhilarated. What was it my grand-mother had always said—"Never be afraid to trust an unknown future to a known God."

My breath stabilized, and I stood straight and tall.

Looking around our mansion, our home, I saw it in a new light. For the first time perhaps, I saw our relationship clearly. Mick was a good person *and* a bad person. Just like us all. But his fame had brought temptations he couldn't resist.

And I thought of the poor dark-haired woman. She must have been driven to insanity to keep stalking him the way she had been for the past few months. How many others were there like her? Too afraid to do anything other than keep quiet. How many hearts had Mick broken over the years?

Sweeping through the kitchen, I kept moving forward until I found the screen door.

I barely felt it hit my back as I exited.

Padding across the soft grass in our backyard, I felt the earth solid and strong underneath me. Without another thought I headed to my secret place.

My spirit was crushed like the violets beneath my feet. I should've known better than to plant them outside. But I wanted them to be a part of my secret gazebo in the woods. Hadn't been back here since Mick's stalker scared Jack and me with all the photos and bright camera flashes. Well, I was scared that day. Can't say Jack was too intimidated. I wish I had his strength of mind. He was sure of his path. And he didn't let anyone detour him. No wonder he was a champion tennis player—the strength of his mind. Not just the strength of his body.

All my married life, I'd been playing second fiddle to Mick's fame. Never wanted to push it too much what with all the kids to take care of. It was my fault as much as Mick's that I'd never cultivated my music career.

But no more. The time to start was now.

Was it crazy to think a middle-aged woman could start a new career in an industry that didn't cater to old people?

Maybe by adding Darla and Angel I could put a fresh face forward. Especially if I wrote the songs. I don't know, they both were pretty good songwriters themselves. Maybe together we could all three make it happen.

I knew one thing for sure. I wasn't going to use my married name to get ahead. I wasn't going to ride on Mick's and Cowboy's coattails. I was going to do it on my own. And I was going to do it my way.

As I walked along, a light breeze lifted my spirits, pulling me into a higher level of thinking. I still had a lot of life in me.

Just the other day, my oldest child told me he thought Angel, Darla and I sounded great when we practiced singing together. This meant a lot to me because he didn't hand out a lot of compliments. He was a good kid. A serious kid. And I knew I could count on him to help me with the younger kids when I had to go on the road. Maybe I could even take little Jamison with me as he wasn't in school yet.

Ouch. A sharp pain went across the top of my right ankle.

Did I just fall? Apparently so.

Otherwise, I wouldn't be lying on my back in the soft grass, looking up at the gray clouds forming in the sky overhead. That's what I get for getting so lost in my thoughts. A swift reminder to pay attention to the real world.

Ouch, I was starting to feel the pain course throughout my back.

And, oh my goodness, my foot throbbed.

Sitting up and twisting around, I saw the leaves were starting to fall in great heaps all over the dying grass. Yes, fall had arrived. Glancing about, I saw a thin wire stretched about six inches off the ground. The ends of it were anchored to two trees, making for a very treacherous situation for anyone walking in the woods.

Was it a trap for animals? Or humans?

I could hardly see it for the leaves. No wonder I had tripped.

Did one of the kids set it up? Or Mick's stalker? I didn't even want to let my mind wander in that direction.

Gingerly, I rubbed my right ankle. It didn't appear broken, but it was starting to swell.

A raindrop plopped on my forehead.

What now? Was it going to rain again? I needed to get to the gazebo fast.

Pushing up with my forearms, I brought myself up on my knees. But I couldn't get up on my good foot without something to hold. I looked around for a big stick. No. Nothing to help. So, I did the next best thing. I started crawling toward the gazebo. Or should I say I crawled and clawed my way to the gazebo. Nothing graceful or lady-like about it. I was in survival mode.

"Why, oh why had I come out here?"

Even as I said the words out loud, I knew why I had come—I found a deep peace in the solitude of being out here in nature. It was a way to heal myself mentally.

As I listened to the wind swish through the oaks overhead, I felt a calmness in my soul despite my physical pain.

My leaving was about more than Mick's wandering ways. It was about me coming into my own. I'd chosen to take a backseat. To let my talent go unused. But I would find a way to be the person I knew I could be. I would find myself—recreate myself. And I'd take my kids along with me.

Within a few minutes of struggling, I had reached the wooden gazebo. Its twisting vines and peeling white paint welcomed me. Slowly, I pulled myself up on one of the wooden steps. Just a few more steps, and I'd be safe from the coming storm. Thunder crashed in the distance.

I looked back at the trip wire. Who in the heck would have set such a dangerous trap?

CHAPTER 34

ARLA

Margaret had not seen me in Mick's office when she rushed down the hallway on her way out the back. Little did she know I had overheard the majority of their fight or that I had caught a glimpse of her tear-stained face as she tore down the stairs. And lastly, perhaps most painful of all, I had literally felt her anger with the slamming of the back screen door.

Love wasn't an easy thing to watch die.

I wish I wasn't a witness.

It only made me question if I was a fool to be falling so hard for Rayne. Would I regret making concessions in my career for his?

The front door opened and closed again. I poked my head out of the office half hoping Margaret had done something as crazy as run around the house and come back inside. But no such luck. Margaret was long gone. The surprise at the front door was Angel.

My face must've looked as stricken as I felt because she rushed toward me.

"Darla, what's wrong? Are you okay?" Her tone was soft and kind. Totally unlike her usual sarcastic self.

I motioned her into the office and softly shut the door behind us. Then I heard Mick descending the stairs. His footsteps heavy and angry sounding.

I put my finger to my lips before handing Angel a handful of paperwork.

Seconds later Mick whipped open the office door, wanting to seek refuge inside.

"Angel," I said in a businesslike manner, "let's work in the kitchen. We can spread our paperwork out on the table."

Mick didn't even acknowledge us as we left. He didn't even question why Angel was standing in his office on her day off. That's probably because he didn't know or care what day it was. Mick's brain was working on his career at all hours every day of the week. It wasn't unusual for him to get up in the middle of the night and work. And I knew for a fact this behavior didn't help his failing marriage.

Mick didn't even glance our way. Instead, he stood silently and sullenly by the open window, letting the cool breeze wash over his heated face. At times like these, I truly believed in the stereotype of redheads having a fiery temper. Certainly, Mick could be a hothead, but his last argument with Margaret took his temperamental antics to another level. It was a good thing Margaret had left. They both needed to cool off.

When we got to the kitchen, I motioned for Angel to follow me out the back door.

"Where are we going?" she whispered with a quizzical look. She must've sensed I didn't want Mick, or anyone else for that matter, to hear what I was about to say.

"Let's walk, and I'll tell you." I took her arm, gently pulling her along. "Why did you come in on your day off? You look nice in this dress. Is it new?"

"Yes, it's new. And I came back for my paycheck. I must've left it on the desk in Mick's office yesterday. He had me doing a myriad of tasks all at one time and my brain got rattled. You know how it is." Angel reached down and took off her shoes. They were flats, but I could tell they were also new. I had on sneakers with my pedal pushers. There was no need to dress up for work today as Mick had wanted me to help him clean out some old, dusty files.

Looking back up at the house, I could see little Jamison standing in one of the upstairs windows. His eyes big and wide. Oh my gosh, he must be devastated hearing his parents fight like two wildcats. For a fleeting moment, I felt the tightness in my stomach that happened whenever my own parents had really bad fights . . . fights not unlike the one Mick and Margaret had just had. Jamison must be scared to death his parents would divorce, leaving him and his brother and sister in the lurch. To a kid a divorce is like a death. Who am I kidding? Divorce is like a death to everyone involved.

Thank goodness, an older child appeared behind him, taking him into their arms. I believed it was Thomas, but I couldn't be sure. Maybe it was Debra.

"Where are we going?" Angel asked as I hurried her along.

"Mick and Margaret just had a whopper of a fight. And Margaret ran out the back without an umbrella or shoes. I tell you, I've never seen her so upset. We need to find her."

"You mean, she just ran off into the woods here . . . without shoes? And it's about to thunderstorm. I actually need to put my shoes back on. I've already stepped on a couple of stickers."

With that Angel stopped abruptly and put both her shoes back on, but not before removing the small burs clinging to the side of her foot. "Ouch!" Angel screwed up her face in pain as the stickers became stuck to her fingers. It took a moment longer for her to free herself of them.

"Hurry, Angel. I think I know where Margaret was headed. Her secret place."

Angel stopped in her tracks.

"Her secret place? Margaret has a secret place? You don't mean the next-door neighbor Jack's house, do you?"

I looked at Angel with disdain.

"No, she's taken to going out to an old gazebo on the property line over there. I only know about it because I followed her once."

Now Angel's face held disdain for me.

"Darla, you followed Margaret? Were you spying on her?"

"Yes," I said tossing my hair, "but I don't like to think of it as spying. I like to think of it as satisfying my curiosity. You know, collecting information. And, of course, I was checking on her to make certain she was okay. Seems she always escapes to the gazebo when something disturbs her. And lately she'd been disturbed a lot what with Mick's female stalker and all."

"I'll say." Angel had started walking fast alongside me again. "Slashed tires. People taking photos of her every move. Actually meeting Mick's female stalker in the woods. And then having to deal with newspaper reports of Mick shooting Ernie in a jealous rage."

A boom of thunder crashed overhead. The sky grew a darker gray. Only a few raindrops splatted here and there, but I could tell it was about to come to a gully washer.

Together Angel and I pushed deeper into the woods. The gazebo was farther out than I'd remembered. Surely I was headed in the right direction.

"Margaret! Margaret!" I yelled out into the whipping wind.

I knew Margaret wouldn't do anything foolish, but I was worried about her mental anguish.

That's when we heard her.

"Margaret! What's that? What are you saying!" I called out.

"Watch out!" We could barely hear Margaret as she called in our direction once more.

But it was too late. Angel and I had already gone head over heels over some kind of wire.

"Sweet Mother of Pearl!" Angel shouted as she fell all catawampus on her butt. While I said a simple "shit" under my breath as I tumbled forward, wrenching my right arm.

"We're coming, Margaret," I screamed out loud in spite of my pain. I could see her waving at us from the old gazebo.

Looking around, I pulled at the wire. It was stuck solid. Pinned between two trees. Jerking again, I managed to pull it free with Angel's help. What in the world? Who in the world? Why in the world would anyone put up a wire trap here?

When we gathered our wits, we continued onward. Angel's pretty dress was torn and muddy. I had grass in my hair. And a bruise was already forming on my arm. A few birds in the trees overhead chirped a warning of the coming storm.

Big, fat raindrops kept plopping down on us. They started to splatter more. Making for a steady rain just as we reached Margaret in the gazebo.

"Do you think you both can help me?" she asked as we moved up the gazebo steps. "I've hurt my foot, and we need to get to that gardening shed just that side of Jack's property." She pointed a little ways ahead.

Lightning cracked overhead, accenting her words.

"The shed will be safer than this open gazebo." Margaret raised herself up on a bench before reaching toward us. "Can you help me up? It's only a few minutes to the shed."

And at that Angel and I pulled Margaret's arms around us before carefully descending the gazebo stairs. Although she wasn't heavy, it was awkward and difficult to make our way across the uneven turf. The grass near the garden shed was knee-high as if the gardener had forgotten it. All I could think of was the old saying, the snakes are always meanest in the tall grass.

Up ahead, the door of the shed looked not unlike a garage door. I tried pulling it up, but it was stiff and hard. I had to hold Margaret as Angel tried to struggle with it. Finally, giving it all the strength she had, Angel got it opened wide. A single window illuminated the old shack inside. Tools and implements, sacks and seeds, potting soil and containers. It had everything a garden would need. Except, of course, a gardener. As Margaret informed us, Jack didn't have one. He mowed his lawn himself. How did she know that? Those two sure were getting to be close friends.

As we moved farther inside, I picked up an old flashlight. To my surprise it shown brightly when I flipped it to the on position. I walked farther still pointing the beam of light this way and that. The back of the shed was L-shaped. Carefully, I turned the corner, flicking the light in front of me. I couldn't believe my eyes. Against the wall was a bed with what appeared to be fresh linens. And carefully folded towels sat near a wash basin. A few women's dresses were hung on a clothesline across the back corner.

Angel and Margaret limped up behind me. None of us saying a word at the unexpected sight.

Ka-boom! Dangerous thunder crashed nearby.

Boom! The shed's door fell down behind us.

In the deadly silence we could hear the metallic click of a lock.

Surely someone did not just lock us inside.

A blood-curdling scream came from deep inside me as a dark figure passed in front of the grimy window.

Someone had been watching us.

"It's her," Margaret whispered. "It's her."

Fear gripped my heart. Each breath hurt as the adrenaline pumped through my veins.

I looked around for a weapon. I didn't have to look far. An axe rested against the wall nearby.

As if on cue, Angel picked up a machete.

Margaret grabbed a pair of gardening shears.

"Lawdy," Margaret whispered again, "this day isn't shaping up at all the way I had planned. I was going to get a jump on my Christmas shopping. Had already called a sitter to watch Jamison. She should be at the house any moment, thank God."

Angel put down the machete and instead put her arm around Margaret's shoulders helping her to the single chair near the bed. One couldn't say Angel was exactly a nice person, but she did seem to know when a person needed her. And she could be counted on to come forward with the kindness needed. Whether that be positive encouragement or a simple heartfelt hug. Clearly, Angel must've had her fair share of tough circumstances to have such heartfelt empathy. Her tough hard shell was just that: a shell.

None of us spoke a single word as the rain fell full force on our ramshackle sanctuary.

My eye caught a tiny glass jar of matches near a lantern. Whoever had been living here had left it conveniently out on a shelf near the door. The batteries in this flashlight would not last long. Thanks to the trespasser living in Jack's old shed, we had everything we needed to make it through the storm. A cold chill ran up my spine. I hoped the squatter living in the shed wasn't Mick's stalker. Surely, she'd left the property after her last run-in with Jack and Margaret at the gazebo. To think of her living out here in the shed was too sad. Not to mention scary. In truth, I had little faith any of the three of us had the moxie to use our makeshift weapons against Mick's stalker. Perhaps she didn't have the guts to hurt us either. We could only hope.

I moved toward the garden shed door and I tried to lift it up with my good arm. Just to check to see if we were stuck in here. No luck. I would try again later with Angel's help. It must've been my imagination that I heard someone lock it. Been reading too many scary stories lately. This was Jack's backyard. No one would lock us in. Unless, of course . . . .

What was that moving outside the window? I moved closer for a better look, but the window was foggy from the humidity in the heavy rain. Outside a few feet from our shed was a man. A tall, thin man with a raincoat and a wide brimmed hat. Upon closer inspection, I realized it was Mick. Oh, thank goodness!

"Margaret, Margaret!" I cried out. "Mick's outside. He must be looking for you."

Margaret tried to move toward me. Angel was helping her.

I turned back to the window. Taking the handle of the axe I was still holding, I bashed out a small pane in the lower part of the wooden window frame and yelled, "Mick, we're over here! In the shed!"

In spite of the wind, he heard me. He was moving toward the window.

Then he stopped and looked back to his left. His face registering fear as his eyes widened.

What was happening? Why was he moving away?

"Mick! Mick! We're in . . ." I stopped mid-sentence as another person entered my point of view from the small window.

I saw him put his hands in the air.

It was the dark-haired woman. His real stalker. And she had a gun.

Rain soaked her dress. It clung to her like a second skin.

Her arms shook in the cold rain as she held the gun in front of her.

Then she fired.

I couldn't believe my eyes. She had fired her gun. But it'd missed Mick.

She steadied herself, getting ready to aim again.

And then someone else fired.

From another location.

The stalker fell to the ground. Blood immediately started to spread on her side.

Mick looked past the woman and cried out, "No, no, no! Give me the gun. I've got to make it look like it's my fault."

Margaret and Angel moved up behind me.

We all three gasped at the same time as Margaret and Mick's oldest boy walked forward. Handing his gun over to his father, Thomas bent down to check the woman.

"She missed." Margaret's words fell softly.

"What?" I said, not registering that Margaret meant the woman's bullet had missed Mick. He had not been hurt.

CHAPTER 35

C OWBOY LARSON

Jail was a hard place for someone like Thomas to find himself. Especially when he was in jail for protecting his father. But he wouldn't in turn let his father protect him. Thomas, as usual, had insisted on telling the truth. He told the police officer who arrived on the scene everything as it really happened.

Now he was in jail. And Mick's female stalker was in the hospital recovering from a shot to the side of her hip. The irony of both him and Mick shooting alleged stalkers in the same place wasn't lost on me. Life was strange indeed.

Leaning back in the hard metal chair, I glanced around the police captain's office. With the exception of a few certificates hanging on the wall, it was completely bare of decoration. I thanked God the captain had taken a meeting with me. Maybe, just maybe, I could get Thomas out on bond. It would be expensive. But Thomas was more important than paying our taxes. And he was definitely more important than paying the electric bill.

The harsh overhead light made everything appear a little greenish gray, including my hands. Holding them out in front of me, I noticed how much they'd aged in the past few years. Crepey skin. Little brown spots. Just like I remembered my dad's hands back in the day. Truth be told, sometimes my hands ached these days, and I wasn't the guitarist I'd been when we had all our hits.

Man, oh man, we needed this album to take off. Not just for the money, but for our egos.

Did I really just think that? What was it Saint used to say when something like that popped out of my mouth?

"That's real sad you can't even brag about it," she'd say. "I know how much you like to brag," she'd say. "As always, it's all about you, Cowboy."

Taking a deep breath, I leaned backwards in the chair again and stared at the ceiling.

Everyone was hurt in the chaos the day before. Everyone except Mick.

Margaret was in the hospital with a broken ankle.

Darla had a sprained wrist.

Angel twisted her back.

Mick's female stalker, Eileen, had a gunshot wound.

And Thomas . . . Thomas was sitting in jail awaiting an uncertain future.

Yet Mick was running around free. Oblivious to the hurt he'd caused. I told him not to come with me today, as we both knew I was the more diplomatic personality. Instead, Mick went to sit with Margaret to see if he could help her physically and emotionally.

I know he was worried. Would she leave him over Eileen? Mick claimed Eileen was a deranged fan who held fantasies about being his lover. That he'd done nothing to make her feel the way she did about him. I couldn't say. I really didn't know the truth. But I did know that through the years there had been others whom he'd done something with.

So had I.

For years, we'd both chased fame and approbation. Then when we got it, we didn't know how to handle it.

Leaning forward in the chair, I put my elbows on my knees and cupped my face in my hands.

A thought that had been nagging at me lately raised itself again.

After we completed this last album, I was going to leave my partnership with Mick. Go out on my own. Might not be a perfect time as Margaret was probably going to leave Mick, too. But from my perspective, there never was a perfect time to do things. I'd just have to gut it up and tell him. Maybe I'd tell him before we recorded the last of the songs we wrote on the camping trip. It'd be the right thing to do. But it wouldn't be the easy thing to do.

The door opened and I stood as the police captain entered.

"Sit down," he gestured at my chair. "Take a rest. We've got a lot to talk about."

Sitting down across from me at his metal desk, he unfolded a newspaper. Photos of Mick and Thomas were prominent on the first page. As was this catchy headline: "Like Father. Like Son."

But that headline couldn't be farther from the truth. Mick and Thomas were nothing alike.

PART 9

A WANDERER'S SPIRIT

CHAPTER 36

McLaren Mansion, Dallas, Texas
Thursday Morning
November 27, 1958

D ARLA

For the first time ever, Macy's Thanksgiving Day Parade in New York City was being shown live on television from 11 a.m. to noon. So, we women were scurrying around the kitchen, getting as much of the Thanksgiving meal done as we could before the start of the parade. Hopefully, we'd get to see a lot of it. Even if we only saw bits and pieces while we were running back and forth from the kitchen to the television set in the den.

I was surprised when Margaret asked me and Angel to attend their big family Thanksgiving meal. She'd even invited my mother, who was actually being civil to me as we worked on making the biscuits.

My mother was a good cook, and I was glad I had her with me today. She always knew how to arrange the silverware and stuff like that. I could never remember. Probably because we never had fancy meals at home when I was growing up. My mother had married down when she married my father, but supposedly they were in love. I guess they were, but they sure did fight a lot.

Across the kitchen, I watched as Margaret hopped around on one crutch. She was instructing Angel as to how to check the turkey to see if it was ready.

When Angel pulled the turkey out of the oven, my tastebuds watered at the heavenly aroma.

Margaret checked it with a thermometer. "Needs more butter and another half hour," she said.

Angel heated butter in a saucepan while Margaret hobbled to the dish rack to get the brush and turkey baster she'd cleaned earlier.

Warm apple pie cooled on a nearby windowsill.

Mick and Margaret's only girl, Debra, sat across from us mixing up deviled eggs.

She looked just like a female version of Mick. Same auburn hair. Same lively eyes. She even worked with an intensity to match Mick's when he was concentrating on doing something well. The only difference was her features were much softer. And her temper didn't have Mick's tendency to flare.

She also had Mick's outgoing ways. But today she was quiet. I felt a pit in my stomach as I knew she must be worried about her brother Thomas. He didn't get to come home as we'd all hoped. The police captain was keeping him separated from the rest of the prisoners because of Mick's fame. But that was the only perk he was getting. They hadn't even set bail. Maybe the guards would let me and Debra in to take him food and have a short visit this afternoon. If they didn't let us visit, the guards might take him the food. Especially if we took them a couple plates as well.

The front door opened. It was Katherine and Clarence. I could tell by their voices they were in the holiday spirit. And that was Cowboy's deep voice coming in close behind them.

I heard Mick recruiting Cowboy and Clarence to help him set up a kids' table by the long table in the formal dining room. I guess I was considered an adult now as I was told I didn't have to sit at the kids' table but, rather, next to my mother and Angel at the big table.

Soon the first-ever live broadcast of the Thanksgiving parade would start on the television. Everyone rushed about trying to get last-minute tasks done so they could see the start.

Katherine's cane clicked as she came down the marble entryway. Turning into the kitchen, she carried a basket containing a fruit salad and a green bean casserole. It was all she could do to carry the load. Quickly, I got up to help.

"Hello, hello everyone!" Katherine was in a great mood. Her face was beaming. "Where are we going to put all this food?" she asked, as we stood holding it.

"If it's already in serving dishes, we could start putting some things on the main dining table once they get the tablecloth on." Margaret opened a drawer and got out some metal trivets. "Don't forget to put these under them to protect the finish from the hot dishes."

Debra stood up and took the trivets. "I'll help. I know what to do." She picked up her plate of deviled eggs and started back to the dining room. Katherine and I followed in a line behind her.

The front door opened again, letting in a blast of cold air.

It was Rayne's mama and daddy, followed by his brother and two sisters.

I knew his mother was Margaret's sister, but I hadn't expected them to drive all the way from Cooper to Dallas for Thanksgiving.

The house overflowed with joyful noise as people of all ages and sizes greeted each other. Little Jamison jumped up in Rayne's mother's arms. She didn't even flinch as she caught him. Clearly, she was a pro at handling kids.

She saw me watching and she came my way.

"Darla, I'm so glad you're here. I'll get to spend a little time with you. Get to know you better."

My heart fluttered. I felt the heat rise in my face.

I wanted to get to know her better as well.

But the sight of her and the rest of Rayne's family only served as a reminder to me that he wasn't here. My heart seized in my chest. I took a deep breath. And I smiled on the outside while I died a little inside. Where in the world was Rayne? And I meant that quite literally, as he could be flying anywhere at any time.

I looked up and saw my own mother carrying plates and napkins. Angel stood behind her with a tray of silverware. The scents of turkey roasting and apple pie wafted in the air around them. Mama smiled and handed me cloth napkins decorated with little pilgrims. "Margaret wants us to set the table so we can watch the parade while everything is cooking," she said. "We've only got a few minutes. So let's hurry."

"Mama," I hesitated, and I don't know why. "Mama, this is Rayne's mother. She's Margaret's sister."

"So nice to meet you." Rayne's mother indeed looked happy to meet Mama. Why was I surprised that everything was going so well?

Just then Angel stepped up to our small group still holding the box of silverware. "Excuse, me," she said, "would someone show me where the knife goes? I always forget which side."

"Oh, gee," Rayne's mother furrowed her brow, "I always forget myself."

Margaret hobbled into the room on her crutch. "How many place settings do we need to make?" she asked, counting on her fingers. "Twenty-one."

Then she corrected herself. "No, twenty. Thomas isn't here." As she said the words, she brought her hand up to her heart. "Oh, dear Lawd. I do hope they are feeding him right today."

Debra glanced up from her work. "Mama, Darla said earlier maybe we can take him a plate. And make some plates for his guards."

Margaret looked at Mick. "Maybe you and Cowboy should go to the jail instead. I don't think the girls will be safe."

"Oh, Mama. Please, please let me go!" Debra's face was completely crestfallen.

Just then, Rayne's brother stepped forward. His resemblance was so close to his big brother my breath caught on the lump in my throat. "I'll take her. I haven't seen Thomas in a year. It'll be good to see him."

"Mick," Margaret said, "maybe you should go, too."

"No," Debra practically screamed, "Daddy's the reason Thomas is in jail!"

An awkward silence held in the air as Debra's eyes brimmed with tears. My stomach tightened and turned on itself as she ran out of the dining room and up the stairs. Margaret tried to go after her, but Rayne's mother set little Jamison down and put a hand on Margaret's shoulder. "Margaret," she said with steel in her voice, "let me take care of this. The girl's right, you know." And with that she hurried up the stairs while we tried to recover below.

I looked around for Mick to see his reaction, but he and Cowboy had gone out back to smoke with Rayne's father. It was doubtful they'd heard anything.

The parade was about to start live on television. But I don't think any of us were ready for it as our excitement had dampened.

Opening the front door, I stepped out into the cool air. Leaves gusted up, swirling around me on the porch. The gloomy weather matched my mood. I missed Rayne so much my heart ached.

CHAPTER 37

Adana, Turkey
Incirlik Air Base
Thursday Late Afternoon
November 27, 1958

R AYNE

I told myself I'd treat Thanksgiving like any other day. But it wasn't working. I missed home. I missed my family. I missed Darla. I wondered what they were all doing right now. They'd never believe my morning. Flying high in the sky right next door to Russia.

It had been hard to get out of bed at 5 a.m. this morning to report to rebreathing to "get on the hose" and suit up. I'd studied and restudied my maps. The routes were color-coded along with marks indicating where photographic and electronic equipment should be switched on and off.

I'd fallen into a routine as far as the overflights went. The only thing different today was the intelligence officer asking me if I wanted to carry a cyanide capsule. No, sir. I didn't want it. My worry was it would break in my pocket and I'd accidentally come in contact with it. But I mean really, if I went down, there'd be little chance of survival. We both knew it.

Thank goodness the flight was over. As much as I enjoyed flying, I'd been amped up a little too much lately. Still reeling from the overflight mission that had crashed recently. We all felt uneasy, knowing it was only a matter of chance that we'd be the next. I suppose when enough time had passed, I'd quit being so antsy.

Maneuvering around a cement outdoor bench, I looked down the runway with my feet planted firmly on the ground.

It was a good day to be outside. Turkey, being near the Mediterranean, had a warm climate almost year-round. The sight of soldiers working and engines rumbling made me feel a little less alone.

Looking at my watch, I got up to go to the one restaurant we always ate at located above a hotel. Not only was it one of the only safe places to eat near the base, but they also served good food. They couldn't match my mother's green bean casserole or Aunt Margaret's apple pie, but still it was definitely tasty.

Who was I kidding? I was as homesick as a new pup being separated from its mother.

Not only was I missing everyone, I was just plain old missing out.

More memories I wouldn't have. More family photos I won't be included in.

I was a long way from home. And I felt it.

CHAPTER 38

Recording Studio, Dallas, Texas
Monday Afternoon
December 1, 1958

OWBOY LARSON

The studio where we were recording was new to us even though their equipment obviously wasn't new. We couldn't book where we usually did. A small slight. But still a slight all the same. If we'd been in our heyday, they'd have thrown out whoever was recording and put us in ASAP.

Mick was smoking heavily again, but he was also singing and playing better than ever.

Couldn't say the same about me. In fact, I'd asked Danny to come in and do a complicated solo I'd written for the last song on the album. Mick didn't say anything about me doing it. And right now he seemed very satisfied with how the music was coming together. His vision of taking our music somewhere new was actually happening, making me glad I hadn't talked to Mick about leaving and going out on my own just yet. There'd be time enough for that later. No need to mess with the successful vibe we had going.

Soon Danny would be here, and we could get the last song under way. Of course, we'd still need to edit. And Mick could be a bear when it came to getting everything perfect. There was a method to his madness —his creative genius—but it always drove me absolutely insane.

There were only thirty more days in 1958. I wanted to finish the year on a high note, so to speak. I felt certain this album, along with the one we'd just cut, was going to bring in enough to pay off any debts we had. Plus, I felt like it would put us back on top.

Already the fiasco with Ernie Koster being shot in the butt had put us high on the radio station playlists. And, of course, on the covers of newspapers and magazines across the country.

But I didn't know how the episode with Thomas shooting Mick's real stalker, Eileen, was going to play out. Whether it helped us or hurt us didn't matter. What mattered was the question of whether or not it would hurt Thomas. He was hoping to be a lawyer one day. Being compared to Mick all his life had made him want to carve out his own path. A very different path. But truth be told, Thomas was a good singer/songwriter. I guess with his mother and father it was in his genes. But he didn't flaunt it, preferring to keep it to himself. Only showing me a few things he'd composed. However, when he did break out his guitar, his skill made it obvious he'd been practicing in private. To make matters worse for him, his voice sounded so similar to Mick's it was hard for even me to tell them apart.

"What are you thinking about so hard?" Mick came over and sat down beside me.

"Just thinking about Thomas. Can't believe they're holding him without bail. Seems the captain didn't want to appear to take it easy on him because he had a famous father." Shaking my head, I reached into my front shirt pocket for a matchstick to chew on. "Surely that fancy lawyer we hired will get him out soon."

Mick hung his head and didn't say anything for a while.

I let him be while I tuned my guitar.

"Danny will be here in a couple hours," I said, glancing up at the clock on the wall. "Why don't you and me go get some lunch. Refuel our creativity."

———

Our favorite place was a little Mexican food restaurant. True Mexican food. With lots of jalapeños and fiery salsa. It was in a bad neighborhood. But I wasn't afraid. Mick had such a bad reputation in the newspapers that I felt like more than a few outlaw types admired him. Suffice it to say no one hassled us. In truth, they never did. Every once in a while, someone would ask for an autograph. That was about the extent of any trouble we'd ever run into in this part of town. And an autograph is certainly no trouble. It would only be a problem if no one ever asked for one.

Mick still wasn't talking. But he was eating chips. I swear Mick had an addiction to chips and salsa. I let him eat a few more before asking him the question I knew wasn't going to go over well.

As if reading my mind, Mick stopped eating chips and looked directly at me.

"What are you thinking so hard about?" he said flatly. It was the second time today he'd ask the question.

I looked at the fountain bubbling in the central courtyard near our outside table. Plants and walkways graced the area around us, making it feel like our own private oasis. The waitress was discreet and only popped by now and then to refill our beers. Or to give Mick another small bowl of salsa. We'd ordered fajitas, and when she brought our sizzling platters, my tastebuds immediately started to water. I was hungrier than I'd thought. This often happened to me when I became immersed in making music. Time stood still. And the next thing I knew hours had passed.

"Mick," I hesitated as I took a tortilla, "what about the dark-haired lady? Your stalker, Eileen? I know she's doing okay physically. Doctor told me that when I went to pay her hospital bill. But I mean what's going to happen to her long term?"

"I didn't press charges if that's what you're asking."

"No, I meant, are you going to talk to her? Maybe work out why she's so fascinated with you. You just haven't told me if there's something to it other than her being a crazy fan."

He gave me a hard look. It wasn't easy to ask hard questions. But the time had come.

"Mick, brother, I'm the one person you don't have to keep secrets from. I'm no saint myself. And, you don't have to tell me everything. Just let me know if this woman has a reason to be doing what she's doing."

Mick stood up.

"Excuse me." He took one more drink of his beer before heading toward what I thought was the men's room.

Imagine my surprise when he never came back.

After fifteen minutes I went to check on him.

He wasn't in the men's room. Or the front lobby.

Trying to seem nonchalant, I asked the front door hostess if she'd seen my friend.

"You mean the famous Mick McLaren? Of course, I saw him. He went right out this door a little bit ago." She pointed to the front of the restaurant. An interesting array of Mexican face masks framed the double-door entrance, making it look more like a Spanish villa than a restaurant.

"Did he say where he was going?" I was almost afraid to ask.

"No, he just said the food was excellent. And he bought one of these pralines." She pointed to a basket near the register overflowing with the candies.

After thanking her, I went back to my table and waited another half hour before paying the bill. It was such a pretty restaurant. Vibrant, happy, colorful. A world away from how I was feeling.

On my way out, the hostess caught my arm. "Cowboy, I have to tell you something. I can't be sure, but I was watching Mick as he walked away, and I think, but I can't be sure—I think he might've jumped on a train that stopped to refuel before rolling out of town." Her big brown eyes pleaded with me. "I think maybe I shouldn't have told you. I know it doesn't make sense." She shook her head so forcefully at her last words that the colorful flower over her ear threatened to fall to the floor.

"No." I patted her hand on my arm in a reassuring way before reaching up to readjust the flower. "It makes perfect sense to me."

I, too, bought a praline candy before walking slowly back to the studio.

Mick was my partner. We knew each other through and through. I can tell you I knew he wasn't coming back any time soon. And I wondered how we were going to finish the album without his vocals on the last track. Much less what I was going to say to Margaret and the kids.

I thought of the hostess at the restaurant with her long dark braid and doe-like brown eyes. She reminded me so much of my late wife Saint. I wish she were still alive to tell me what to do. Because I sure as heck didn't have a clue.

In the distance, a train blew its horn.

Wonder if Mick knew where he was headed. Or if he even cared.

CHAPTER 39

D ARLA

I sat holding the postcard Rayne had sent from who knows where. Bold printed letters on the back read "MISSING YOU!" Looking at the little X's and O's he'd drawn, my heart seized as I realized I probably missed him more than he missed me. As I turned the black and white postcard over, I looked for a clue as to his location. There was none. Just a beautiful photo of a vase of roses. It prompted a memory of one of my grandmother's favorite sayings: "If they are roses, they will bloom." So we would see about our love. If Rayne and I were meant to be, our love would bloom. It would either happen or it wouldn't.

Watching a single plane flying high above me on this beautiful December afternoon, I wondered—would Rayne be home for Christmas? I dared not even wish for it. But wouldn't it be wonderful? Maybe if I didn't think about it too much . . . put too much weight on it, it would happen. But honestly, I'd learned in my short life that things rarely turned out the way I wanted. I would settle for any visit from Rayne. Because even if it wasn't an official holiday, being with him would be a holiday for me.

I sighed to myself. How could it be only a few weeks until Christmas? This year had flown by for me. It was one of the most pivotal times in my life. So much had happened. So many life-altering choices made. I said a silent prayer as I gazed up at the overcast Texas sky. *God, please help me make the correct choices in the days ahead. And, God, please if you can see fit, please get Thomas out of jail. He's not the type to be in there and I'm afraid he'll be hurt.*

CHAPTER 40

McLaren Mansion, Dallas, Texas
Monday Evening
December 1, 1958

ARGARET

A slight drizzle of rain fell outside. Mick had not come home from recording. And I didn't know if that was a good thing or a bad thing these days. Sure, we'd fought over his female stalker, but I hadn't thrown him out of the house. True, that decision needed to be made, but I was hesitant because of the children.

The doorbell rang.

Who could it be this late in the evening?

I supposed it wouldn't hurt to answer the front door. After all, we did have a guard shack.

"Who is it?" I called out as I approached the big oak door.

"It's Thomas."

"Thomas!" I threw the door open wide. "Oh, Thomas!" I wrapped my arms around him. He'd lost weight in the short time he'd been incarcerated.

"Mama!" He hugged me back with a sorrow so deep I could feel it.

"Come inside. Get out of this misty rain." I pulled him through to the den. "Why didn't you use your key?"

"I didn't have it on me when they arrested me." He stopped talking and pushed his damp hair out of his eyes. "Mama, did you hear the lady I shot survived, but she may walk with a limp for the rest of her life? I feel so bad."

"No, Thomas, no." I put my hand on his shoulder. "You saved your father's life. She was going to kill him. I saw it through the shack window. She shot at him."

"Maybe so . . . but she missed."

"Only because she was shaking. What was to keep her from shooting again?"

He moved away from me. "I didn't want to hurt her."

"I know. We all know that. Please, Thomas, you must turn the page and get past this unfortunate incident. Don't let it define you. Your life is just beginning."

Debra came running down the hall from the kitchen. "Is that Thomas I hear?" She practically squealed with delight as she turned the corner and saw him standing there. His face lit up with the sight of her. "Jamison!" she called out. "Come here, now! Thomas is home!"

As Jamison clambered down the stairs, my heart lifted. Things were going to be okay.

Brrring! Brrring!

I hurried to pick up the phone. "Hello, this is the McLaren residence . . . Yes, Cowboy. When are you and Mick going to finish up there at the recording studio? Yes, yes, I'm sitting down." I lied. I was standing in the hallway. But I pulled a nearby chair over and plopped onto it. "Is something wrong? What's wrong? Please tell me."

Cowboy's words rang hollow in my head.

"I don't understand. Did you two have a fight? Where would he go? Why would he go?"

Cowboy talked some more. I stared at the photo of our family hanging on the opposite side of the hallway. We were all dressed in our Sunday best. Every one of us was smiling.

"Yes, Cowboy, I'm okay," I lied, but I didn't know why because I was not fine at all.

Laughter floated back to me from the kitchen. I would tell the children in the morning. No need to spoil their happiness tonight. Worry rose in my heart as I thought about Mick riding the rails. I didn't like him much at the moment, but I still loved him. Cowboy and I must've finished our conversation because I heard myself saying goodbye.

Then I walked into the kitchen and celebrated my eldest child's homecoming.

CHAPTER 41

McLaren Mansion, Dallas, Texas
Monday Afternoon
December 22, 1958

**D**ARLA

Margaret had called a practice session with Angel and me. Tomorrow the three of us would be making our big debut at the holiday show in downtown Dallas. Truly it wasn't more than a Christmas tree lighting and a few singers taking a makeshift wooden stage with a microphone. But it would be our first time singing together as a trio in front of a real live audience. Cowboy had gotten us the gig. He seemed more committed than ever to being a music producer now that Mick had taken a walk.

My heart was racing at the thought of singing in front of so many people. I'd never sung with a trio before, only by myself. I hoped I wouldn't mess up.

Angel had tried to mend the new dress she had tore the day we were caught out in the storm. It looked okay, but it didn't look new anymore. I couldn't help but notice when she entered the room wearing it that there was no longer any sass in her step. No flouncing of her blonde locks. I'd never tell Angel that Cowboy told me this, but he'd said all their relatives up in Oklahoma were dirt poor. When I'd ask if that included Angel, he said she, too, was poor as a church mouse. But he hoped her career would take off. That's why he'd asked her to come to Dallas. Angel always appeared so polished and put together, one would never guess she lacked for anything. Certainly not confidence.

I stole another glance at her expensive new dress. By the looks of it, she must've shelled out most of her monthly salary. But now with the obvious repair it couldn't be considered very nice anymore.

Margaret must've noticed Angel's damaged dress too because she went to the tree and took a big gift out from under it. "Here," she said with a twinkle in her eye, "I think you need to open this gift before Christmas."

Angel's eyes grew big and wide as she took the fancy gift box and went to the sofa to sit down. Carefully, she opened it, saving the golden bow, ribbons and paper for another use. A soft gasp escaped her as she pulled out a new dress.

She stood and held it up to herself.

The new dress was just as gorgeous as the one she'd damaged.

"Oh, Margaret! It's beautiful."

I ran to touch the fabric. "Angel, it brings out the blue in your eyes. It's absolutely perfect for you."

I knew Margaret was experiencing financial difficulties as it had cost the family a fortune to get Thomas out of jail, and to pay the female stalker's hospital bills. Not to mention the tax problems Mick and Cowboy were experiencing. I couldn't believe Mick had walked out when they were so close to finishing their latest album. He knew how much they needed the money. Now Margaret had gone and bought Angel a replacement dress. It was just like Margaret to do so.

Margaret smiled for the first time in ages.

"Please go try it on so we'll know if it needs to be altered before our show. You can use the room Katherine stays in when she's here. Down the hall and to the right."

When Angel left the living room, Margaret looked at me. "Did you know today is the winter solstice? The shortest day of the year. And the longest night."

"No, I don't really know scientific things like that," I said, thinking the night before had seemed like the longest night to me as I lay tossing and turning. I still hadn't heard if Rayne would be home for Christmas.

"Don't worry. I'm not super smart about things like that either. I heard it on the radio." Margaret smiled yet again. "And I also heard Alvin and the Chipmunks' new song, 'Christmas Don't Be Late.' Have you heard it?"

"Who hasn't heard it? I think they're playing it every hour. If only we could be so lucky as to have one of our records played half as much."

Angel had returned in the new dress. Whirling around, she put on a show for us. "It fits perfectly. No need for alterations." Then to our surprise she started singing in the high-pitched squealing voice of the Chipmunks. She sounded just like Alvin.

Margaret howled with delight. And I couldn't help but laugh so hard I snorted. Which made Margaret start giggling all over again. Every time she stopped laughing, Angel would start impersonating Alvin the Chipmunk again.

Little Jamison appeared in the doorway. "What's going on in here? Are you practicing 'Christmas Don't Be Late' for the big holiday show? It's my favorite song."

I couldn't wait for Rayne to be home so I could tell him about what'd just happened. I had so many things to tell him. Please, please, Rayne, come home for Christmas.

———

Later that night back in my own house, I tossed in my bed until the wee hours of the morning. Between thoughts of Rayne and pre-holiday show jitters I couldn't fall asleep. Yes, Margaret was right. It was definitely the longest night of the year.

CHAPTER 42

Recording Studio, Dallas, Texas
Monday Afternoon
December 22, 1958

C OWBOY LARSON

Danny was doing a great job on the guitar solo. And Thomas was doing a great job of standing in for Mick. I'd convinced him to help me out. Reminded him his mother needed the money our album would make, especially with Mick out of the picture.

When we first started the recording session, he'd asked, "Do you want me to try and sound like my father? Or just sing in my own voice?"

Since I intended to introduce him on the album as if it'd always been planned, I said, "Do it in your own voice." Which, to my surprise, ended up sounding more like Mick than Mick had sounded lately.

Years of smoking and drinking and wild living had not helped his vocals.

As I listened to the results of our session, I had to admit Thomas was a good singer in his own right. I'd told him to make the song his. As a result, he'd rearranged a few things. Danny, being the quick study he was, followed right along with him.

Hours passed as the two perfected the song. I helped in my own way—by staying out of it.

The people in the recording booth gave Thomas and Danny well-deserved praise.

"So, Thomas," I asked as we were wrapping things up, "do you think you want to go into the music business?"

"Might as well," he replied as he put his guitar back in its case. "Probably not going to make it as a lawyer with my background. I mean, honestly, I probably won't even be able to get into law school with my criminal history. Can't believe Dad's lawyer wouldn't let us tell the world Eileen was Dad's real stalker. Didn't want their relationship getting out in the press. Said Daddy and you didn't need more bad news. Especially right after Dad shot Ernie Koster in the butt. So now it looks like I just overreacted and shot one of Dad's silly female fans. Both shootings make me and Dad look like gun-toting idiots. And I get a criminal history and mugshot to boot. I know the lawyer got the charges knocked down, but he didn't get everything erased off my record."

Danny stepped forward. "Thomas, it seems like you were enjoying yourself today. As my grandmother would say, you have the music in you." He was trying to change the subject to something cheerier, I supposed. "Not everyone can play and sing like you do. It's a gift. Add to that the fact you get to record and do things like this because of your famous father. Well, that's a head start on the rest of us."

I, too, could tell Thomas had really enjoyed the session.

"We'll see," Thomas said quietly. "So far, from my point of view, having a famous father has been both a blessing and a curse. You never know what he's going to do next. Or not do in this case."

What Thomas said was true. And it was just this attitude that had taken Mick so far. There was a reason he had made it to the top in such a high-pressure business. He was a bit of a nutcase. And, in truth, so was I.

Looking up at the clock on the wall, I said, "Guys, let's hurry. I need to get Danny to the bus station. I promised I'd have him home well before Christmas."

As we scurried down the dimly lit paneled hallway of the studio, a well-dressed woman stepped out of a side office. "Danny. Thomas. Don't forget your paychecks." She turned to me. "Cowboy, your record label sent them over. They also asked if you had any word from Mick yet."

"No." I thought about adding more. Instead, I just said, "No, I don't."

As she handed Thomas his paycheck, she added, "Young man, you sounded just like your daddy in there. He'd be so proud."

She didn't see the slight look of annoyance register on Thomas's face. As soon as it came, he hid it again. I was beginning to recognize that, just like Margaret, Thomas was a master at hiding his true feelings.

———

Usually, Mick and I celebrated after finishing an album. Champagne. Steaks. That sort of thing. In the early days it was a case of Jax beer. Maybe fajitas. But tonight, I'd gone straight home after taking Danny to the bus station and dropping Thomas off at the overly decorated McLaren mansion. In addition to lights, garlands, wreaths and bows, Margaret had even setup a life-size manger scene complete with Baby Jesus, Joseph and Mary.

In comparison, my apartment downtown was dark and lonely. I'd tried to cheer it up with a small Christmas tree. But it wasn't working, I felt no festive spirit. From years past I learned it was better not to fake being happy this time of year and, instead, just endure it.

The late-night knock on my door had been preceded by a baby's cry. I swung the door open fully expecting to see the neighbor lady from down the hall asking for help with her newborn.

Instead, it was Mick. And he was holding a baby! A baby I'd never seen before with auburn hair. A baby carriage sat by his side with a small bag of baby items inside.

Shoot a monkey! The last thing I was prepared for was Mick to show up again. Never in a million years did I think he'd come back. Much less right after I'd finished recording our album.

I watched in amazement as he gently bounced the baby up and down in the air before bringing it to his chest. Within a moment the little one quieted. As Mick held the infant in his arms, he tucked a soft blue blanket around it.

Suffice it to say, I'd never been so dumbfounded in my life.

It was an absolute shock to my system.

My heart started pounding so hard I got dizzy.

Boom. Boom. Boom. Blood pounded on my brain.

The dim hallway lights made the scene surreal.

I didn't want a surprise tonight. I wanted to read the newspaper and go to bed early.

Pushing the door open wide, I took hold of the carriage's handle and steered it into my tiny den. Mick followed without a word. From years of snooping reporters and nosy fans, we knew better than to speak openly out in the hallway.

As Mick made himself and the baby comfortable on the couch, he looked up at me and asked for a towel.

Still speechless, I brought him one right away.

My brain couldn't quite work out why Mick had a baby with him. All I could do was stand with my mouth agape as I watched Mick put the plush towel under the babe before reaching into the carriage for a diaper. He looked like an old pro as he undid the safety pins and took them out before maneuvering the child around.

"Cowboy, you don't happen to have any baby powder, do you?" His eyes held a faint glimmer of hope. "Margaret always reminded me to keep 'em as dry as possible so they don't get diaper rash."

"It would seem Margaret has taught you a thing or two over the years," I said sincerely. "Unfortunately, no. I don't have any powder of any kind."

He proceeded to expertly change the diaper as he talked. "I know we need to finish the album before the end of the year to make our contract deadline." He jostled the baby around as he put the safety pins back in. "I don't have to tell you how much we need the money."

I watched him work a moment more before responding. Anxiety rose in my chest. I took a deep breath before responding.

"We did make our deadline. The last track was completed this afternoon." I sat myself down in a nearby chair and crossed my legs. Mick's face registered surprise as he looked up from what he was doing. I continued, "Thomas filled in for you on vocals. He did a great job. In fact, I'm going to give him credit on the album. Danny hit it out of the park, too. He was incredible on his guitar solo."

Mick's eyes clouded over. "I'm sorry I missed it," he said softly as his voice cracked.

I sank down in my seat. I could tell by his tone, and the look on his face, that he really was sorry he'd missed the recording session. However, I wasn't going to let him off the hook so easily for leaving like he did. And what about this baby? In time I'm sure he'd expound more on where the baby came from. I think I already knew. Just didn't want to hear him say it out loud. What were we going to tell Margaret? She was his wife, but she was also my friend. I didn't want Mick to hurt her anymore than he already had at this point.

Leaning forward, I held out a finger for the baby to grasp. I had to admit he was a cute little fella with his auburn curls and chubby cheeks.

"Would you like a drink?" I said as I pulled a bottle of whiskey out of my kitchen cabinet pointing it in his direction. "To celebrate our latest collaboration."

He nodded.

And I got a second bottle out of the cupboard for myself.

No need for glasses. We *clinked* our two whiskey bottles together.

In unison we ripped off the protective paper tabs and unscrewed our bottle caps.

"To us!" he said.

"To us!" I replied.

Together we tipped them back. The swig of whiskey calmed my nerves. My breathing finally returned to normal even if our worlds never would.

Deep down inside I'd come to the realization both our lives were but mere vapor trails shooting across the sky. I didn't know why either of us spent so much time and effort trying to leave a mark on this ever-changing world. Our fame was irrelevant.

Mick put the cap back on his whiskey bottle. He left the bottle on the side table as he picked up the baby. "Say," he said cradling the child, "would you mind if we slept here tonight? I plan on going home after the holiday show tomorrow. But first I want Margaret to have her time to shine. What I've got to tell her can wait."

"Are you sure you want to tell her anything? Without even knowing your whole story, I can think of a few options that include not ever telling her." I squirmed around uneasily in my seat.

Mick gazed at the baby in his arms. "No, I need to tell her. I need to try to be a better man for both her and my kids." He paused before adding, "All my kids."

PART 10

BETTER DAYS AHEAD

CHAPTER 43

Adana, Turkey
Incirlik Air Base
Tuesday Morning 4:35 a.m.
December 23, 1958

AYNE

The jump seat wasn't the most comfortable to sit in, but I wasn't going to complain. When they told me a supply plane was headed to Texas and they needed an alternate pilot, I said yes immediately. Apparently one of the regular pilots was still recovering from a bad case of food poisoning. They had sent me along in case the two pilots needed a backup. It was hard to believe after one long plane ride and one short bus ride that I'd be home for Christmas. There had been no time for phone calls or letters. I packed a bag and hopped onboard.

And, as usual, I started to daydream of Darla. It was amazing how fast life could change. As I went to bed the night before, I'd been in the dumps about not getting leave for the holidays. Then, next thing I knew they're shaking me awake and telling me to get dressed.

Just as they closed the plane's doors for takeoff, my commander looked at me with a big grin on his face. "Merry Christmas!" he yelled over the roar of the plane's engine.

"Merry Christmas!" I yelled back as I waved goodbye.

CHAPTER 44

Downtown Dallas, Texas
Holiday Show
Late Tuesday Afternoon
December 23, 1958

ARGARET

Darla and Angel were nervous as two long-tailed cats in a room full of rocking chairs. I wasn't much better. The crowd was a little larger than expected this year. The sound crew was in the process of adding more speakers farther out from the simple wooden stage. A velvet curtain served as a backdrop. Cowboy stood near me, peeking out around the curtain at the crowds. I thought he might've been a little worried about the crowd being so large. But no, he was cool as a cucumber. Guess twenty years of being in front of audiences had made him very comfortable with large crowds.

Red, green and gold holiday decorations gave the downtown Dallas atmosphere a cheery pop of color in spite of the gray skies. At least the forecast was clear of rain. It looked like the weather was going to hold through the night. That's good. Because the tree lighting was scheduled to happen later, right after the holiday concert of singers and musicians.

I straightened my skirt. And my shirt. Tapped my foot. And took yet another deep breath. We were one of the first acts up.

A lady with a clipboard signaled it was time to take the stage.

Checking my hair one last time with my hand, I silently said a prayer for our success. That the crowd would find favor with us.

The announcer was speaking our names. He called us the Southern Songbirds. Never heard that before, but I liked it.

I walked out first. Followed by Darla. And then Angel.

I heard the crowd cheer as we gathered at the single microphone.

Then the crowd quieted in anticipation.

My heart hammered in my chest. And I felt a little unsteady.

The music started. "Silent Night." I took yet another deep breath to steady my nerves.

We had arranged the music in a unique way, and we sang it in rounds.

Looking out over the audience, I could see Katherine and Clarence sitting front and center. I focused on them. Their smiling faces made me feel calm. Peace came over me. Finally, I found the strength of my voice.

There were only a few rows of seats. The rest of the crowd was standing. But I didn't glance out over the audience again. I focused on the front row. Admiration shone in Katherine's eyes and it gave me confidence. When we finished, the crowd clapped as they murmured approval. A few made catcalls at Angel and Darla. They both looked so pretty in their party dresses.

After a moment, I spoke into the microphone.

"Ladies and gentleman, we'd like to do one more. It's a new song. Maybe you've heard it on the radio."

The crowd quieted. The music started and we sang the song Darla had selected for us: "Blue Christmas." It had just come out on Elvis's new album. I don't know how the backup musicians got the sheet music so fast. Maybe they were playing by ear.

The crowd went wild. Darla was correct. It was the perfect song to sing.

When we went backstage, Cowboy smiled as he gave each of us a big bear hug.

"Fantastic," he cried out. "How do you like your new name? When I signed you up for this event, they made me give your group a name. Didn't have time to check with you. We can change it if you don't like it."

"I like it," Angel said as she flounced her shiny blonde hair.

"It works for me." Darla's eyes sparkled. Clearly, she was floating on cloud nine. And well she should be after our performance.

"Yes," I said, "it works for me, too."

The announcer was introducing the act behind us. We all turned as if on cue and stopped talking. They were walking out. And the music started. It didn't stop for the next hour and a half as act after act followed. It took a good thirty minutes for my racing pulse to return to normal.

———

Cowboy took us to the record label office after the show. He said they had a surprise for us. I didn't expect the surprise to be a party for Ernie Koster. He'd mostly recovered from his injury, and they had decided to throw a little party for him to celebrate the re-release of his songs on a compilation album.

In addition to holiday decorations, the record label office was also adorned with a big sign reading "Congratulations, Ernie!" A large round cake sat on a table along with plastic plates and forks. A few bottles of champagne were on ice.

When they brought Ernie in, we all yelled, "Surprise!"

And by the look on his face, it worked.

Cowboy sidled up to where Darla and I were standing and said, "I'm so happy that Rayne brought it to Mick's attention that Ernie was living on the streets." He stopped talking for a moment and ran his hand through his thick hair.

Darla chimed in. "Yes, Rayne did a good thing when he told Mick about Ernie. However, when Mick asked the studio to give Ernie a job, I don't imagine Mick meant for the studio to give Ernie the job of pretending to be his stalker."

We all three laughed at her words. And I took yet another sip of champagne.

I had to admit Mick had done some good things in his life. But he'd also done some bad. Shooting Ernie in the butt could be construed either way as the publicity had brought attention back to Ernie's music along with more attention to Mick and Cowboy's upcoming album. Honestly, Mick had told me he couldn't have planned it better if he'd tried. Fans were going on a waiting list to be first to get their new album when it goes on sale. Crazy, but true.

Where was Mick? My thoughts started to turn dark as a flicker of anger made my heart hurt. He should be here for Ernie. He should've been at the holiday show for me.

I heard another champagne cork pop. Champagne began to flow. The head of the record label stepped up to a lectern and gave a speech about how well Ernie's album was doing. Next, the interns started cutting the cake. And more corks popped. I'd never really had much alcohol in my life, and perhaps I drank a little too much, a little too fast. I swear I became downright heady.

Ernie made everyone laugh as he accepted a glass of bubbly along with a framed copy of his compilation album. Holding it up, he exclaimed, "Imagine making money off your music when you can't sing or play no more. Thank you all! Thank you for saving me! Life can turn on a dime, can't it? I never dreamed of the light shining on me again. And it's not just the money. It's the simple fact that people are listening to my music again."

Another record exec stepped forward and presented Ernie with a bonus check.

Ernie wasn't the only one who had tears in his eyes.

Then, when I thought things couldn't get any better, Cowboy addressed the crowd.

"I have one more announcement on this day of celebration. Our newest act . . . the Southern Songbirds," he gestured at Angel, Darla and me, "have been given a recording contract. And I'm going to produce their first album."

Everyone cheered and clapped.

I was so dumbstruck by the news I almost fell over. Darla choked on her champagne. And Angel had to thump her on the back to help her quit coughing. A record contract at my age. Talk about a second chance. My breathing was shallow, and my head was spinning. Things went black as I heard someone say, "Oh, no! Margaret's fainted."

———

Back at our house, in my bed, I wondered how Cowboy, Darla and Angel had gotten me home. Not only had I fainted, but apparently, I was so drunk when they revived me, I could hardly walk. In fact, I still was not in my right mind. My head ached so. Was this what a hangover felt like?

"Brrring! Brrring! *Who could be calling at this hour? Please someone make it stop. My head couldn't take anymore.*

"McLaren residence." I could hear Darla answering the phone in her most professional voice. Then, all of a sudden she was squealing like a schoolgirl. Finally, composing herself, she said, "Cowboy, it's Rayne! He's at the bus station. Any chance we can go get him?"

Cowboy took the phone from Darla. "Hey there, Rayne. What area of the bus station are you at?" I could hear Ryane's deep voice answering him, but I couldn't make out his words. "Yes, we'll be there as fast as we can. Yes. In my Cadillac with the longhorn steer ornament on the hood." Cowboy was laughing as he said, "should I bring Darla with me?"

Darla made a face as she jumped up and down, taking the phone back.

"Rayne, Rayne. I can't wait to tell you. Cowboy got me, Margaret and Angel a recording contract. I'm a real singer. Yes, indeed, I am flying high. We all three are. In fact, Margaret is downright drunk. I'll tell you more when we pick you up."

Then, in her excitement, she abruptly hung up.

"Oh, no! I didn't say goodbye," she exclaimed.

"Let's go pick up Rayne," I heard Cowboy say as he put on his coat and hat. "Angel, can you stay here for a while? Just to help Margaret in case the kids need anything."

"I'm fine," I said. But secretly I was glad Angel stayed by my side. It'd been a long day. And Katherine wasn't back yet. Strange. I know she was with Clarence, so I wasn't worried, but she was usually back by this time. In another hour it would be midnight. Christmas Eve. My sister and her family would be coming into town. Perfect. We could surprise them with Rayne.

Sighing contentedly, I said, "This has been one of the best days of my life."

Angel didn't say a word.

In a few minutes, I glanced at the overstuffed chair and ottoman she was lounging in. She had fallen asleep with a smile on her face. I got a blanket to cover her. Then I went to check on the kids with my footsteps wobbling just a bit. I thought of the old saying, "A man works from sun to sun, but a woman's work is never done." Even if she's drunk as a skunk.

CHAPTER 45

R AYNE

I saw them before they saw me. Really, how could I miss a convertible Cadillac with a longhorn steer ornament on its hood slowly moving through traffic? Add to that the fact Cowboy was wearing a shimmery gold shirt with silver fringe. And Darla was wearing an incredibly beautiful dress. The very sight of her tugged at my heart, reminding me of just how much I'd missed her while we were apart. I was so sorry I'd missed her big debut with Angel and Margaret at the holiday show.

Slowly, I made my way through the crowd at the bus station and lifted my arm high in the air, waving in their direction.

Darla saw me first. She hopped out of the Caddy, and not unlike a Hollywood movie, she ran toward me practically leaping into my arms. It was such a relief to finally hold her again. I wrapped my arms around her softness, still holding my duffel bag full of clothes and a few small gifts for Darla. I'd already mailed a big box of presents to my family back home. I'd held on to Darla's gifts in hopes of delivering them in person next time I saw her. One in particular had to be delivered in person—a small red velvet box.

The air was cold, but the night was clear. Darla's eyes sparkled and danced in the bright station streetlights. Her sweet perfume heightened my senses making me pull her even closer.

"Rayne, I can't believe it's you." She held me tight as she threw back her head laughing. Her white teeth flashing. "Come here. Let me kiss you." Her lips were soft and warm despite the chill in the air on this blustery winter night.

"I missed you." It was all I could get out before she kissed me again. This time even more passionately. In the background Cowboy's horn mooed. People were gathered around his car asking for autographs.

"We better go help him," I said as I put Darla back on her feet. We walked back to the Caddy holding hands. It took more than a few minutes to get through all the overzealous fans. A police officer had been called in to help direct traffic.

Soon we were in the backseat of the Caddy. I wrapped my arms around Darla, holding her tight. Our bodies warmed by the liquid fire of our kisses.

Cowboy ignored us as he navigated downtown, flying through the darkness of the backstreets of the city. The radio blared a country love song. One of Cowboy and Mick's actually. The radio's bass pounded so deep, it pulsated through my entire body. I could see Cowboy smiling to himself in the rearview mirror as he sang along.

It felt good to be home.

CHAPTER 46

McLaren Mansion, Dallas, Texas
Saturday Evening
December 27, 1958

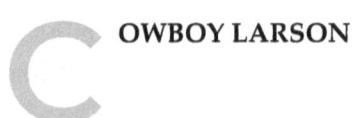OWBOY LARSON

Mick told Margaret the truth about him and Eileen, his true stalker.

From the kitchen, the kids and I could hear patches of what Mick was saying to Margaret in the den.

He started off calmly by telling Margaret it was meant to be a one-night stand. But it turned into a short-term fling. Then Eileen got pregnant. He paid her off.

I wondered if the kids, who were sitting around the kitchen table with me, could make out what was being said between their parents, and, if so, how it was affecting them.

Mick continued, only this time pleading. We could feel Margaret's tears in our hearts.

He said, "The initial money hadn't been enough. Because of her mental state, Eileen wasn't able to hold a job, much less take care of a newborn. Add to that her widowed mother was ailing and could barely take care of herself. But in spite of things, she was helping Eileen and the child as best she could."

In short, Mick told Margaret he kept getting pulled back into the baby's and Eileen's lives. He told Margaret he'd tried more than once to walk away. But Eileen started stalking him. Acting crazy. Saying she was going to kill him.

Mick had gone to the police; however, he had no proof. And he really didn't want to put her in jail.

Suffice it to say, nothing was done.

That is, until the night Thomas shot Eileen.

Mick's voice softened as he continued explaining over Margaret's sobs.

Even though Eileen would recover, he knew she wasn't ready to be a mother. For the past few months before the shooting at the shed, the baby had been living with Eileen's ailing mother while Eileen came and went with different men. In fact, she'd already left the hospital before the doctor was ready to release her. She'd gone off to the coast to visit her cousin.

That's when Eileen's mother called Mick. She didn't have the health, or the funds, to take care of the child.

Mick told Margaret he wanted to do what was right. So, he left and went to get his son.

"Please forgive me." Mick's voice was hoarse and hardly audible. Then it increased in strength. "Margaret, I'm trying to be a better man. A better father. A better husband."

From the safety of the kitchen table, the kids and I heard him beg for Margaret's forgiveness over and over again in the den. I held my breath as I waited for Margaret's reply. Every muscle in my body tensed as I strained to hear.

Silence ensued.

Mick had pushed Margaret too far this time.

The kids and I listened as Margaret threw anything and everything that would break against the fireplace mantel. Including some of Mick's most precious music awards.

She yelled, "How could you? How could you?"

She screamed, "Get away from me! I hate you!"

She cried as her world fell apart. "Don't touch me! Get away from me!"

And all I could do was stay in the kitchen with the kids.

Before too long Katherine snuck around the corner to join our safe refuge.

Thank God for Katherine!

She took the baby I was holding from me and rocked him in her arms. Debra sat nearby staring at her tiny new half-brother. Thomas held Jamison, who looked like he was going to cry. The overhead lights flickered as they cast a warm, golden glow over the kitchen counter-tops and table. Outside, a few raindrops hit the screened windows and back door. The clock over the sink ticked loudly as the seconds fell away.

And then, after about ten minutes, it seemed from the sound of things Margaret had calmed down. Or perhaps she'd run out of things to throw. We heard her steady voice say, "I'm not raising another baby. The kids are just now old enough for me to tour. It's my time to shine and you're not going to take it away from me."

With that we heard her determined footsteps cross from the den into the foyer before she slammed the front door behind her. It rattled with finality.

I looked back up at the kitchen clock.

It had been a short fight. Not much said. Not much could be said.

Thank goodness Mick had waited until two days after Christmas to break the news. Because it really had been a wonderful holiday what with Rayne being home and his family coming in from Cooper to visit. For the first time in years, I'd experienced true joy.

But it had been dampened by the fact I knew heartbreak was waiting in the wings. I'm just glad we all had two more happy, fun-filled days before the mental anguish started. The strange part, I don't think Mick realized how many people he'd hurt or was hurting. I looked around the table and counted at least six, including myself. Seven if you counted the baby.

Thomas sat perfectly still holding Jamison. Finally, he spoke, his voice flat with no emotion. "I don't think I'll ever get used to the drama in this house. When I was young, I used to get really upset like Jamison here when our parents fought. Seems like my emotions were always raw, waiting for the next big thing to happen. The next shoe to drop, so to speak. My heart would hurt so badly I'd be afraid to draw another breath as I listened to the harsh words they'd throw at each other. Now I'm emotionally numb. I can't feel a thing."

"I know what you mean," Debra said as she sat down near Thomas and Jamison. "Days like this are why I'm never getting married."

Katherine watched over the baby, softly cooing as she rocked him to sleep.

I wondered where Margaret had gone. And if she was coming back. My gut feeling was she went next door to the neighbor Jack Donovan's mansion. He seemed to have become very close to her while we were away writing at the cabin.

Katherine broke my reverie as she said aloud to no one in particular, "I could raise this child. I want to raise him."

No one spoke a word. Silence filled the room as we all stared at Katherine and the baby.

I must say, Katherine looked absolutely serene. So, indeed, only six of us were upset, not seven. No, make that five—the baby was still cooing and gurgling under Katherine's soft caress.

CHAPTER 47

Driving to Dallas, Texas
Monday Evening
December 29, 1958

ARLA

I could hardly believe my eyes. Please, if I'm dreaming, don't wake me up.

Holding out my left hand in front of me, I admired my new wedding ring as it sparkled in the car's interior light. Did we really get married? The day before seemed like a dream. Mama was going to be so mad I had eloped. Or maybe not. There was no money for a wedding. And she really did seem to like Rayne. Seems like they'd taken to each other the first time they met.

Reaching out, I took hold of Rayne's right hand. I hoped he didn't have trouble driving, what with me hanging all over him. He smiled, but his eyes stayed on the road. Staring straight ahead.

Fields of winter wheat flew by as we drove along the well-worn highway. Not too many people out today. All at home celebrating with friends and family, I supposed.

It had been a great Christmas just a few days earlier at the McLaren Mansion. I was so glad they invited both Mama and me again like they did for Thanksgiving. It was much better to be in a big group, and Rayne's family had come to town, making everything just perfect. I'll never forget the overjoyed look on his parents' faces when they realized he'd made it in for the holidays. His mother had been so pleased when Rayne and I decided to drive to their house afterward for a few days. It'd been the most glorious last few days. With the exception that Mick was still missing. Where could he have been all this time? I really thought he'd make it back before Christmas. I could sense Margaret's worry, even though she tried to hide it from the kids. They were so used to their father traveling it probably hadn't hit home with them that he might not come back.

Stop it! I told myself. I'm not going to think sad thoughts. Only happy thoughts. I was going to get every ounce of joy I could out of life.

When Rayne proposed the day after Christmas, I thought he might be kidding. But no, he had a ring and everything. I have to admit, I'd never been so surprised in my life. We had gone out on the front porch of his parents' home for some air. And as I walked in front of him to the far end of the porch to sit in a glider, I heard him say, "Darla, I know we've only known each other a short time. But when you know it's right . . ."

Without thinking, I'd whirled around to look him straight in the face. Instead, I elbowed him in the chest, sending the small velvet ring box he was holding flying unopened on the ground.

"Oh, no!" I said as I got down on my knees to retrieve it. "Oh, no. Oh, no. Oh, no. I'm such a klutz!"

"I know," he said taking the velvet box from my hand. "It's one of the many things I love about you." Slowly he pulled me up before opening the box to reveal a diamond solitaire set on a golden band.

I gasped.

"Darla Darling. Will you marry me?"

"Oh yes, oh yes, oh yes!" Tears flooded my eyes.

He took the ring and put it on my hand.

It was a surreal moment.

Rayne said he knew it was fast, but he wanted to get married before he had to return to base. Said he'd be able to bring me over to be with him some of the time. So, of course, I said yes to his whirlwind plans. How could I not? I thought about him every waking minute of every day. I absolutely knew he was the one. I felt like I'd known him my whole life, even though it'd only been a few short months.

His parents were our witnesses at the courthouse. It wasn't too busy there as most of the offices were closed between the holidays. What employees who were working all gathered round and threw rice as we left. Everyone seemed happy for us. Rayne's sisters and brother had arranged a small gathering of family and friends at their house. The girls had even baked a cake. It was a little lopsided, but I told them it was the most beautiful wedding cake I'd ever seen. And I meant it. The day had been so wonderful. I had even fit into Rayne's mother's wedding dress.

I leaned my head on Rayne's shoulder. Thankful that this car had a bench seat.

The night before we had stayed at a small motel for our honeymoon—The Town House Motor Hotel. A flashing neon sign read "Vacancy" over the one-story strip of rooms. Another sign boasted "Refrigerated Air." The motel also offered a pool with colorful umbrellas, metal tables and chairs near the front motor court. I had doubted if we'd use either one this time of year. But still fancy for a roadside motel.

My body warmed as I thought of our first night together in the tiny but clean room. Just the basic necessities. White sheets, green cotton bedspread. A Bible on the nightstand.

How did I deserve to be this happy? Closing my eyes, I relived our first married kiss. And our most recent one.

Floating in a daydream, I glanced at the city lights as we neared

Dallas. The ambient glow lit up the sky. So far from the country we'd just been driving through. Many of the houses we passed still had their holiday lights blazing bright. Usually I got a little blue this time of year. As if reading my mind, Rayne spoke.

"And to think I thought I was going to be on base during the holidays. Life is so good. And I'm so happy to be married to you. I know it was fast, but sometimes you just know. Plus, if we're going to have a long-distance relationship . . . well, at least you can visit more, and I can tell you more if you're my wife."

A thrill ran through me as I realized that, as his wife, I could stay on base a few times a year when I wasn't touring. I'd never lived anywhere exotic before. Not unless you count Dallas and Fort Worth as exotic. I guess one could consider Dallas and Fort Wort exciting, but not exactly exotic.

Traveling to Turkey to see Rayne in early spring was too much. How would I ever say goodbye to him the day after New Year's? Then I reminded myself to think about that later, Darla. You'll be busy with the recording contract Cowboy managed to get for us.

Rayne pulled into a gas station. It had a store attached. Going inside to get some sodas and chips, I left Rayne to check the oil. The cashier asked me, "Is that your husband out there?"

"Yes," I wondered how she knew Rayne was my husband. Then I saw her looking at my ring. It wasn't big, but it was a sparkler.

"He's waving, trying to get your attention."

I went to the door and stuck my head out. "What is it?"

"Get Moon Pies for Cowboy and Mick."

My heart sank. Had no one told Rayne about Mick? Surely he noticed his absence at the holiday celebrations a few days ago. Once back in the car, I debated talking to Rayne about Mick. But didn't want to ruin the romance. Didn't want to think about anything but happy thoughts. So I decided not to pursue the subject.

But Rayne did.

"Don't worry, Darla. Mick will come back. He likes to ride the rails, and he knows how to take care of himself. That's how he got to Dallas from Houston years ago. Just ask my mother to tell you all about Mick and Margaret's wild tale of riding the rails. Or ask Cowboy, he was with them. In fact, that's how the three of them met."

So he did know about Mick leaving. Cowboy must've filled him in on Mick's latest escapade.

As we turned onto the quiet residential street, I could see the big iron double "M" gates of the McLaren Mansion.

"Look," I yelled excitedly, "Mick's out in the front yard playing with Jamison."

"See, what'd I tell you? I knew Mick would come home. Good thing I brought Moon Pies for both him and Cowboy. It's their favorite."

As we pulled up the drive, we saw Margaret coming from around the back of the house. Her hair was a mess and her face was puffy from tears. Jamison stopped playing with Mick and ran to her. Arms outstretched, he called, "Mama, Mama! You're back!"

We continued watching from the car as Margaret picked up little Jamison and marched right past Mick. She didn't have to say a word. The look on her face said it all as she headed toward the next-door neighbor Jack's house with Jamison in her arms.

Rayne leaned over and gave me a soft kiss on the lips. "See, I told you Mick would come back."

"Yes," I said, "but it appears Margaret has left."

It may not have been the right time to announce our marriage. In fact, I was pretty sure it wasn't. But I couldn't resist telling Angel and Katherine once we were alone. They both were so happy for me. After gushing over my ring, Angel asked if I wanted her to fill me in on everything that had happened at the mansion while Rayne and I were gone. I said I did. It was obvious she was bustin' at the seams to tell me. Her animated face glowed with excitement as she warned me the news was going to be shocking so I needed to prepare myself.

But there was no way I could've prepared myself for the real-life soap opera she was about to reveal.

A newborn. I couldn't believe there was a baby boy. But, yes, he was real. And he was sleeping in a basinet in Katherine's room.

Then, as if things couldn't get any crazier, later that afternoon, Margaret came back from next door with little Jamison. And she very loudly kicked Mick out. Screaming and yelling, she had a real honest-to-good hissy fit as she tossed his clothes out over the upstairs balcony to the front yard below.

Later, through the grapevine at our recording studio, Angel and I heard he went to live in Cowboy's downtown apartment. Sleeping on the couch. Mick that is, not Cowboy.

CHAPTER 48

McLaren Mansion, Dallas, Texas
Tuesday Afternoon
December 30, 1958

ARGARET

To say things had been tense in the house was an understatement. I couldn't believe I threw Mick out of his own house. But I was glad I did. He'd be okay. Like an alley cat he'd land on his feet.

I took a deep breath and stretched out on the armchair and ottoman near our bed.

A mourning dove cooed outside our bedroom window, oblivious to the fight that'd just happened.

I stared at the ceiling, noticing for perhaps the first time the intricate swirls in the plaster above.

No longer would I bargain my life away to please someone else. I reckoned this was just as much my house as it was Mick's, maybe even more so as he was always on the road. He could sleep in the garage for all I cared. I was staying here. Holding my ground. For once doing things on my terms.

Mick could go straight to hell.

Throwing myself across the bed, I began to cry for the umpteenth time since Mick brought home the baby and confessed. How could he? As my heart seized, I considered that I had played a part in his deception by never confronting him. Wanting to keep a perfect family. Wanting to keep security. Wanting to keep success. But no more. I would get past this. My heart would heal.

Did I throw Mick out on the street? Yes. Was I going to let him back in my life? I hadn't decided yet. I didn't want to keep him away from the kids. Especially when they would need him more than ever if I went on the road. Only time would tell what would happen to our family. It didn't have to be decided today.

Sitting up on the bed, looking at my reflection in the vanity mirror, I chastised myself. Margaret, get up and put your big girl pants on. You're not the first to experience heartbreak. You have things to do to get ready for the New Year's Eve show Wednesday night. I couldn't believe Cowboy had gotten us the gig. But it was true—the Southern Songbirds were going to ring in 1959 performing at one of the fanciest hotels in Dallas.

Getting up from the bed, I walked around the room before opening the balcony doors and going outside.

The fresh air revived my spirits.

I needed to find it in myself to congratulate Darla and Rayne on their marriage. Angel couldn't keep their secret. And why should she? Just because our marriage was crumbling doesn't mean the two of them should hide their love. The way I looked at it, at least someone in the world was happy. Which meant I, too, had hope for better days. In fact, maybe my best days were ahead. Just needed to tread through some pain to get to them. God willing, I told myself, I'd not only live through this mess, but I'd actually triumph in the process.

Downstairs in the den someone had put on Alvin and the Chipmunks. Jamison, no doubt. I smiled to myself as the music floated up from below. Yes, the kids were going to get through this, too.

Now what to wear for our New Year's performance? Or, more importantly, what to sing for our New Year's set?

CHAPTER 49

Downtown, Dallas, Texas
Train Station
Tuesday Late Afternoon
December 30, 1958

OWBOY LARSON

The outside air was crisp and cool. Families gathered around loved ones as they said their goodbyes. A few people wept tears as they hugged and patted each other on the back. Others smiled and laughed, getting in a few last precious memories before taking the trip back home.

Katherine stood looking extraordinarily beautiful in a powder blue coat. Her bright eyes shone with love as she looked down at the baby she was carrying in a basket. Clarence stood nearby with her suitcases and trunks loaded on a dolly.

She was going back to Houston. And she was taking Mick's child with her.

Mick stood nearby looking hapless. His hands shoved in the pockets of his overcoat.

"Are you sure?" he whispered as he leaned his tall form closer to her.

"Yes, I'm sure." Katherine smiled up at him. "Mother is going to be so happy to have another grandchild nearby. You do know our big brother's children are almost grown? Having a little one to play with will lift her mood. Give her something to look forward to each day." She stopped talking for a moment and put her hand on Mick's chest. "Honestly, I think this is best for everyone. I've been wanting to go back to Houston. It's where we grew up. We have a lot of friends and family there. And I can do my work for you and Cowboy from Houston as long as I have a phone and the U.S. mail." She laughed as she said those last words.

Mick looked up at the sky, eyes brimming with tears.

I hadn't seen Mick cry in a long, long time.

Finally, he choked out, "And I think it's best for Margaret. It wouldn't be easy for her to see my child every day. Even if she didn't hold anything against the baby, it'd be a constant reminder of my betrayal."

Katherine's mood softened. She handed the baby's basket over to me before enveloping Mick in a heartfelt hug. The kind of hug that only siblings would understand. She'd always welcomed Mick back in her life again and again. He could never do anything so wrong as to lose her unconditional love.

The train whistled in the background, alerting us its departure was imminent.

The smell of diesel mixed with popcorn and cotton candy. *How could I be hungry at a moment like this?* Behind us vendors shouted out one last call for their wares before people started to board.

"Mick," Clarence said as he arranged the luggage on the dolly before taking a step forward. "Mick," he repeated, "I'm going with Katherine. I want to be where she is, and you don't need me anymore."

While I was surprised, I wasn't shocked. I knew how much Clarence and Katherine cared for each other. Still, it couldn't have been an easy decision for Clarence to leave a good-paying job to follow her and the baby. But love doesn't make sensible decisions. Love follows the heart and believes everything will work out for the best.

The train whistle blew one more time as a line of people had already started boarding.

Katherine reached into her purse and brought out their passenger tickets.

I jostled around the baby in the basket as she reached to take it from me with her free hand.

"Please, Mick . . . I need you to understand. I want to go home. Mama won't be around forever. We'll see you again soon. And, of course, you can always come visit us in Houston. Lord knows you know how to catch a train."

Then Katherine turned to me and smiled.

"You come too, Cowboy. You know we think of you as family. You're always welcome."

Turning back to look at us one more time before she departed, she winked and said, "See you on the radio!"

As we walked back to the Cadillac, Mick said more to himself than to me, "I am doing the right thing for the baby, aren't I? And for Margaret? I just want to do the right thing for everyone involved instead of just what's right for me."

Putting my arm around his shoulders, I gave him a brotherly hug. I did think he was doing the right thing, but I also knew he didn't need me to answer. Because really in this situation there were no right answers.

Taking the matchstick I was chewing on from between my front teeth, I carefully steered him to the popcorn and cotton candy vendors where I bought a big bag of popcorn for the two of us. I must say, the salty, buttery snack did make us feel better. Especially after Mick produced a flask of whiskey that I'm sure he'd been hiding for just such an occasion. Silently we drank and munched our way back to the Cadillac.

Mick looked at me quizzically.

"What?" I said.

"I feel a song coming on."

"Hold that thought. I've got pencil and paper in the Caddy."

CHAPTER 50

AYNE

"Happy New Year," I whispered to Darla as we kissed at midnight.

In the distance fireworks exploded in the night sky against a twinkling background of stars.

Inside the hotel, the New Year's Eve show and party were still going strong. Silver and gold balloons littered the floor. Champagne corks were popping. And people were using their noise makers to great effect. Earlier, the Southern Songbirds had sung a fantastic set. The crowd couldn't have loved them more. Nor could I. I thought my heart would melt when they sang "All I Have to Do is Dream."

Silently I made a pledge to myself to support Darla's career as much as I did my own.

Time stood still for us, even as the clock on the nearby church struck midnight.

Magic filled the air as the bells in the church tower pealed loudly.

Reaching up, I removed a few paper streamers from Darla's hair before leaning in to kiss her again. This time longer and deeper.

I held Darla's body close to mine as we moved to the music flowing through the balcony doors from the reverie inside.

Yes, this last year had wrought many life changes and had challenged me in ways I'd never thought possible. *Who knew what 1959 would bring?* After all, I always did say things went better for me in years that ended in odd numbers. But maybe I'd have to rethink that philosophy after the year I'd just experienced. Good . . . and bad . . . 1958 had been spectacular. I discovered my dream job. And I found Darla.

In the background, I heard Angel and Margaret singing "Auld Lang Syne." A true reminder that time passes . . . and things invariably change.

I hugged Darla again, grateful for the time we were getting to spend together.

But a lump formed in my throat at the thought of the following day when I'd be on a plane going back to my secret life. A place where my real last name was never uttered. How was I going to explain this alternate reality to Darla? I didn't know, but I did know I would be able to tell her more now that she was my wife. And I would be able to have her with me more. Who knew where we'd go from here? Would I stay in my contract with the agency? Would her singing career take off? There were no definitive answers. There never are in life. I was satisfied just to take things one day at a time.

"Oh, look!" Darla snuggled closer as she pointed upward. "A shooting star. You know what the old folks say, 'It's an angel hitching a ride on a star back to heaven.'"

Or a stealth U-2 spy plane, I thought to myself.

Just then a tuxedoed waiter came around the French doors leading to the balcony. Moving toward us with his silver platter extended, he offered crystal flutes of sparkling champagne.

"To us," Darla said as we held our glasses up toward the night sky.

"To us," I said.

The way I was feeling tonight . . . I couldn't fly any higher.

ALSO BY GINA HOOTEN POPP